PRAISE FOR

Just Stay Away

"Nobody believes Craig when he insists nine-year-old Levi is the source of the mayhem in his life—which is regrettable, as Levi might be a troublemaker worse than *Baby Teeth*'s Hanna (so says the author of *Baby Teeth*). *Just Stay Away* is a tense page-turner that literally had me reading with my shoulders hunched."

—Zoje Stage, bestselling author of *Baby Teeth* and *Mothered*

"Cancel your plans and find a good chair because once you start *Just Stay Away*, you won't be able to stop. A psychological game of cat and mouse evolves between a writer and his daughter's creepy new friend in this superbly plotted, fantastically immersive domestic thriller. From the characters to the writing to the pitch-perfect ending, Wirt delivers on every level."

—Mindy Mejia, bestselling author of *Everything You Want Me to Be* and *To Catch a Storm*

"A relentlessly creepy and dangerously addictive read, *Just Stay Away* will have you checking your locks and jumping at shadows once you've finished. Using the unique perspective of a stay-at-home dad, Tony Wirt expertly crafts an atmosphere of ever-increasing isolation, claustrophobia, and gaslighting to ramp up from a sinister simmer into a full-blown nightmare. In doing so, Wirt explores gender roles, masculinity, and boyhood in the profound ways you find in the best of the genre. An absolute must-read—if you dare!"

—Brianna Labuskes, *Wall Street Journal* bestselling author of *A Familiar Sight*

"In *Just Stay Away*, Wirt flawlessly weaves tension into everyday domestic life. The protagonist, Craig, finds himself in a suspenseful game of cat and mouse with a neighborhood child that will leave you wondering, What would you do to protect those you love?"

—Elle Grawl, author of *One of Those Faces* and *What Still Burns*

Praise for *A Necessary Act*

Underground Book Reviews 2017 Novel of the Year, Reader's Choice

"I literally could not put this book down. As far as thrillers and crime novels go, it ticked every box for me, whilst also managing to be unique in its concept and style. Great characters, genuine bellyaching tension, and an ending that both surprises and satisfies . . . and yet is left wide, wide open . . . I truly hope there is more to come."

—Underground Book Reviews

"*A Necessary Act* grabbed me by the throat and refused to let go—even after I turned the last page!"

—C.H. Armstrong, author of *The Edge of Nowhere*

"This book is filled with creepy and suspenseful moments that are sure to get anyone's heart pumping. Just leave the lights on."

—*Rochester Magazine*

JUST STAY AWAY

ALSO BY TONY WIRT

A Necessary Act

JUST STAY AWAY

TONY WIRT

This is a work of fiction. Names, characters, organizations, places, events, and incidents are either products of the author's imagination or are used fictitiously. Otherwise, any resemblance to actual persons, living or dead, is purely coincidental.

Published by Thomas & Mercer, Seattle

www.apub.com

ISBN-13: 9781662513770 (paperback)
ISBN-13: 9781662513787 (digital)

Cover design by David Litman
Cover image: © Suthep Wongkhad / EyeEm, © Jose A. Bernat Bacete, © Thurtell / Getty Images

Printed in the United States of America

To Erin and our girls. I promise it wasn't like this.

Chapter One

Craig leaned back in his ergonomic desk chair and stretched his arms toward the ceiling. He'd been hammering away at the keyboard for at least an hour and gotten some decent stuff down. Nothing that would change the literary world forever, but at least good enough to feel the warm glow of accomplishment.

His eye caught the Project Statistics tab, but he quickly tore his attention away. He stared out the window, hoping something out front would distract him from the temptation of that arbitrary mark of progress.

Nothing good came from clicking that button. The right move—the productive move—was to ignore it, keep writing, and worry about word count later.

Or, even better, not worry about it at all.

But that little progress report was a pesky itch. Once it got into his head, he had to scratch it.

He clicked: *415 words.*

All the delusional satisfaction he'd built up leaked out of him like he'd known it would, making room for a fresh wave of frustration. He'd talked a big game about writing this book for years. Some writers hid what they did, not wanting to face the embarrassment of failure if things didn't work out. Craig did the opposite. He broadcast the fact that he was making a go at writing in part to keep himself from quitting when it got tough.

He *had* to succeed, because everyone would know if he didn't.

And so far, he hadn't.

If he was honest with himself, Craig had to admit he had rarely made anything more than a half-assed commitment to writing. Some nights, some weekends. Maybe a strong start at NaNoWriMo, a.k.a. National Novel Writing Month, in which writers sprint to finish a first draft in November, but Craig always seemed to peter out after the first week. In his defense, a family and a full-time job were ready-made excuses to put the dream of being an author on the back burner.

Then, at the start of the COVID pandemic, he lost that job, which wasn't so bad because he hated it anyway and losing it gave him the chance to stay at home with their daughter, Alice. But just as the world was getting back to normal, Courtney was offered a job up in Rochester and their family made the move from Iowa City.

Once they got settled, Craig floated the idea that maybe he should stay home with Alice and finally fully commit to writing. Courtney pocketed a nice raise with her new job, so she could keep them going until Craig sold a book.

She had always encouraged him and loved the idea of him finally giving it a real go, and Alice was thrilled to have her daddy around all day.

Craig just hadn't anticipated how hard it was to write a book with a seven-year-old bouncing around the house.

He'd set a goal of 1,500 words every morning—a goal that was still reachable if he kept going without worrying about everything going on around him. Do that and the first draft of his book would be done in time for MinnLit, the Minnesota Festival of Literature, in Minneapolis, where his college friend Zoe had convinced him to preregister for the agent pitch session.

Aside from his wife, Zoe had been his biggest cheerleader. They'd worked together at the student paper, but while Craig moved on to media relations, she'd become an editor at a midlevel publishing house. Even though Zoe mainly handled romance novels, she was an invaluable guide to the sometimes secretive ins and outs of the publishing world. So when she'd insisted the pitch session was the most effective way to land an agent, Craig had signed up.

The cost was steep, especially for a guy who wasn't bringing in any income yet, but Zoe had said it was a rare opportunity to bypass the lonely slog of sending out unsolicited query letters that inevitably end up in an agent's bottomless slush pile and praying for an intern to pluck yours from obscurity.

Unfortunately that opportunity only mattered if he actually had a finished manuscript to pitch. At the pace he was putting words onto paper, it seemed like a fantasy.

Craig pushed back from the desk and rolled over to the turntable spinning along the far wall. It was a Marantz 6200, the crown jewel of his meticulously curated writing office—a splurge he'd told Courtney was essential because proper writing music was incredibly important. She had no problem with his office investment, although she teased him about his concept of the word *essential*.

If you put as much thought into your book as you did your writing music, you'd write a worldwide bestseller and we'd be able to retire to the Bahamas.

She probably had a point, but Craig's daily music selection *was* fairly scientific. It had to be upbeat to push him forward, ideally matching the mood of whatever scene he was writing. An action scene needed to feed off something aggressive like the Replacements or Hüsker Dü, but if his main character needed to wallow in his own misery, only something like the Cure would get Craig into that headspace.

Needing a boost, Craig pulled out his copy of *The Low End Theory* and dropped the needle. He wheeled back to his laptop and closed his eyes again, letting the jazz-infused hip-hop beats of A Tribe Called Quest wash over him.

Time to work.

"Daddy?"

He sucked in a deep breath, pushed aside his creative frustration, and put on a smile before spinning around toward the office door.

"Yeah, honey?"

Alice had snuck her head around the door, as if she wouldn't be as much of a disturbance if she didn't cross the threshold. "Can I have a yogurt drink?"

"Yeah, sure," Craig said. She thanked him and slid back out of sight.

He didn't want to say anything. She was seven and trying to do the right thing by asking before taking, and she certainly wasn't trying to be a bother.

And yet . . .

"Hey, Alice, come here a second."

Having been invited, she swung the door open and stepped into the office with a smile. Always a smile, because she was possibly the sweetest girl on the planet. Her light-brown hair was pulled back into an unintentionally offset ponytail of her own making, and the purple shirt she wore advised him to *Be Kind*.

It was good advice, and Craig allowed his love for his daughter to soften the reminder he had to give her yet again. "You know, kiddo, if you want something to drink, you don't need to come ask me. You're a big enough girl that you can just go get it for yourself. Remember, Daddy's working on his book, so maybe only come get me if it's something really important, okay?"

Alice smiled, her first adult tooth peeking out of her gums and already looking way too big for her sweet little face. "Sorry, Daddy."

"It's okay, kiddo. I just need to get a lot of work done today, and if I have to stop, sometimes it's hard to get started again, you know?"

"Okay, I won't bother you again." Alice disappeared and pulled the door shut behind her.

Before Craig could turn back toward his laptop, there was another small knock.

"Yes, Alice?"

"Can I watch TV?"

The office window framed a perfect summer day. The grass was an impossible green, and the few clouds in the sky kept the sun from making things uncomfortable. A neighborhood kid rode past on his bike while a pair of robins seemingly cheered him on from the birch tree in their front yard.

It was too nice a day to waste inside. They both should be out there playing, chalking up the driveway or hunting butterflies in the backyard. Unfortunately, if he was serious about being a writer, he needed to put the work in. Four hundred fifteen words wouldn't cut it. If he let Alice put a movie on, he'd get about ninety minutes of uninterrupted writing. Maybe he could finish this chapter and even take a bite out of the next.

"Sure, babe."

Alice skipped away, and Craig swiveled back to the keyboard. He'd make it up to her after lunch. Play with her out back or walk up to the park for a bit.

He started typing.

Chapter Two

Craig leaned against the deck railing and took a pull from the bottle of beer in his hand. The remaining sunlight glowed pink over the trees in the distance, and a stray mosquito buzzed around his head as he waited for Courtney to weave her way back through the smattering of people standing around making boring work-party conversation.

They'd had to attend these types of events every now and then between their two jobs back in Iowa City, but since moving north, it felt like they were doing it every weekend. Xenida, the huge medical-research firm that recruited Courtney, apparently believed employee morale was built exclusively in bosses' backyards.

Parties like that hadn't been so bad back in Iowa because at least Craig knew some of the people there. Up here it was a dizzying array of new faces he could barely remember if he'd met before, all talking about medical metadata and clinical-management algorithms. Numbers and statistics had never been Craig's forte, but in his years with Courtney, he had gleaned just enough to follow along, so long as she kept it relatively big picture.

That wasn't happening with these folk, so Craig was relegated to the most banal chitchat before they moved on to someone they could impress with serious research numbers.

"So, what do you do for a living, Craig?"

Without fail it was the first question he got at these things. Just a bouquet of awkwardness tossed in his general direction. If he said he didn't have a job, that he stayed home taking care of their daughter, it opened a floodgate of *Mr. Mom* jokes and questions about watching soap operas and eating bonbons all day—as if that happened outside a hack joke from 1974. That's why he always said he was a writer, even if he hadn't published anything yet.

Unfortunately, that answer had proved problematic as well. If they couldn't pull out their phone and find your book on Amazon, it was hard to be taken seriously. Just another delusional hobbyist, sitting around the house his wife paid for.

How much of that was stuff they actually believed and how much was Craig's insecurities and self-consciousness was up for debate. Either way, he danced around the questions as politely as he could before spying Courtney over by the cooler and excusing himself.

She smiled and gave him a knowing wink as he approached. "How's it going over there?"

"It's fine," he said. "That guy Jeff said that when I finish my book I shouldn't sell it to Hollywood for a movie, but go to Netflix and have them make it into a series."

"His name's Jake, by the way, but it's still a *really* good idea." He loved that she perfectly matched his sarcastic tone. Not mean, but enough to let him know she was on his side. "I'm surprised you didn't think of it."

"The future is in streaming, apparently." Craig finished off his beer and dropped the bottle in a cardboard box under the little table next to them. "That's assuming I can beat Jake to the punch, because . . . and you aren't going to believe this . . . but *he's* always thought about writing a book. He's got a best-seller idea, but since 'nobody reads anymore,' he isn't doing anything with it."

Courtney rolled her brown eyes hard enough for the both of them. "Oh, I'm sure. I've read Jake's reports . . ."

Craig basked in the love and support radiating off his wife. Her new job required his presence at boring backyard parties, but he knew it was the reason he was able to chase his dream.

For that he was grateful. The fact that she was willing to make fun of her new coworkers with him was just the icing on the cake.

"I wonder what Alice and Kaitlin are doing." Craig looked out over the expansive back lawn and briefly wondered how much whichever VP owned the place pulled in after taxes. "She was so excited when I told her who was coming over tonight."

Their house might not be even half the size of this place, but they'd really lucked out with their neighbors. Dan and Kaylene had been nice and helpful from the day they moved in, but the real prize was their teenage daughter, Kaitlin, who had been willing and available to babysit from the get-go. Alice absolutely idolized her. Shortly after they had moved in, Kaylene brought over a huge garbage bag full of Kaitlin's old clothes for Alice, and Craig had never seen their daughter so excited.

"I told them they could eat dinner downstairs and watch *Frozen II*, but she said she already watched it this morning." Courtney snuck some playful accusation into her voice. "She sneak a movie on you?"

"No, I told her she could." They had talked about limiting screen time during the summer, especially on days when the weather screamed for outdoor activities. Craig wasn't trying to hide it from his wife but had kind of hoped that little nugget of information would have slipped past her unnoticed. "She was coming in every fifteen minutes asking me if she could have a snack or to tell me about something super cute the cat did. I didn't want to be mean or hurt her feelings or anything, you know, but I was getting nothing done. Finally she asked if she could watch TV, and I said fine. I wasn't going to, but I honestly needed some solid writing time without interruption. But after lunch we went out back and played on the swing set for a long time. My arms are probably going to be sore from how many times I pushed her."

Courtney punched him in the shoulder and grabbed a fresh beer out of the cooler next to them. "It's fine." She grabbed a second bottle and handed it to Craig. "I appreciate that you're the one taking care of her all day and handling the rest of the house stuff at the same time, all while finding the time to write your book. A TV break once in a while isn't the worst thing. I trust your judgment."

"Thanks." Craig gave her shoulder a squeeze before popping the top on his beer. He looked around for a garbage can before dropping the cap on the table. "And don't worry, it won't be an everyday thing. I can handle it. Promise."

A middle-aged man in a Tommy Bahama shirt walked up and snuck between the two of them to grab a beer. Courtney perked up and put on her socializing-with-work-friends voice.

"Eric, have you met my husband, Craig?"

"Nice to meet you, Greg." Eric switched his beer to his left hand and extended his right over to Craig as his eyes sparked with recognition. "Oh . . . you're the Mr. Mom, right?"

Craig stole a quick glance over Eric's shoulder and saw his wife give him a supportive wink.

"Mr. Dad, actually." Craig couldn't help but put some extra squeeze into his handshake. "Courtney is the mom in our family."

Eric looked legitimately confused.

"*Craig* is a writer," Courtney said. "So he can be at home with our daughter and work on his book at the same time. It's perfect."

"A writer, eh?" Eric said. "Have you written any books I've heard of?"

Eric looked like the kind of guy who had heard of exactly two books, neither of which he'd read but had maybe seen the movie.

"Still working on my first."

The man's eyes were already wandering over the backyard crowd behind them. "Yeah, well, you'll have to give me a signed copy when it comes out."

Craig was pretty sure none of the first seven responses that came to mind would be beneficial to his wife's career, so he agreed and forced a smile as Eric wandered back into the crowd.

Courtney slid next to Craig and leaned into his ear.

"Thank you," she whispered and gave him a kiss on the cheek. Craig felt the warmth of her love trickle through him and let it blot out the annoyance that swirled inside him.

Chapter Three

The only noise bouncing around the office was the clack of Craig's keyboard. Side B of *Lodger* had stopped spinning a while back, but he'd been too focused to notice that he'd written through the entirety of David Bowie's Berlin Trilogy.

He just kept going, without interruption.

Eventually, as he typed his way to the end of that day's second chapter, his stomach sent up a warning flare. He glanced over at the clock and found out why.

It was 1:12 p.m. He'd been going nonstop all morning.

He slid his cursor up to Project Statistics: 3,396 words.

Holy shit.

Craig was so excited about his morning output, it took him almost a full minute to wonder where Alice was. He closed his laptop and emerged from his writing enclave to a silent house.

A few days ago he'd ordered a cat leash for Felix. It arrived yesterday afternoon, and he surprised Alice with it after breakfast. He'd figured if they could go on a little backyard adventure together, it might keep her from watching television all morning. And anything that kept her outside would keep Courtney happy and give him time to write.

It obviously worked.

Craig headed toward the kitchen and noticed a white, orange, and black ball of fur curled up in a warm spot of sunlight. Felix was still wearing the bright-pink harness, but the leash was not attached.

"Alice?"

Felix glanced up at him for a second, then rested his chin back atop his paws. If he knew where Alice was, he wasn't saying.

"Alice?" Again, no response. Craig's footsteps echoed around the kitchen. "Where you at, kiddo?"

Right as the first flare of nerves shot up from his stomach, movement from the backyard caught his eye through their sliding glass door.

Alice was out on the swing set, pumping her legs back and forth with a look of joy plastered across her face.

Next to her, doing the same thing, was a boy Craig had never seen before.

He watched them for a bit, Alice's mouth moving constantly in a way that made Craig smile. Instead of calling her in for lunch, he headed out onto the deck.

The afternoon air was warm, but the breeze that snaked its way through the trees kept things from getting hot. Their house was on the end of a cul-de-sac in a neighborhood where the lots weren't fenced, so the backyards blended into each other in a vast, kid-friendly swath of green. One thing that had attracted them to the place was the thick patch of woods that marked the back edge of their property, which, according to Google Maps, was about the size of a city block. Courtney loved the rural feel it gave the house, and it afforded them more privacy than one would expect in the middle of town.

He was down the deck steps and halfway across the yard before Alice noticed him.

"Daddy!" She dragged her feet across the bald patch of dirt under her swing and came to a stop. As she ran to him, her face was flushed pink from either the sun or the excitement coursing through her little body. "I met a new friend."

She crashed into him with a fierce hug that warmed him more than any summer day could.

"That's great!" Craig picked her up and whipped a quick 360 that brought out another scream of delight. "Can you introduce me?"

Back on the ground, Alice grabbed his hand and pulled him toward the giant play set the previous owners had left behind. The wood was weathered from years of use, but the thing was a rock-solid beast. Two swings and a dangling buoy stretched out from a covered clubhouse, accessed by a ladder on one side and a climbing wall on the other. A slide stuck out on the far side, with a trapeze bar hanging off an extended beam next to it.

Alice's friend still went back and forth on the other swing.

"This is Levi. He lives over there." She waved her hand in the general direction of the woods.

"Well, hi, Levi. It's nice to meet you." The kid kept swinging and didn't acknowledge Craig's greeting. He was pumping his legs hard, hands tight around the chains and a look of aggressive determination under a tangle of dirty-blond hair that swayed in and out of his face. He swung hard a few more times to gain altitude, then let go at the apex.

Craig took a step back and pulled Alice along as the kid flew through the air and landed a few feet in front of them.

Like a gymnast, Levi took a moment to steady himself before thrusting his fists into the air.

"WORLD RECORD!"

Craig chuckled as the kid's voice echoed off the woods behind them. "Impressive."

Levi ran back and hopped on the swing again. He was pretty skinny, but the beginnings of wiry muscles pulled taut on his legs as he pumped back and forth. His shins had a dirty crisscross of scratches across the skin, and the leather boat shoes he wore without socks seemed an odd choice for playing in the backyard. Didn't matter much to Craig, however. This was the first neighborhood kid he'd seen Alice play with, and friends were always welcome.

"So which house do you live in, Levi?"

He ignored the question and started pumping his legs again, apparently content to live in his own little Swing Olympics.

"Okay, then . . ." Craig looked down at Alice. "You ready to have some lunch, kiddo?"

"Can Levi have lunch with us too?"

Craig was happy she had someone to play with, but he wasn't sure he was ready to start cooking for the neighborhood, especially kids who refused to talk to him. "Levi's parents may already have lunch ready for him, but I tell you what. Maybe we should get the pool out this afternoon, and Levi can come back with his swimsuit on? How 'bout that?"

Alice squealed in delight, so Craig looked back to Levi, who was once again hitting top altitude on the swing. "Sound good to you, Levi?"

The kid launched himself off the swing again and arced toward Craig. He scrambled back in time for Levi to land exactly where he'd been standing. The close call sucked the breath out of him, and he could do little else but stare at the weird kid standing at his feet. He appeared only an inch or so taller than Alice, but probably had at least a year on her.

Levi looked up at Craig for the first time and met his gaze for an awkward second.

"Yes."

Craig caught up on his breathing and watched in bemusement as the kid disappeared back into the woods.

Alice wolfed down her peanut butter–and–potato chip sandwich, then scrambled up to her room to change into her favorite swimsuit. A minute later she bounced down the steps and practically dragged her dad into the backyard.

Craig pulled out the inflatable wading pool and put his lungs to work blowing it up.

"You want to run and get the hose?" he asked between puffs.

Alice took off around the side of the house as Craig looked up to see Levi emerging from the woods. He looked even skinnier without a shirt on, each rib jutting through a bare chest that looked painfully white above his crisp red swimming trunks. Craig couldn't help but chuckle to himself at the sight of the kid. He'd had no clue if Levi would show up or not, but there he was in all his bony awkwardness.

"Hey, buddy," Craig said. "You ready to swim?"

Once again, Levi didn't respond, so Craig went back to work on the pool. He could feel the kid's stare on him as he huffed, and it was unsettling enough that he capped the nozzle well before the ring was full.

"Hi, Levi!" Alice dragged their hose around the corner of the house, and Levi's expression changed. It was like he'd switched his personality back on when Alice showed up, and Craig found himself relieved to get those eyes off him.

Whatever. Nothing strange about kids being more comfortable with other kids. Besides, even if he seemed a little odd, kids needed other kids to play with.

Alice pulled the hose over to the pool and started the water.

"We gotta get some sunscreen on you," Craig said. "You care if I get you while you fill?"

"Sure," she said.

Craig snatched the yellow can off the ground and sprayed an oily mist across his little girl's back. She had Courtney's fair skin, and he'd learned his lesson earlier that summer when he'd forgotten to reapply every forty-five minutes at their athletic club's pool. Poor kid had looked like a cooked lobster by the time he'd realized his mistake. Craig had spent half the night rubbing aloe vera on her shoulders and listening to her cry about how her sheets hurt.

"C'mon over, Levi!" Alice shouted to her new friend as she tossed the hose away, pool filled to the extent her patience would allow. "Let's get in."

Levi hopped off the swing and walked over to the pool. Craig looked at the kid's pale shoulders and held the can toward him. "You want any sunscreen, Levi?"

The kid ignored him again and stepped over the inflated side into the water.

"We've got the lotion kind if you like that better . . . you can put it on yourself," Craig added, fully aware that a grown man rubbing lotion on someone else's kid could definitely be seen as problematic.

Levi refused to make eye contact. Craig shrugged. Wasn't his kid. If the boy didn't care about sunburns, he certainly wasn't going to hold him down and force him. "Your call, but if you change your mind, it's right over here."

Craig turned back toward the camp chair he had set up under their huge oak tree. He'd brought an iced tea and the latest Nick Cutter novel out back. The kids would probably be fine without him keeping an eye out, but when water and someone else's kid were involved, it was better to be extra careful.

Besides, there were definitely worse ways to spend an afternoon than reading in the backyard.

Well, the iced tea could be a beer.

Craig sat back in the chair and cracked his book as the kids splashed away. Whatever shyness Levi had around adults melted away with Alice. She was a stream of stories as they played, and Levi laughed alongside her even though they probably meant nothing to him.

After about fifteen noisy, blissful minutes, Alice hollered over to him. "Daddy, can we get more water?"

Craig peeked over the top of his book and saw the kids standing barely ankle deep in the pool, having managed to splash out about half the water.

"You bet." He dropped the book and pushed up from the chair. "Let me go turn it on."

He ducked around the corner and turned the spigot on again, then followed the hose back to the pool. The kids were busy splashing each other, so Craig grabbed the end of the hose and squeezed the handle, sending a jet of water toward their feet.

Alice laughed and started high-stepping as the stream hit her toes, prompting Levi to do the same. Craig swung the hose around, dousing their legs, then flipped a little stream of water up toward Alice's face. She squealed with laughter and jumped back out of the way.

"Oooooh, gotcha," Craig said, sending another spurt of water at her.

Alice screamed, hurdled the side of the pool, and ran off into the yard, constantly looking back with a not-so-subtle invitation to chase her. He stalked behind her like a zombie, sending off squirts from the hose whenever he got close enough. Every time the cold water hit her back, Alice would fire off a high-pitched shriek that echoed through the neighborhood. The neighbors probably thought they were murdering someone back there, but Craig didn't care. He was having a blast with his daughter.

When Alice ran out of range, he turned back toward the pool to check on her friend. Levi stood calf deep in the middle of the wading pool, watching him.

Craig shot a little spray of water toward him as an invitation to play, but the kid just stared as the droplets fell in the water in front of him.

"Daddy . . ." Alice was running around the periphery of the yard, intermittently weaving closer, begging to be chased again. Craig turned back to his daughter but could still feel the boy's eyes on him, as if he were a rat in a lab. A puff of breeze hit the mist of water blowing back from the hose and sent a shiver through him.

"Can't get me!" Alice flew past and ducked behind the oak. Craig sent a steady stream into the tree trunk and heard her laughing from behind it.

"All right, kiddo, you win." He dropped the hose next to the pool and stepped around toward the oak tree. "I think I'm going to read a bit more, then maybe—"

A sharp blast hit Craig just below his right eye and enveloped his face in water. He stumbled backward and threw his hands up to protect himself. The water pressure stung his palm and sent a shower cascading back around him, enough that he could barely see Levi with the hose in his hand.

The water kept working around Craig's guard to deliver a painful shot in the face. He pushed against it and approached Levi, until his foot caught the edge of the pool and toppled him forward. Craig landed with a splash at the boy's feet, the stream of water shooting past him into the backyard. He snatched the hose out of Levi's hand and tossed it aside.

The kid's piercing laugh filled the backyard as Craig pushed himself up and wiped the water from his face, then reached down and picked up the hose.

He'd been using the *Shower* setting when chasing Alice around.

It was now on *Jet*.

"You okay, Daddy?" Alice had come back around the tree and was standing outside the pool. Craig let the water drip off his face and took a steadying breath. His cheeks stung, and he realized how lucky he was that first blast hadn't hit him in the eye.

"Yeah, kiddo, I'm all right." Craig looked down at Levi, who hadn't moved from his spot or stopped laughing since he'd taken the hose from him. People talk about the beauty of a child's laugh, but Levi's had all the warmth of a tornado siren. "You got me good there, buddy. But you've got to be a little careful when you're dealing with people's faces, okay. That hose has a lot of pressure on some of those settings. You could hurt someone if you got them in the eye or something."

Levi's face showed no remorse or any embarrassment at getting lightly chastised by someone else's parent. He examined Craig with those bright-blue eyes. It felt like Craig was on the wrong side of a one-way mirror, Levi behind it, observing him. Taking mental notes on his behavior.

Craig shook his head and let the water and nerves drip away. "Why don't you guys do something else for a bit?"

Alice took the cue and ran back toward the play set. "Come on, Levi, let's swing!"

Levi turned to follow her, but not before Craig noticed a smirk on his face. He waited until the kids were pumping away on the swings before following the hose back to the spigot and shutting the water off. If they wanted to swim any more, they'd have to make do with what they had.

They played in the backyard for another half hour before Alice asked for a snack.

"Can we eat it out here?" she asked.

Levi stood in the background, about ten feet behind her. Craig couldn't shake the creepy feeling that he was lurking.

"You know what, kiddo? It's probably time for Levi to head home and for us to go inside. I've got some things I need to do." Craig didn't actually have anything to do, but wanted to take the excuse to pull the plug on that afternoon.

"Okay." Alice wasn't old enough to hide her disappointment, but she was good about listening to her parents. "But can Levi come back tomorrow?"

Craig looked over at the kid. Still standing. Staring. Almost as if he were daring him to say no. And, if he was honest with himself, Craig wanted to say no, but there was no good reason to deny his little girl another day with her new friend.

"Yeah, I guess that's fine."

"YEAH!" The offer cleared all the sadness from Alice's voice and gave Craig a surprising spike of optimism. He thought back to all the good writing he'd gotten done that morning. If Levi could keep Alice occupied again, maybe he'd get another couple of uninterrupted hours tomorrow.

"Sounds good," Craig said. "Sound good to you, Levi?"

The boy looked at him with the same smirk Craig had seen after he'd blasted him in the face with the hose. He nodded and took off across the yard.

Alice shouted after him.

"Bye, Levi!"

They headed in through the basement sliding glass door under the deck, walking past the pile of sticks Courtney had asked him to clear out multiple times. Craig glanced back toward the woods and saw Levi standing at the tree line, watching them go inside.

The sticks could wait another day.

Chapter Four

"So tell me about this Levi kid." Courtney spoke around a mouthful of wintergreen foam as she guided an electric toothbrush across her teeth. Alice had told her all about her new friend Levi at the dinner table, to the point they'd had to remind her multiple times to stop talking and eat her chicken.

Craig pulled on a faded Interpol T-shirt and stepped back from their bedroom into the bathroom. "I don't know much, really. He just kind of showed up."

"He just emerged from the woods?"

Craig laughed. "Yeah, pretty much."

"Levi of the Forest."

Courtney cracked herself up, and Craig loved that about her. She was smart enough to crunch piles of metadata into new ideas for cancer treatment, but still goofy enough to paint the image of a feral neighborhood boy emerging from the trees to play with their daughter. Craig thought back to their first date—sitting in a dive bar, talking over a basket of chicken wings that had grown cold because he couldn't stop laughing long enough to eat. He reached over for the toothpaste and squeezed some out on his toothbrush, contemplating his luck. "But, seriously, I don't really know how he ended up here. Alice was out back with Felix this morning—"

"Oh my god, how much does she love that leash?" Courtney said.

"Yeah, that was a good purchase," Craig said. "Anyway, she was out in the backyard all morning, and I got *so* much writing done. Like, actual *good* stuff. It was freaking amazing. If I can do that every day . . . oh man."

Courtney rinsed her mouth out and spit into the sink. "Was she out there all morning by herself?"

There wasn't any accusation in Courtney's words, even though the lizard part of Craig's brain looked hard for some. He was defensive by nature—had been since childhood—but he knew it and always kept his guard up against the insecurities that lurked inside. Not only did it help him keep healthy relationships, but it was one of the many traits he'd identified in himself that he was determined not to pass down to Alice.

Besides, his wife had every right to ask about—and give her opinion on—what their daughter did. Craig's being at home with Alice all day did not make him more of a parent than she was.

"She's old enough to play outside by herself, and she knows to stay in our yard. A little time in nature, away from Dad, is probably good for her," Craig said. "And of course she wasn't by herself. Levi of the Forest emerged from the trees to be her woodland companion."

"Yeah, I guess." It was obvious she'd rather have Craig back there with her, but she seemed willing to concede the point. "So you got some good stuff down today, huh?"

Craig pulled the toothbrush out of his mouth to talk, happy for the change in subject. "Best day I've ever had. I mean, it was *amazing*. Words were flowing like a garden hose, and most of it was actually decent. I was so in the zone I had to make myself stop for lunch. Honestly, I could have kept going all day, but I'd promised Alice we'd get the pool out, so I shut it down to go hang with her."

That last part wasn't nearly as subtle as he'd wanted, but Courtney appreciated it anyway. She leaned over and kissed him on the cheek before heading to the bedroom. "That's awesome. I can't wait until you're super famous and I can retire and hang out with you guys all day."

"Well, if I get super famous, I'll have to be working on the next bestseller." Craig finished his teeth and followed his wife into their bedroom. "It's a vicious cycle, you know. When you're a big-timer, the fans always want more, and you have to feed the beast. That's why I'm gonna be one of those obscure writers that most people haven't heard of but have, like, a cult following. That way I can release a book every ten years or so and then get super famous after I die when everyone says I was their favorite all along."

Courtney was already propped up on her side of the bed, reading last month's copy of *Fast Company*. Craig pulled his socks off and slipped under the covers beside her.

"So this Levi kid, he's okay?" she asked. "You're cool with Alice being out back with him alone?"

Craig tried to answer right away, but something held him back. His face tingled where the hose had blasted him earlier that day, and the manic laughter coming from the kid echoed inside him.

The kid is fine, right?

Sure, he didn't talk much, and that stare was kind of unnerving, but kids were weird, especially around adults they'd just met. Hell, the first time they had Dan and Kaylene over for dinner, Alice kept a blanket over her head for the first hour. They probably thought she was an odd duck too.

Craig realized an awkward silence was stretching around the room.

"Yeah, no worries," he said. "The kid's fine."

And he was. However awkward he'd seemed at first, around Alice he'd seemed normal. She had spent all dinner telling Courtney how much fun they'd had together, and couldn't wait to play with him again tomorrow morning.

A spark of anticipation lit in Craig's gut at the thought of another solid block of writing time, chasing away whatever doubts tried to hide out in the corner of his mind.

—

The warm water of unconsciousness swirled around Craig as he floated down in a much-needed river of sleep. His eyes fluttered open for a second, as they did multiple times a night before he sank back into a deeper sleep. But this time, instead of the black canvas of a dark bedroom, they caught the blurry outline of a kid standing beside their bed.

Every muscle in his body seized, and he lay frozen. The only part of him capable of movement was his heart, which beat like he'd mainlined Red Bull. Craig's blood vessels pulsed in his temples as he stared, his imagination, fueled by a lifetime of Stephen King books, running wild.

A broken word cracked the quiet of night.

"Daddy . . ."

Alice's voice sent a wash of relief through him and loosened his chest enough to allow the breath that had been trapped inside to whoosh out. He felt around for words but had to wait for the adrenaline to seep from his system before his brain could reboot into coherence.

"Hey, kiddo." Craig's whisper was hoarse with sleep. His daughter's face began to take shape in the dark in front of him, and he chided himself for thinking it could be anyone else.

"I had a bad dream." It had been a while since Alice had woken him up in the middle of the night, but her voice told him there were tears he couldn't see.

Craig propped himself up on his elbow, and Courtney rolled over with a grunt behind him. She had her weekly staff meeting in the morning, which meant she'd have to be up and out the door early. He glanced at the alarm clock next to the bed and eased himself out from under the covers. "I'm sorry about that, sweetie." Now that he had control of his voice, he kept it as quiet as possible so as not to disturb his wife. "Let's head back to your room so we don't wake Mom, okay?"

Alice's hand found his as they walked around the foot of the bed, and he could feel the tears she'd wiped away before coming to get him.

The door was still open from when she'd come in, and a faint glow crept in from beyond. Their master bedroom sat at the top of the main stairway, with an open walkway leading to a guest bedroom on the right and Alice's room to the left. A night-light glowed from an outlet in the hall for just such an occasion. It combined with the light coming in from the front windows downstairs to cast everything in a midnight-blue tint.

Alice was quiet as Craig led them back to her room, a chandelier to their right hanging over the open entryway below. He glanced down at the locked front door as they passed.

Another night-light, this one in the shape of a butterfly, glowed from Alice's room as he ushered her back. She climbed onto her bed and held her favorite stuffed bunny, Pete, under her chin.

"So you had a bad dream, huh?"

He could see her nodding in the pink glow of the room.

"Do you want to talk about it?"

Alice hesitated for a moment and then started talking about bad guys locking her in a house that was full of traps that she had to get through to get out. She was talking about falling in a pit of hypodermic needles when Craig realized where the story was coming from. As a kid, scary movies had always fascinated him but were always too much for him to watch. It wasn't until he'd gotten to college that he'd been able to watch horror movies without them severely impacting his sleep. Courtney had no interest in them, especially as they'd gotten more terrifyingly violent in recent years, but Craig still found himself watching every now and then when he was alone.

That's how he realized his seven-year-old daughter was talking about the *Saw* movies.

How the hell does she know anything about those?

Craig gave Alice a big hug and assured her she was safe and nothing like that was ever going to happen to her. He felt her melt into his arms and cry a little more as they sat on her bed. They talked about fun things they could do tomorrow and remembered cute things Felix had done that day. Craig considered going off to find the cat and bring him up to her bedroom, but there were a million hiding places in their house where he could have curled up for the night.

At some point Alice yawned and Craig figured her nightmare was far enough behind them she'd get to sleep again. He tucked her in tight and made sure Pete the Bunny was there for her to hug if things got scary again. It was time to head back to his room and get some sleep of his own, but there was one thing he couldn't let go. He knew he shouldn't ask. It was pointless, because he already knew the answer.

But he stopped in the doorway and turned back. He couldn't help it.

"So that scary stuff you were dreaming about . . . Where did you hear about that?"

The room was silent for long enough Craig wondered if she had fallen asleep already.

"Levi was telling me about his favorite movies that he watches on YouTube, but . . ." She paused again, and Craig wondered if he'd ruined all the calming work he'd done over the last twenty minutes. ". . . they don't sound good, and I don't want to watch YouTube."

He went back to her bed and sat next to her. His hand found her forehead in the dark, and Craig swept her light-brown hair back. "Don't worry about it, kiddo. Sounds like he was watching movies that weren't for kids, huh?" He took his hand back as she nodded. "And you don't have to watch YouTube if you don't want, but you know what? There are all kinds of things to watch on YouTube, not just scary movies. In fact, you know what the most popular thing to watch on YouTube is? Kitty videos."

Even in the dark, he could sense her face change.

"Really?"

"Yep. There are millions of cat videos on there, doing all kinds of silly stuff. One time I saw one of a cat that liked to ride around on the Roomba. If you want, maybe we can watch some during breakfast tomorrow morning?"

She nodded so hard Craig could feel the *Saw* movies tumbling from her head.

"Okay, you get some sleep, and tomorrow we'll watch a whole bunch of silly cat videos."

He kissed her on the nose and headed back to his room. With his eyes fully adjusted to the dark, the walkway seemed even brighter on the way back.

Craig left their bedroom door open just in case the Jigsaw Killer slipped back into Alice's head. Then he crept around to his side of the bed as quietly as possible.

Who the hell lets their kids watch movies like that?

If Levi was watching them on YouTube, though, it was probably without his parents' knowledge.

Okay, who the hell lets their kid dig around on YouTube like that?

Craig was glad Alice was young enough they didn't have to worry about the perils of the internet yet, but it was only a matter of time.

"Everything okay?" Courtney's voice was caked in sleep as he slid under the covers beside her.

"Yep. Just a bad dream."

"'Bout what?"

With the way Courtney hated horror movies, he could only imagine her reaction to Levi pumping Alice's head full of gore. Might put a quick end to their backyard playdates—and his writing time. Craig never hid anything from his wife, but the middle of the night wasn't the place to have those conversations anyway.

"You know . . . typical kid stuff. She's fine now."

Courtney rolled over and fell asleep before the echo of his lie left the room.

Chapter Five

Craig was about to start another chapter when he noticed the time. He liked to write until noon, but he'd blown past his daily goal over an hour before and was at a natural stopping point, so he figured he could close down his laptop a bit early and give Alice a little extra attention before lunch.

He pushed back from the desk and closed his eyes, reveling in the warm glow of unprecedented productivity.

It was amazing what a quiet house could do for a writer's output.

Writer.

Almost hard to believe it was really happening.

Before this week, he'd spent hours in the office, listening to records and staring at a blinking cursor until Alice would pop in with a question or pick her noisiest toy to play with just outside the door. Each time he'd swallow the frustration. She was just a kid and wasn't trying to keep him from working, but . . . ugh.

Then Levi came out of the woods.

Craig popped out of the office and drank in the quiet. Alice had gone outside almost immediately after breakfast, eager to meet up with her new buddy. He looked in all the sunny spots around the living room but didn't see their cat anywhere.

Alice probably had him leashed up outside with her.

Craig was digging a bottle of juice out of the refrigerator when a shriek snapped him out of the productive glow he'd been basking in for the last week. He hustled over to the window above the sink and looked out over the backyard.

Alice and Levi were standing around the play set, but his daughter was bouncing around, pulling at her friend. After a second, she moved enough that Craig saw what they were looking at.

Their cat, Felix, was dangling from the play set, writhing around at the end of his leash.

Craig dropped the bottle on the counter and sprinted out onto the deck. The cat yowled and hissed as Craig flew down the wooden steps that led to the backyard. Alice was tugging on the back of Levi's shirt, panic painted across her face.

"He doesn't like it." Her voice was almost quiet, like she had to push it through her fear. "Put him down."

Levi pulled his shoulder away from Alice and kept his eyes locked on the dangling cat in front of him, knuckles white around the handle of the leash.

Craig almost stumbled into the sturdy wooden legs of the play set as he scrambled to a stop. "What are you *doing*?"

Alice's eyes begged for help from behind, but Craig got no reaction from Levi, who just raised and lowered Felix from the trapeze bar like a live piñata. The harness held the cat tight around his front shoulders, so it didn't look to be hurting him, but it was painfully obvious to anyone within earshot he sure as hell didn't like it.

Craig reached out to scoop Felix into his arms, but the poor cat lashed out with his claws.

"Shit!" Craig jumped back and pressed a hand over the four angry red lines on his forearm.

He turned back toward Levi, who still held the leash while the hint of a serene smile snaked across his face.

"Give me that."

Levi waited until Craig's hand was an inch from the leash before letting go. Felix dropped to the ground but managed to twist himself around and land on all four paws. The cat tore off across the yard, dragging the leash behind him while Alice screamed his name in pursuit.

Craig turned back to Levi, struggling to process what he'd seen. The kid met his eyes with a slightly confused expression, as if he were unsure what Craig was so worked up about.

"Daddy, come help me with Felix." Alice had chased their cat over to the concrete slab under their deck, near the sliding glass door into the basement.

"Give him some space, sweetie." Craig kept his eyes on Levi as he headed over to his daughter. Felix was holed up between the house and a big plastic bin they kept the backyard toys in. "He's probably really freaked out, so don't get too close. I don't want him to scratch you."

He glanced down to see tiny bubbles of blood seeping up along the marks Felix had left on his forearm, the sight of which sent up a flare of pain. Craig reached over and pushed the sliding glass door open, and the cat immediately darted inside. His tail was puffed up like a feather duster, but he didn't seem injured. Alice's face was bright red beside him, and she was breathing like she'd run a marathon. "What were you guys doing?" Craig asked.

"I had Felix on his leash, and we wanted to swing, so I tied the leash to the ladder so he didn't have to go inside." Her eyes swelled with tears as her words came faster. She was at least as upset about the incident as Felix was. "But Levi said we should let Felix swing, too, and he put the leash around the bar and pulled him up, but Felix started meowing, and I was afraid he was going to get hurt."

Craig knelt down and put his hand on Alice's shoulder. "It's okay, honey, I'm sure Felix is just fine. He's just scared because cats don't like stuff like that, you know?"

"I'm sorry, Daddy." She wrapped her arms around his neck, and the tears flooded out.

"It's okay, sweetie. It's okay. Felix is going to be fine. We're just lucky the harness goes around his chest and not his neck. Just give him some time, and he'll calm down and be back to normal." Craig pulled back so he could look in Alice's face. He wiped a tear away with his thumb and kissed her on the forehead. "Why don't you go inside and check on him? Don't get too close right away—he might want a little space, kind of like when we brought him back from the vet, remember? But you go check and see if he's okay. If he wants, you can give him a couple treats."

Alice sniffed a drip back into her nose.

"What about Levi?"

Craig looked back toward the swings. Levi was in the same spot he'd left him, staring across the lawn at them.

"I'll talk to Levi," Craig said. "You go check on Felix."

He stood up and gave her another kiss on the forehead before sliding the door open again. Alice disappeared inside, and he could hear her calling for the cat as he turned back toward Levi.

The boy held uncomfortable eye contact as Craig walked back across the yard.

"Hey, Levi." At six feet tall, Craig had to sit on the bottom rung of the ladder that led up to the clubhouse so he could get eye to eye with the boy. "You know you've gotta be careful with animals, right? I'm sure you weren't trying to hurt him, but a whole lot of bad things could have happened there."

The kid stood silent awhile, then spoke as if he'd just woken up. "Can I see your arm?"

It threw Craig for a second, but then he held out his forearm. The skin alongside the scratch marks had swollen up, and a smear of blood streaked across them. "Yeah, Felix scratched me pretty good. That's why you've got to be careful and not mess around with animals. Even pets. When they're scared, they don't know how to react the way we do, so they can scratch or bite."

He looked down at the tracks on his arm. They weren't too deep and itched more than they hurt at this point. "Cat bites and scratches can be nasty. They get infected easy, and then you've got to go to the doctor."

Levi looked up to Craig's face.

"Are your scratches going to get infected?"

"Um, I don't know. I hope not." Craig rubbed the blood away. "But I'll have to go in and clean them out either way."

Before Levi bolted toward the woods, Craig thought he saw a look of disappointment on the kid's face.

"Levi—" Craig was actually surprised when the boy stopped short of the trees. He walked over to Levi so he could use his caring-dad voice. "If you're going to play down here, you've got to be careful with Felix, you understand? We can't do that kind of stuff with him."

"I won't." Levi turned around slowly, his eyes dancing with a different level of understanding. "Promise."

"Okay . . . thanks." Craig didn't know why he thanked the kid, but it's what came out. He watched the boy weave through the trees back into the woods as Alice called to him from the house.

He turned to assure her he was coming, but the corner of his eye caught Levi turning right—away from his house and farther into the woods—just before he disappeared.

Alice's voice came across the lawn again. *"Daddy!"*

"Yeah." Craig turned away from the woods and rubbed the returning pain out of his forearm. "Coming, kiddo."

Chapter Six

Craig hoisted an armful of brush and dumped it into the old wheelbarrow Courtney's dad had let them have when they'd moved in. About fifteen jagged edges poked along the scratches Felix had given him the day before, sending a little reminder of pain up his forearm. He pulled off one of his work gloves and rubbed the sting out of his wound. The swelling was gone, but that little fur ball had gotten him good.

Courtney had been politely reminding him for at least a week to take care of that crap, but he'd been so wrapped up in his book that he'd kept forgetting. He'd even planned on getting more writing done when she took Alice out shopping for new sandals that afternoon, but figured that might be pushing it. Besides, now that Alice had Levi to hang out with, he could count on quiet writing time during the week and didn't really need to take advantage of an empty house on the weekend.

Craig wheeled the brush around the swing set and glanced at the spot where poor Felix had dangled from his leash.

Where *Levi* had dangled poor Felix from his leash.

He hadn't told Courtney about what happened. He was going to, but by the time she was home, Alice had calmed down and didn't say anything about it, so Craig figured there was no sense in bringing it up. Felix wasn't hurt or anything, and the kids had just made a stupid choice.

Not Alice.

Yeah, that was Levi's idea, and Craig couldn't shake the feeling that there was something a little off about him. That said, weirdness had a broad spectrum, and it was hard to tell where any particular boy slotted in based on a few afternoons and one bad decision. Especially coming off a pandemic that had basically locked them away from the world. How much social development had been lost over those two years?

Craig dumped the sticks about ten feet back into the woods. Their Realtor had told him their property ended at the tree line, and Craig wasn't sure if this section of woods belonged to the houses on the other side or if it was some weird neutral zone that nobody held a claim to. Either way, he couldn't imagine anyone getting upset about a few extra sticks tossed back there.

He peered through the woods, the trees and brush thick enough to give a shiver of claustrophobia. Craig hadn't done much poking around in there during the few months since they'd moved in, and decided to wander back a bit. He tromped through the bushes and fallen branches, threading among trees until he stumbled onto a thin path cutting through the forest.

He glanced back the way he'd come but could barely see Alice's swing set standing beyond the edge of the tree line. Ahead of him, he saw nothing but leaves and branches, but knew it couldn't be too far before he came out in the backyard of one of the houses on Deer Ridge. The path continued into the thick of the woods to his right and angled up toward the neighboring block to the left.

Levi's neighborhood.

He started up the path, stepping over bushes and fallen branches as he went. The foliage was still thick ahead of him, but eventually Craig crested a bank and stood at the end of the woods where the path emptied out into the backyard of a massive house made of glass and angles. A huge deck wrapped around the back, towering over a heavily manicured yet somehow spartan lawn.

It had to be where Levi lived. And if so, it was no surprise he spent so much time down at their place. This was a house designed for adults, not kids. Outside toys and swing sets didn't fit the aesthetic.

To Craig's left, an elaborate stone patio covered a good third of the yard. Multiple cocktail tables were arranged between a huge outdoor fireplace and a barbecue setup the likes of which Craig had never seen.

He took a few steps over to get a better look. A grill that looked like it could handle about ten racks of ribs and a brisket for dessert was built directly into the stone countertop. Bags of charcoal, bottles of lighter fluid, wood chips to add that smoky flavor: all had their dedicated place.

Craig's eyes drifted over the patio, and he realized as impressive as it was, it looked completely unused. The grill gleamed in the afternoon sun, no soot or fingerprints to be found. Not one of the charcoal bags sat half-full with the top folded over. Even the lighter fluid had fresh-from-the-store plastic wrap around the nozzle.

He could almost smell the epic meat tornadoes he could whip up with something like this in his backyard, and these people hadn't so much as grilled a hot dog.

The scrape of a sliding glass door pulled Craig out of his barbecue fantasy, and he turned to see a woman step out onto the deck. Her black hair was tied back tight, and her face glistened with sweat. The gray yoga top she wore showed quite a bit of tan skin through a complex tangle of straps. She looked to be somewhere in her forties, with a face that could intimidate you into thinking she was pretty.

It took a full second before Craig realized he was openly staring up at her from the backyard, and he scrambled down behind the counter before she noticed him. He pressed his back into the rough stone and prayed she hadn't seen him hide. Maybe he should have stood there and given a friendly wave, introduced himself as a new neighbor, and complimented her on their amazing setup.

Too late for that.

Now if she spotted him, he was a grown man creeping around in her backyard. He'd be lucky if she didn't call the police. Craig shrank farther down and pulled his feet in close. He didn't dare stick his head out but listened hard for any sign that she'd seen him. Luckily, she'd been holding her phone when she came out.

Craig waited, fighting off the instinct to take off toward home. A stranger bolting from your backyard was just as creepy as seeing one lurking around your outdoor patio.

He gave it a few more silent minutes before poking his head up over the counter.

She was still there, standing at the edge of the deck, eyes immediately locked on his.

Before he could do anything, her scream shook every tree in the forest and ripped through the backyard pergolas of her upscale neighborhood.

Panic coursed through Craig's veins as he stood up from behind the counter, hands raised in front of him like he was surrendering to the police.

"No, no, no . . . sorry if I scared you . . ." His voice sounded too loud and aggressive for an apology, but she was twelve feet above him and still screaming. He cut around one of the tables, but his foot caught one of the chair legs, which almost sent him tumbling onto the flagstone below. Craig righted himself and put on his most nonthreatening smile. "I'm your neighbor and I was just . . ." What *was* he doing, if not creeping around her backyard? His mind raced for an excuse, something to put her mind at ease, but the files were empty.

"I'm *really* sorry if I scared you." Craig stepped off the stone and into the yard so she could see he wasn't trying to come after her but wasn't trying to hide anything either. "I'm Craig Finnigan. We moved in a few months ago, back on the other side of the woods."

The screaming stopped, leaving a ghostly stain on the air, and the woman stared down at him with eyes he couldn't quite read. The initial fear seemed to be morphing into anger.

"This . . ." Craig put every bit of friendly into his voice. "Is this Levi's house? Are you his mother?"

Her eyes darkened at the mention of Levi's name, which made perfect sense since the stranger who'd crept into her yard was now name-dropping her kid. "You need to leave."

"Yeah, sorry. I'm Alice's dad." He used his daughter's name like a shield, but it offered no protection. "Levi has come down to play in our backyard a few times."

"I'll call the police." She threw her words down on him like rocks.

"No, no . . . I can leave. I just . . ." He put a lid over his boiling frustration. He'd obviously frightened her more than he'd realized, and it would probably be best to retreat and regroup. He could introduce himself to her another time, in another light, when he was a neighborhood dad and not some creep in her backyard. "Again, I'm very sorry I frightened you. Sorry."

Craig took a handful of steps toward the woods before turning back around. "My wife, Courtney, and I are right through there if you ever—"

Levi stood under the deck, staring at him. Not really hiding, but somehow blending in with the shadows. Craig looked at him for some sort of validation, but the kid stared back as if he were content to enjoy the show playing out in front of him. They stood in an awkward staring contest for another moment before Craig turned back and hurried into the woods.

Just a few steps into the trees, something grabbed Craig's foot and sent him sprawling onto the ground. An arrow of pain shot through his right wrist where it had tried to break his fall and taken the brunt of his weight. He rolled over and saw a small chain snagged around his ankle. It stretched over to a metal tube that had been lying just off the path, near a fallen log.

He pushed himself up and saw a puffy gray tail sticking out from the end of the tube.

It was a squirrel trap, and it obviously worked. Craig looked around the trees above him. Alice loved watching squirrels hop from branch to branch and scurry around the backyard. She'd named at least six of them—or given the same one six different names—and would squeal with delight whenever one climbed onto their deck.

The little gray rodents were everywhere. You'd need dozens of traps to make a dent in the population. And aside from occasionally raiding a bird feeder, what did squirrels do to warrant extermination? Although considering the level of patience and understanding Levi's mom had just shown him, Craig could definitely picture some kill-'em-all Cruella de Vil vibes coming from up there.

He nudged the trap back off the path and into some of the underbrush. As far as he knew, Alice didn't go back into the woods, but he didn't want to take a chance of her stumbling across it.

Chapter Seven

Craig stared at his laptop in disbelief.

The air around him crackled with excitement, and his stomach felt like he was just about to barrel down the first hill of a roller coaster. He read the email from Zoe again because he must have misunderstood it the first time.

—

> You have that manuscript ready yet? If not, you better get cracking cuz I was talking to Jennifer DiAmato (JDMA Lit) about a project and she randomly mentioned she's looking for small-town thriller with an edge type stuff. So I told her about what you're working on, and she was VERY interested. She's not doing the pitch meet but said she'd meet up for coffee Sat AM to talk and take a look. She doesn't take many new clients, so you better make sure you get that thing polished up. Don't make me look bad!!! No matter what, you owe me drinks forever for this. GOOD LUCK AND GET TO WORK!!!!!!

—

A giggle slipped from Craig's lips, which were stuck in an almost drunken grin. A quick Google search of Jennifer DiAmato did nothing but dump gasoline on the fire inside him. No wonder Zoe had used all caps in that email. DiAmato was big time, representing major-league authors Craig wouldn't dare compare himself to on his best day.

The agency website confirmed she was closed to new queries, but somehow Zoe had gotten him a face-to-face meeting with her.

Now he just had to make sure he had something good to show her. A rough draft wouldn't cut it.

A thread of panic cut across the excitement flowing through his system. Craig pulled up the calendar app on his phone and looked for the little dot in August.

Thirty-one days.

It could be done if he kept at it. He could have the first draft completed by the end of the month and then have enough time to do a round of edits if he hurried.

But he'd *really* have to hurry.

Zoe had gotten him a foot in the door to a very exclusive club. One that could make his entire literary career, so even if he had to write during every free second he had from now until MinnLit, he would do it.

The excitement crept back in as he read down the list of authors DiAmato represented on the JDMA Literary website. If he got his name on that list, no one would doubt he was legit. He'd be right up there with the big dogs.

"Woo-hoo-HOOO!"

His celebration echoed back into the empty house and was loud enough he wouldn't be surprised if Alice and Levi had heard it in the backyard.

He pulled up his manuscript and dove in for the day, a fresh wind of motivation at his back.

—

Craig could feel the pull from his laptop as he ushered Alice downstairs the next morning. He'd been thinking about his book all night, barely able to sleep as new character wrinkles and plot twists popped up in his brain like mushrooms. He'd never done drugs but couldn't help but wonder if this was what the beginning of addiction felt like.

But while he itched to get writing, Alice dragged her feet.

She couldn't decide what to wear, didn't know what she wanted for breakfast. Meanwhile Craig's book was calling to him from the office.

He was practically shaking with anticipation by the time she forked her last bite of the toaster waffle he'd selected for her, and had the plate halfway to the dishwasher before she finished chewing.

She mumbled something behind him, but Craig was in too much of a hurry to hear.

"What's that, kiddo?"

"Can you play outside with me today?"

He slotted the plate among the rest of the dirty dishes and grabbed a soap packet from under the sink. "You know I'd love to, but I've got a lot of writing to do today."

Alice stared at the empty table and hid her feelings about as well as any seven-year-old. Craig glanced out the window and confirmed Levi was already on the swing set. "Hey, Levi's out there waiting for you. Better hurry!"

None of the excitement he pumped into his voice made a dent in Alice's disappointment. "I want to play with *you*."

A pang of guilt hit his stomach. "And you know I love playing with you, but remember that agent I was telling you about who wants to read my book? I've got barely a month to get it done and make sure it's *really* good, so I'm gonna have to work super hard to get it done in time."

Alice didn't look impressed. He'd wondered if that thing with Felix would put a damper on the kids' friendship, but they'd played yesterday with no problems. Maybe Levi was a little weird, but Craig had talked to him about their behavior expectations. Craig wasn't concerned. As much fun as it would be to spend the morning outside with Alice, he really needed the quiet time.

"How about this . . ." He paused and smiled with anticipation. "If I get some good work done this morning, maybe we can go to the pool this afternoon?"

The dour cloud was blown away as Alice practically jumped at the suggestion. Her squeals of anticipation warmed Craig's heart.

The pool fixes everything.

"But I have to get a lot of writing done beforehand, okay?"

Alice's eyes sparkled just thinking about her favorite chlorine wonderland. "We'll stay outside all morning and be super quiet. Promise!"

"You don't even have to be quiet," Craig said. "I can't hear you back there when I'm in the office with my music on, so you don't have to worry about that at all."

He hadn't even considered that until he heard the words come out of his mouth. He hadn't heard Felix's yowling the other day until he'd gone out to the kitchen, because he'd been squirreled away in his office, buried in his book with music blasting around him. What if something went wrong back there?

Craig glanced out the sliding glass door and figured he could leave it open with the screen. If he kept his music down to a reasonable level and didn't close the office door, he'd hear if something bad happened. And he'd make sure to pop his head out every now and then, just to be safe.

"We'll stay outside the whole time until you come and get us. I won't even come in to go to the bathroom or anything."

Craig chuckled and gave his daughter a squeeze. "You can come inside and use the bathroom anytime you want, goofball."

He hugged her again and sent her out back to spend the morning with Levi while he churned out another 2,500 words in a quiet house.

Just after noon, Craig called Alice in for lunch and made a peanut butter–and-jelly sandwich while floating in a postproductivity glow. She scarfed it down and ran upstairs for her swimsuit before Craig even sat down with his own lunch, then practically danced around the table waiting for him to finish eating so they could leave.

The Southeastern Minnesota Athletic Club pool could be frustratingly busy during the summer, and with temperatures sitting in the nineties that afternoon, it was absolute madness. But Alice had given him a full morning of quiet, so he owed her.

Craig didn't know if it was the pristine blue skies or the leftover endorphins from his writing, but they had a blast. Usually he would tire out before Alice and spend a good part of the time relaxing on the deck while she swam, but that day he matched her enthusiasm. The two of them splashed around in the shallow end for a bit, then carved out a little spot in the chaos where Alice could practice her cannonballs off the side.

On the other side of the pool, a steady stream of kids splashed out of the towering waterslide into a small roped-off area.

"Looks like fun," Craig said. "Want to give it a try? I bet you're big enough."

Alice looked over at the slide like it was something she'd never considered. "For real?"

Craig could hear the bravery mustering in her voice.

"Yeah, let's give it a try." Another kid splashed out of the tube. "I'll wait down at the bottom just in case you need help, okay?"

A nervous smile spread across her face. "Okay."

They walked over to the slide together, and Craig sat down on the edge of the pool when Alice got in line. She waved to him about seven times as she waited on the stairs, and he wondered if she would actually go through with it.

She hesitated at the front of the line, but eventually disappeared into the tube. About ten seconds later, she splashed down with a scream in front of him, and from that point on, they did nothing else the rest of the afternoon. Alice climbed those stairs countless times and squealed with delight every time she flew out the bottom of the slide.

Craig laughed along with her and let the experience wipe away the residual guilt he felt about ignoring her that morning.

The towel Craig had put on the seat underneath him had turned cold by the time he pulled into the driveway, and the whole car smelled of the chlorine they had marinated in all afternoon. Alice had bounced in her seat the entire ride home, trying out all the stories she wanted to tell Courtney that night.

Dan Newton was digging in his mailbox at the end of their driveway and waved as Craig climbed out of their SUV.

"Why don't you run in and change out of your swimsuit," Craig said to Alice as he waved a pruney hand toward their neighbor. "I'm going to grab the mail."

"Okay, Dad."

He watched with a smile as she ran into the house, so glad he'd taken the time to hit the pool that afternoon, then turned down the driveway toward their mailbox. Dan was still standing there, holding his own mail and obviously waiting for Craig.

"Hey, Dan. How goes it?"

"Not bad, you guys doing okay?" His neighbor's voice was cheery, but his eyes were a little awkward.

"Yep, all good." Craig figured if his neighbor wanted more than small talk, he'd bring it up himself. "Took Alice to the pool this afternoon. Figured it was a good day for it."

"Yeah, it's a hot one," Dan said, still dancing around whatever conversation he wanted to start. "So, hey, I was gonna ask you something . . . You have some kind of run-in with Cassandra Ryan?"

Craig stared blankly, as the name meant nothing to him.

"Something in her backyard?"

The pieces fell into place with such a loud click he was certain Dan had heard it.

Levi's mom.

Good lord, how had Dan heard about that? Was the rumor mill in this town so desperate for gossip that a little misunderstanding got treated like breaking news?

"I mean, I was tossing some old sticks back in the woods and decided to walk around a bit—you know, just kinda exploring. Ended up walking a path that emptied out by their house, and she saw me." Craig studied his neighbor's face for sympathy. "Must have scared her. I tried to introduce myself, you know, let her know I wasn't some creep or anything, but it wasn't a big deal."

I'll call the police.

"How the heck did you hear about that?" Craig hoped his voice sounded casual enough.

Dan motioned back toward his house. "Kaylene is on one of those neighborhood Facebook groups, and Cassandra was posting about some guy sneaking around their backyard. Didn't name any names, but didn't make it too hard to figure out when there's only one new guy on the block."

A wave of frustration crested through Craig. He'd hoped the incident would just be an embarrassing bump in the road. Something he—*they*—could look back on someday and laugh about. But now this woman had taken their misunderstanding online, where mix-ups and false impressions metastasized into major transgressions and outright crimes with little regard for facts.

"Don't worry about it." Dan could obviously read what was going through Craig's head. "I'm sure it will all blow over. Everybody knows what Cassandra Ryan is all about."

"What do you mean?"

"Oh, you know how those Deer Ridge wives are."

Craig caught a little whiff of misogyny rolling off his neighbor, but didn't say anything. "I don't, actually."

"I mean, it's mostly doctors and bigwigs up there. Wives don't do much but sit at home and look for something to get upset about. Then take into account who *her* husband is, and, well . . . Has Courtney dealt with him at all?"

"I have no clue who you're talking about."

"Ope, sorry," Dan said. "She's married to Stephen Ryan, head of neurology over at the hospital. Does all kinds of research, gives talks all over the world. Kay used to deal with him when she worked at Merck. Everyone over there basically treats him like a deity, which is good because that's pretty much how he sees himself."

"Sounds like a fun family."

"Deer Ridge, man. It's another world up on that hill."

Craig thought about the nice houses on their block. Never in his life would he have imagined *this* not being the rich neighborhood. Heck, Dan owned his own landscaping business and didn't appear to be hurting for cash in the least.

"Yeah, well, like you said, hopefully it just blows over. Her son comes down to play with Alice pretty much every day, so at some point I guess she'll realize I'm not some creep."

Dan shifted his weight and leaned in toward Craig. "I'd keep an eye on their kid if I were you."

Craig tried to pull back into a more comfortable personal space. "Why?"

Dan glanced around as if he were afraid of eavesdroppers. "Well, last summer Kay caught him peeping in on her."

"Yikes," Craig said. He wanted to be shocked, but he was more surprised that he wasn't. Not that he condoned it in any way, but boys that age were—for lack of a better word—curious. "What did you do?"

"He took off when she saw him. She wasn't changing or anything, so that's good, I guess. But still . . . it's a little creepy. I'm just saying be careful, is all."

Dan wasn't wrong about Levi being a little strange, but between what Craig had seen from the boy's mother and what his neighbor said about his absent, egomaniacal father—that could definitely contribute to some personality quirks. It would be stranger if the kid *weren't* a little weird.

"Well, I appreciate that," Craig said. "The kid is a bit of an odd duck, that's for sure, but Alice likes playing with him, and if I'm perfectly honest, when he comes down, it keeps her out of my hair so I can write."

Dan's eyes lit up, probably happy to change the subject. "Oh, yeah, how's the book coming along? You going to be famous soon?"

"Ha! We'll see." It was then that Craig realized how well his writing was going, because he wasn't annoyed by the same joke every writer gets whenever someone asks about their work in progress. He thought about the meeting Zoe had set up, and an electric spark crackled in the back of his mind. It was probably best to play it cool, keep his cards close to his vest and wait until he actually had something to brag about. Building up premature hopes did nothing but give you a higher ledge for people to witness your fall if things don't work out.

"Actually, I've got a meeting with a big-time agent next month to look over my book."

"Really?"

He could see the impressed look in Dan's eyes and wanted to spread it on his morning toast.

"Yeah, she handles a bunch of bestsellers and apparently doesn't take on many new clients anymore, but she said she was interested in just the type of thing I'm working on, so . . . you know . . . we'll see what happens."

"That's fantastic," Dan said. "I'll have to tell Kay when she gets home that we're gonna have a famous author living next door."

Craig felt some heat on the back of his neck and tried to play it cool. "I mean, you never know what's going to happen. She may take one look and say it's total crap. It's a subjective business. Nothing's guaranteed."

"But if she's a big-timer and she's interested, that's a good thing, right?" Dan clapped him on the shoulder and let out a hoot. "Just don't forget us little people when that thing gets made into a movie."

"Promise." Craig swallowed a smile and headed over to his own mailbox. He dug out the day's haul and looked over at Dan, who was already halfway up his own driveway.

He understood why Dan felt the need to warn them about Levi, but Craig wasn't sure what he was supposed to do with that information—aside from making sure to keep their curtains shut. The kid obviously had some boundary issues, but those were not uncommon for kids that age. Craig had probably done a lot of things that would be considered creepy when he was a boy.

What was he supposed to do, ban Levi from his backyard? He was literally the only friend Alice had, and he wouldn't take that away from her just because the kid was a little awkward. Especially if the poor guy wasn't getting any guidance at home.

He heard Alice's laugh filter around the house. She hadn't said anything bad about Levi, so why should he worry? Kids had a way of sniffing that stuff out, often better than the adults.

Letting the boy play down here with Alice would probably do him some good. Sometimes all kids needed was someone to spend a little time with them, especially when nobody else in their lives would.

The thought jarred loose a memory Craig had buried long ago, but he pushed it aside and headed up to check on his daughter.

Chapter Eight

All the lights on the first floor were out when Craig came down from tucking Alice in for the night.

"Courtney?"

Her voice came in from the deck. "Out here."

Craig looked out the sliding glass door and saw his wife sitting in a chair, feet up on their patio table, beer in hand. He smiled, headed to the fridge, and dug through cans in the bottom drawer until he found their last Surly Furious IPA.

The sun had set a while back, but a dark-pink haze hung on the horizon as a reminder. A citronella candle flickered in the middle of the table, doing its best to keep the mosquitoes at bay.

"I figured it was a beer-on-the-porch kinda night," Courtney said.

Craig couldn't argue with that logic. The temperature had dropped as the sun set, and the stars were beginning to peek out above the trees. He cracked his beer and pulled a chair next to his wife. She had changed into shorts and a T-shirt after saying good night to Alice, her dark hair thrown up into a sloppy bun.

"Between that meeting Zoe set up and Alice going down the water-slide, you guys have had a pretty big couple days."

"It's kind of crazy." He could still feel the vibration of excitement in his chest. "I mean, it's an amazing opportunity. I'm so freaking lucky Zoe happened to be talking to her."

Courtney let him gush about it a bit, even though she'd heard the whole story multiple times. Craig eventually realized he'd been talking about himself more or less nonstop since he sat down, so he figured he should ask about her day.

She talked about the project she was on. Things were progressing well, but it was turning into a lot more work than Courtney had expected when they moved up here. Her days were ending later, and it didn't look like the workload would let up anytime soon.

Eventually they switched over to Alice's adventures at the pool and her countless journeys down the slide.

"I'm glad she went for it," Courtney said.

"She was a little hesitant at first, but she saw other kids her age doing it, and I think that was the push she needed."

Courtney took a sip of her beer. "Yeah, she needs some friends. Once she starts school in the fall, she'll meet a whole bunch of new kids. But she seems to be doing okay for now, doesn't she?"

"I think so," Craig said. "Especially lately. She's been playing outside with Levi every day."

Courtney curled her toes around the edge of the table and swatted a persistent mosquito from her forearm. The remnants of sunlight were gone from the horizon, letting the stars twinkle to their full potential. The house was dark behind them, but the moon shone down enough they could see all around the backyard.

"Yeah, she was talking about that tonight." Courtney spoke casually, but the way her sentence dropped told Craig she was holding something back.

"What?" The silence hung as his wife considered whether it was a topic worth pursuing. "Say what you want to say . . . it's fine. What's on your mind?"

Courtney hesitated long enough for a distant owl to add its opinion; then she blew out a long breath. "She was talking about how excited she was to go swimming—which is great—but mentioned that you agreed to go because she stayed outside all morning."

"No, no . . ." He swallowed the guilt that bubbled up from his gut and kept his tone light. "I told her we could go to the pool if I got my work done. *She* said they'd play outside the whole morning and be super quiet and not even come in to go to the bathroom, and I told her that wasn't necessary and she could come in whenever she wanted." Craig laughed. "She doesn't have to pee in the woods for me to work."

But she *hadn't* wanted to play outside that morning. The pool offer was a way to push her out there. What would he have said if she'd insisted on playing inside? Technically, he wasn't forcing her out back, but he wasn't really giving her any other options. Craig tried to push those thoughts aside.

Courtney didn't say anything for a second, then eased back in. "What if you wrote after dinner? I'm going to be working on this San Diego presentation pretty much every night, but I can move out to the kitchen and let you have the office if you want to write in there. That way you can do stuff with Alice during the day."

"I tried writing at night back in Iowa City, remember? For whatever reason it doesn't work for me," Craig said. "I don't know why, but my creative juices just flow much better in the morning."

"Okay. Just an idea." Courtney waited again. "It doesn't have to be every night either. If you have a day you want to do something with Alice, you can still get something done that night if you want."

"We had a lot of fun at the pool this afternoon." Craig hoped it didn't sound too snarky, but wanted to put an end to the conversation.

The longer Craig sat there with nobody talking but the crickets, the more guilt seeped in. Was he being selfish, making Alice play outside every morning so he could work? He *was* making a strong effort to spend time with their daughter when he was done and had assumed that was enough. When he was a kid, his mom basically pushed him out the door at 9:00 a.m. and didn't expect to see him until dinner.

He figured he was doing *much* better.

"I know I've said it a million times today, but it's such a crazy amazing opportunity," he said. "I can't blow it."

"I get it, but don't put too much pressure on yourself," Courtney said. "Like you said, who knows if she will even like it? And if she doesn't, that's fine. You don't have to sell a book to make sure there is food on the table."

"But I *want* to contribute, not just be some lazy layabout."

Courtney put her beer down and turned to Craig. "Honey, you contribute every day. You're here with Alice. You're making lunches, dinners. Doing laundry. If you weren't here, the place would literally fall apart. Don't for one second think you aren't doing most of the work in this family, and don't for one second think I don't realize that."

Craig leaned his head back and blew out a breath. "I know, but . . ."

He felt her squeeze his arm. "You're going to write an amazing book. I know this. All I'm saying is don't put all this pressure on yourself. We're going to be fine."

Craig put his hand on top of hers and looked over to find her brown eyes. She'd always been there for him, and he was determined to prove her right.

Courtney winked and turned toward the backyard. "So which one is Levi's house?"

"It's right up on the edge of the woods, but you can't see it from here." Craig pointed toward the woods in what he figured was the general direction. "If you head into the woods from behind the swing set, eventually there is a path. Take a left and head up, and it comes out right in their backyard."

He hadn't told her about the incident with Levi's mom, because he'd assumed it was nothing but a mix-up that would soon be forgotten.

But if it was nothing, there's no reason not to tell her about it.

A mosquito buzzed in his ear, and Craig swatted at it.

"How do you know?" Courtney asked. "You been snooping around in the woods?"

Did she know? If Dan and Kay had heard about it, how long before Courtney would? She wasn't a Facebook user, but rumors seemed to fly quickly in this town. Would it be better to tell her his side of the story now so she wouldn't be blindsided when she heard it from someone else?

"I was back there the other day dumping those sticks, then just kind of explored around a bit. You can see where Levi cuts through down the hill. If he keeps coming down through the woods the same way, he's going to carve a new path that empties out right behind the swing set all by himself."

"Levi of the Forest," Courtney said. "Beating a path to our door."

Craig took another drink from his beer and let the night speak for him.

"Some nice houses up there," Courtney said. "Levi might be rolling in it."

"Dan said his dad is head of neurology or something."

Courtney looked over at him. "Stephen Ryan? Wow. He's a big deal."

"You know him?" Craig asked, happy to steer the conversation away from the Ryans' backyard.

"Haven't met him, but I've heard of him. Like I said, he's a pretty big deal. Xenida has a huge thing going with neurology, so we've got people over there all the time. It's basically what they hope our project becomes in a few years."

"I guess Kaylene's company worked with him for a while. Said he was kind of a prick."

Courtney laughed. "That wouldn't surprise me at all. Tends to go with the job description a lot of times."

Craig finished off his beer and considered how another would affect his writing the next morning when Courtney sat forward in her chair.

"What is it?"

Her face didn't show any concern, but she was staring intently at the woods. "I thought I saw something move behind the swing set."

Craig looked down into the dark but couldn't see anything out of place.

"Could've been a deer," he said. "We see three of them back there almost every morning."

Courtney shook her head. "No, it wasn't a deer."

The play set was visible in the moonlight, but the shadows behind it blended into the woods and offered a lot of hiding places to whatever was back there.

If there was anything back there at all.

Courtney stood up and walked over to the railing. She stared into the dark for a minute, then let loose a high-pitched whoop.

A dark spurt of movement flashed from behind the play set, followed by the crash of underbrush as whatever was back there tore off through the trees.

"What was it?" Craig assumed raccoons, foxes, and deer all wandered their backyard at night.

"Don't know, but it sure sounded big." The crunch of its escape faded, and Courtney turned away from the railing. "Oh well. I'm going to head in."

She patted Craig on the shoulder as she pulled the sliding glass door open and went back inside. The kitchen light flicked on.

Craig took one last look toward the woods, but the light glowing out of the windows behind him made anything in the backyard impossible to see.

He gave up and followed his wife inside.

Craig's eyes snapped open as his body washed ashore from the nightmare he'd been drowning in. Careful not to wake Courtney, he gently slid his half of the sheet off and let the cool air of their bedroom raise goose bumps on his sweaty skin.

Threads of his dream were pulled across his mind, but he didn't grab at any of them. His memories were enough that he knew he didn't want to remember any more of the nightmare. It had been a long time. Long enough he'd hoped the boy would never invade his thoughts again, but Craig should have known better.

Some ghosts can't be exorcised.

He rolled onto his side, and his alarm clock told him just how middle of the night it was. The house was silent, allowing the ringing in Craig's ears to take center stage as he tried to fall back asleep. He didn't know if there was any science behind it, but nobody ever had two dreams in a night, right? It was one dream, wake up, shake it off, then back to sleep until morning.

At least that's how it had always been for him, even when nightmares had been a regular thing.

Craig returned to his back and stared up at the ceiling.

It made total sense that the dreams would come back, no matter how long it had been. Weirdo kid shows up, wants to play.

Levi even looked a little like him.

He closed his eyes as if he could just will the memories out of his head. Shake it like an Etch A Sketch and erase the lines that had been cut from existence.

They'd offered counselors at school after it had happened, but that wasn't an option. His friend Andy rolled his eyes at the suggestion. Why would anyone in their grade need to talk about what happened to some little kid? Craig agreed, and by the time he realized that maybe he *should* talk to somebody, everyone in school had moved on.

Everyone but Jacob Westerholt, obviously.

Chapter Nine

"Need any more juice, kiddo?"

Alice sat at the kitchen table, mouth full of pancake, and shook her head. A thick dribble of maple syrup hung off her chin, and Craig watched her wipe it off with the back of her hand. He grabbed a washcloth, ran it under some water, and brought it over to his daughter.

"Just in case you need it."

The morning was still a little gray. Storms had rolled in the night before, and while the rain had stopped, the clouds were stubborn. When he'd heard the rain pounding against the bedroom windows around 3:00 a.m., Craig had worried the storm would continue through the morning and keep Alice inside for the day. He'd thought up a juicy little twist for his book and was itching to get it down.

When he woke up again with Courtney's alarm and the storm had passed through, he was relieved he'd get the chance. It was probably still soggy in the backyard, but a little mud never hurt anyone.

Craig had just grabbed himself a banana when the doorbell rang. The sound surprised him since it was way too early for any deliveries or visitors.

He left Alice to finish up in the kitchen and answered the door.

Levi stood on the front stoop.

"Hey, buddy," Craig said. "How are you doing?"

He stood solid, the normal fidgeting of a boy his age absent.

"I want to play with Alice."

Craig glanced at his watch and saw it was barely 7:30 a.m. His daughter was still in her pajamas. "Well, Levi, it's kind of early, and she's not quite ready to play yet. But she can come out in a little while. Is that cool?"

Levi didn't respond.

"You know, buddy, she still has to get dressed and stuff, so why don't you come back after a while, okay?"

The kid held eye contact long enough that it became uncomfortable, then turned away.

"Fine."

Craig stood in the doorway and watched him leave. A pair of brand-new white sneakers were stuck on the end of his scrawny legs, caked in mud from the trek through the woods. Craig could imagine Cassandra Ryan's reaction upon seeing that.

Poor kid.

He closed the door and headed back to the kitchen, where Alice was polishing off the last of her breakfast.

"Who was that?" she said.

"It was Levi. He's ready to play with you." A whiff of disappointment crossed Alice's face. "Come on, that'll be fun. Won't it?"

She slid out of her chair and picked up Pete the Bunny. He had been her go-to stuffie since she was born, and usually didn't leave her side until she was dressed for the day. The old guy had been loved to death and was pretty threadbare. "I want to play dollhouse."

Alice's reluctance sent a little warning flare up in the back of his head. "You like playing with Levi, right? He's a good friend?"

"Yeah, but it's yucky out today."

He'd known this day was coming. No matter how much Alice liked playing out back, eventually she was going to want to do something else. Something that didn't mesh with his writing schedule.

Craig looked over at the calendar. MinnLit was twenty-nine days away, and his writing pace had slowed a bit over the past few days. He needed to keep pushing.

"Oh, it's not too bad out. Besides, the sun will be out soon, and it will end up being a really nice day."

"We always play outside," Alice said in a voice that told Craig his weather-related argument wasn't helping. "I want to play dollhouse today. I'll be quiet. I promise."

Shit.

He picked up her syrup-drenched plate and carried it over to the dishwasher. He didn't want to make her do anything she didn't want to do, but if he didn't get this draft done and polished, he'd blow a golden opportunity.

All they had to do was get through his meeting at MinnLit and everything would change. By then Alice would start school and he'd have all day alone in the house to write.

They just had to push through until then.

"Maybe you can play outside during the morning, and then after lunch we can do something fun."

She didn't look convinced. He didn't want to force her out back, but he needed some quiet time.

"Tell you what . . . if you play outside this morning, this afternoon we can go out for some ice cream. Deal?" He hoped the mention of an ice cream run would perk her up, so he stepped on the gas. "What do you say, huh? You can get a double scoop if you want. Cookie Monster *and* birthday cake?"

As much as he wanted to frame it as a fun chunk of daddy-daughter time, Craig knew better. It was bribery, plain and simple. Unfortunately, he had no other ideas.

Out of the corner of his eye, Craig noticed Levi hadn't gone home but was waiting by himself on the swing set. "Look, Levi's already out there waiting for you, kiddo. Better hurry up and get dressed, huh?"

Alice looked out the window at her friend, then turned back to go upstairs. But she definitely moved with more resignation than excitement.

He reminded himself that she always loved playing back there and once she got going she'd have a blast. But the guilt was like a rock in his shoe. Every step he took it was there, reminding him of its presence.

And he couldn't seem to shake it out.

—

Craig struggled to shake the disappointment on Alice's face that day, and it stemmed the flow of words enough that he didn't hit his goal until almost one o'clock.

To her credit, Alice had done her part, and he hadn't heard a peep from her all morning. Hopefully that meant she'd been having fun out back with Levi. The sun had never really broken free of the clouds like he'd promised it would, and it still looked relatively dreary outside.

Craig headed out back to find the kids, but the yard was empty.

"Alice?" His voice echoed back from the trees.

Craig wandered down to the swing set, half expecting Alice and Levi to come sprinting around the corner of the house at any second.

There were plenty of fresh, muddy tracks all over the play set—on the ladder, down the slide, all around the swings—so they'd been there not that long ago.

A shriek cut through the woods and ripped through the damp air.

"Alice?" His voice was much louder this time—worry elbowing its way to the front of his mind and pushing him into the trees.

Muffled voices came from up ahead, and Craig crashed through the underbrush toward them. Random branches and exposed roots threatened to trip him up, but he navigated his way as quickly as he could before eventually bursting out on the path he'd found the week before.

Alice and Levi walked toward him along the muddy rut.

"Hey, guys, everything okay?"

"Yes." Levi offered no other explanation, his voice curt and emphatic, like he expected no more questions. Craig didn't see any injuries or tears as they got closer, so the buzz of fear in his gut fizzled out.

"I thought I heard a scream."

"I fell off a log," Alice said. "There's a bunch of logs over there, and if you fall off, you get eaten by crocodiles, and I almost made it to the end but fell."

"And the crocodiles bit her head off."

Craig tried not to wince. He took a quick scan of Alice, who was a little dirty but otherwise no worse for wear.

"Okay, then. You guys must be starving. I was writing so much I didn't realize it was so late."

Alice nodded, and Craig glanced down at Levi. His parents obviously weren't too concerned about getting their boy any lunch, considering he was still down here with Alice. Levi's mom was probably too busy talking shit about Craig on Facebook to worry about lunch.

An idea sparked in Craig's head and brought a smile to his face.

"Tell you what . . . Alice and I had talked about getting ice cream this afternoon. What if we *all* went out for lunch first? We could go grab some burgers, then get ice cream afterward? How's that sound?"

Levi looked at Alice as if he were more comfortable answering her than her father. She nodded, and a tiny smile crept across Levi's mouth—it had probably been a while since an adult showed any interest in him. Craig couldn't control the kid's family situation, but if he could be a positive influence while he played with Alice, then that was something he was willing to do.

A lot of his odd behavior was probably nothing more than a plea for attention, and Craig certainly wasn't going to ignore a kid who just wanted a little attention.

"How about this—we'll head home and change while Levi goes and cleans up and asks his parents if it's okay. That work?"

Levi headed home without a word. Craig was legitimately interested to hear what Cassandra Ryan decided. It was not just a way to do something nice for her son, but something of an olive branch to her. A way to show no hard feelings remained from the misunderstanding in the backyard, and to prove to her he was a good guy.

And if she said no, that would be fine also. He'd made the effort to extend his hand—if she knocked it away, that was on her. If her reputation was what Dan said it was, all he had to do was let people see who he really was and let them decide whom to believe.

Craig offered his hand to Alice, and they started back home through the underbrush. He felt the warmth of vindication, able to get a ton of work done and still be a good dad. Not that he'd done it to prove anything, but he had to admit he'd enjoy listening to Alice tell her mother all about their spontaneous trip during dinner.

Craig tramped down the underbrush and held a branch aside for his daughter.

"So what were you guys doing back here?"

"Just playing."

Craig took a big step over a fallen log. He'd have to be careful about man-eating crocodiles.

"Does Levi play back here a lot?"

"Yeah. He's got a fort. There's this fallen tree back there, and he put up a bunch of branches along each side."

"Cool. What's he got in his fort?"

Alice kept her eyes on the ground as she walked so she could step around the branches. "He wouldn't let me go inside, because it's secret. But I didn't want to anyway because it smells bad."

The dank, earthy smell of decaying leaves and dirt pretty much covered the woods back there. A skinny sapling snapped back onto Craig's shin as they continued through toward their backyard. They eventually emerged and headed up the deck steps, where they took off their shoes outside the patio door. Alice ran upstairs for new socks and was back down just as Craig saw Levi emerge from the woods again. Craig and Alice stepped out the back door to meet him.

"Your parents say it's okay?"

Levi nodded. He hadn't changed out of the dirty collared shirt he'd been wearing, and his shoes and socks still had a lot of mud on them.

It would probably make a hell of a mess in his back seat, but their SUV was due for a major cleaning anyway. There were probably enough crumbs to reconstitute nine boxes of granola bars back there already, so a little mud wasn't going to change things.

"All right, then. Let's do it. Levi, do you have any food allergies I should know about before we go?"

He looked up at Craig, a little confused, and Alice jumped in before he could answer. "Daddy and I are both allergic to fish."

"That's right," Craig said. "We've got to be careful, don't we, Alice?"

"If we eat even just a little bit of fish or even if they cook my food with the same stuff they used for fish, my throat will swell up shut and I can't breathe until Daddy gives me a shot. It's called anna-plaxis."

"Anaphylaxis," Craig corrected.

"The shots are automatic, and you just hit a button on top and *POP*. We keep them in the drawer by the table so they are right there just in case, and we have to bring one when we go out to eat because they don't have them there. Can I show him, Daddy?"

Craig chuckled. "Levi doesn't need to see our EpiPens, kiddo."

Alice absolutely loved telling people about their shared allergy. He and Courtney had worked hard to normalize it for her so she never felt embarrassed or tried to hide it, because a mistake could legitimately kill her. She might draw out their restaurant experience by explaining every detail to whatever poor waiter drew their table, but it would keep her safe as she got older and didn't have her parents around all the time to ask questions.

Luckily, fish didn't turn up in that many unexpected places, and they'd already scouted out plenty of restaurants that didn't have seafood on the menu—a plus of living in the Midwest. Craig felt sorry for parents dealing with severe allergies like eggs or peanuts, because those things could hide in anything. He couldn't imagine having to negotiate that minefield. "But that's why we always have to be very careful and why we always ask about our friends, too, just in case. So, anything you can't have, Levi?"

He shook his head.

"Okay, then," Craig said. "Let's boogie!"

Chapter Ten

The burgers were hot and greasy, and the fries were crisp. Between bites, Alice told the story of seemingly every time they'd gone out to eat while Levi stuffed his face like a man fresh out of prison.

After lunch, they piled back into the car and drove across town to Alice's favorite ice cream shop. She explained every flavor to Levi, and they both ended up getting a double scoop with Cookie Monster and mint chocolate chip. The sun still hadn't broken free of the clouds, but it was warm enough to dribble melted ice cream down the kids' hands as they ate at one of the picnic tables alongside the parking lot.

Craig went back for another handful of napkins before they got in the car and headed home.

While still a boy of few words, Levi's shyness had melted away as the day progressed. He seemed totally at ease talking with Alice and even answered some of Craig's questions with more than a single syllable. Craig had danced around the topic of his parents, trying to get a sense of how involved they were, but didn't have much luck. He did learn his dad was currently in Europe at a medical convention, which made Craig feel that much better about taking the kid out.

Craig wove his way through a few residential streets and turned onto Deer Ridge Road. Massive houses made of sharp angles and hedges lined the street, protected by a phalanx of mature boulevard trees that seemed to wave through any passersby who dared linger too long.

Their house might be just on the other side of the woods, but this was a distinctly different neighborhood.

Levi's place was up on the left side of the street, and the shrubbery hid the police car until Craig pulled into the driveway. Two uniformed officers were at the front door, talking with Levi's mother.

All three turned toward his SUV as Craig rolled to a stop behind the cop car. He stared back, hoping nothing bad had happened, and offered an awkward nod. He'd planned on introducing himself to Levi's mom—*well, reintroducing*—but she obviously had something going on, and whatever it was, it was none of his business. He'd talk to her another time.

"Well, Levi, I hope you had fun today."

For some reason the kid didn't take the hint to leave.

"Why are the policemen here, Daddy?" Alice's voice was more curious than nervous.

The cops kept looking at him, maybe waiting for him to leave so they could continue speaking without random strangers eavesdropping.

"Don't know, kiddo. I'm sure it's fine." He glanced back at the kids. "Why don't you hop out, Levi? Thanks again for coming with."

He didn't say anything but popped open the door and slid out from the seat right behind Craig.

The kid's feet had barely hit the ground when his mom pushed past the closest police officer and stormed across the lawn.

"What the hell are you doing with my kid?" Her dark eyes locked on Craig, the brows etched above them sharp and angry. It was so unexpectedly hostile that whatever answer he could give dried up in his mouth.

She knelt down in front of Levi like she was inspecting him for damage, then practically threw him behind herself toward the front door. "Get inside."

"What's the matter, Daddy?" He could hear the panic in Alice's voice filtering up from the back seat. Craig didn't have an answer as he opened the door and slid out from behind it. He could see red blotches of rage on the woman's otherwise fair skin, her dark eyebrows practically lightning bolts above her eyes. The cops, seemingly as surprised at her reaction to Craig's arrival as he was, had snapped back to duty and started down the stairs.

"Sir, I'm Lieutenant Roger Shaw." The cop's voice had a practiced calm to it, like a teacher trying to keep a classroom discussion from going off the rails. "Could we get your name?"

"I'm . . ." Craig's brain was still not putting the pieces together. "I'm Craig Finnigan. Alice's dad?" He looked at Levi's mom for recognition, but got none and went back to the cop. "We live just through the woods back there. We're just dropping Levi off."

Having the cops next to her did nothing to calm Levi's mom down. "Dropping him off? Jesus Christ, I've been looking for him for hours."

"Oh . . . I'm sorry." Craig glanced at his watch, still not getting it. They'd been gone a little longer than he'd expected, but nothing crazy. He looked at Alice in the back seat, and she was absolutely terrified. "We went for ice cream after lunch, and I guess that took a little longer than I expected. Sorry about that."

Lieutenant Shaw opened his mouth to say something, but Levi's mom was faster. "Who the hell do you think you are that you can just take my kid out for lunch without even telling me about it?"

The reality of the situation finally broke through for Craig. Of course she was pissed. He would be, too, if his kid took off without telling him. "Oh, man . . . I told him to go ask you if it was okay. I'm so, so sorry. You must have been freaking out."

The apparent misunderstanding did nothing to calm her down.

"You would, too, if some stranger decided to take off with your kid without saying anything."

Craig looked at the cops, then back to Levi's mom. "Like I said, I'm so, so sorry for the mix-up. He told me he'd asked you and you said it was okay."

"Don't try to blame him for your fuckup," she said.

Lieutenant Shaw reached in to grab the reins. "Okay, let's calm down a bit and figure this out." He put his cop eyes on Craig and put some interrogation in his voice. "You say you took the boy out to lunch?"

"Yes. I had promised my daughter we'd go out for ice cream today if I got a lot of work done . . . I'm a writer, and I'm trying to finish up this book . . ." The cop listened, even as Craig felt himself rambling and sweat broke out across his back. "Anyway, when I went out to get her for lunch, she was playing with Levi and asked if he could come with for lunch. I said sure, as long as his parents said it was okay. So I told him to go home and ask while we went inside to change . . . Alice was muddy from playing outside all morning . . ." He paused and took a deep breath in an effort to get back on track, but his nerves were shooting off fireworks inside his head. "So, anyway, Levi came back, and I *specifically* asked if his mom said it was okay, and he said yes, so we left."

Craig searched the cop's face for understanding, but it was like white-on-white text. "I realize now I should have checked with her myself to make sure, and I am really sorry about that. It won't happen again."

Lieutenant Shaw and his partner exchanged a look before he turned back. "It sounds like this can be chalked up to an unfortunate miscommunication."

Cassandra Ryan wasn't about to let it go and brought out the big gun Craig feared she'd been holding in reserve. "I saw this guy creeping around our backyard the other day, and now he takes off with my kid, and you aren't going to do anything about it?"

Both cops' expressions changed at that.

"That true?" Shaw asked. "Were you in their backyard?"

"I wasn't back there creeping around or anything." The back of Craig's shirt stuck to him as the situation spiraled. A bead of sweat formed on his temple, but he was afraid that wiping it away would make him look more nervous. "I was cleaning up brush in our backyard and dumping the sticks in the woods. We just moved in a few months ago, and I'd never really looked around back there, so I guess I was just kind of exploring."

"In the Ryans' backyard?" Shaw's voice had much less understanding than Craig would have liked.

"No . . . I mean, I ended up following a path that came out by their house . . . the same one Levi uses when he comes down to our place to play, I'm sure." He wasn't sure what effect he wanted from that statement, but whatever it was, he didn't get it. "Anyway, I was up there, and I saw her on the deck, so I tried to wave and introduce myself—"

"You were staring up at our house from the patio." Cassandra turned back to the cops. "I caught him peeping up from behind the grill."

"I absolutely was not. I—" Both cops' eyes had hardened, and the situation was suddenly very real. Craig closed his eyes for a second to gather as much calm as he could find. "Yes, I was over by their grill. Like I said, I was following the path and it dumped out into their backyard, right by their outdoor patio. It's huge . . . really cool . . . and I wandered over for a second to check it out. I wasn't thinking about how that would look. I just . . . I wasn't thinking. But when she came out onto the deck, I realized how bad it would look to see me back there, so I panicked. I hid. Probably should've just owned up to it and explained myself right then, but I was embarrassed."

Cassandra ignored him and turned to the cops. "After I caught him, he wouldn't leave, and I had to threaten to call the cops, which I *obviously* should have done right away."

Craig was dying to jump in and defend himself, but it seemed like every time he opened his mouth, things got worse. He wanted to point out that if she was so concerned he was some sort of predator, why did she let her kid play down in their yard every day, but he held back. If he wanted the cops to believe him, matching her aggression would be a bad look. Better to stay calm and look like the bigger person.

"I can't say what happened the other day, but for now everybody is back where they belong, and I'm sure we can all agree nothing like this will happen again, right?" Lieutenant Shaw asked.

"Absolutely." The tension in Craig's chest eased. They believed him. "Again, I'm sorry for the misunderstanding. I promise it—"

Levi's mom let out a frustrated curse and turned back toward the house without another word. Craig and the two cops watched her until the door slammed shut.

The other cop let out a chuckle of exasperation, but Shaw cut him a quick glare. Craig wasn't sure what to say, if anything at all. He'd already explained himself and apologized numerous times.

Sometimes it was best to keep your mouth shut.

"Do you mind if we ask you a couple more questions, Mr. Finnigan, just so we make sure this whole thing is straightened out?"

"Of course." Craig wasn't sure how much more he could say to straighten things out but didn't want to be argumentative in any way.

"How do you know the Ryan boy?"

"He comes down and plays with my daughter, Alice, pretty much every day."

"And he was down there today?" Those were the first words he'd heard from the other cop. He was younger, with a thin black mustache across his lip. The gold bar over his uniform pocket said Officer Perez.

As Craig patiently and tediously went over the morning for the cops, a car passed by on the street and the driver almost broke his neck trying to figure out what was going on in the Ryans' driveway. Craig hadn't considered how this would go over in the neighborhood rumor mill, but was sure Cassandra was already blasting her side far and wide.

But Craig had the truth in his corner. Hopefully that meant something.

After he finished, Lieutenant Shaw glanced back at his partner and exchanged a look they must have developed over years of working together. "All right, like I said before, I think we can chalk this up to a misunderstanding and move on."

Craig let out a breath he hadn't realized had been inside him since they pulled up and saw the police cruiser. "Thank you so much."

Shaw nodded and glanced back toward the house.

"I'd just be very careful around the Ryan boy, okay?"

Craig turned toward Alice sitting in the car, still looking like a bundle of nerves. It wasn't fair that she'd miss out on her only neighborhood friend because his mom had overreacted to a simple misunderstanding.

And if she couldn't play with Levi, what the hell was he going to do about his book? He couldn't lose his writing time to this.

"Is it okay to still play with him? Alice, I mean . . . not me. Obviously." Craig forced a laugh at his slip of the tongue, but it just made him sound more awkward. "She plays with him every day. He's the only friend she has in the neighborhood."

"That's up to you, I guess, but if it were me, I'd give it some time." Shaw looked back over his shoulder again as Officer Perez started back to the car. "My advice is to tread lightly around the kid. Stephen and Cassandra Ryan hold a lot of sway in this town, and you saw how upset she was. Legally, I don't think you did anything wrong, but they can still make your life difficult if they want."

Craig thanked the officer again and headed back to his car, where Alice remained in her back seat booster. It wasn't until he'd hit the ignition and was backing out of the driveway that he noticed the wet sheen in her eyes.

"What's the matter, kiddo?"

She wiped her face on the front of her shirt. "I was scared you were going to jail."

He held her eyes in the rearview mirror as they drove out of Deer Ridge.

"No, sweetie, it was all just a misunderstanding with Levi's mom, and the police know that. She didn't know where he was and was scared, which is totally understandable. If you disappeared on me, I would freak out too. I should have gone and talked to her myself before we left instead of trusting Levi to do it."

"But he said he told her. I heard him say it," she said. "Why didn't he tell his mom that he told you?"

It was a good question. Just like that day in their backyard, Levi could have spoken up and taken him completely off the hook.

Was he afraid of his mother?

"Well, she was pretty mad, and the cops were there. Maybe he was kind of scared to tell the truth, you know? Maybe he was afraid he would get in trouble, so he didn't say anything."

Alice pulled back and looked Craig dead in the eye. "You always get in more trouble if you don't tell the truth."

Craig smiled at his daughter parroting the words he'd told her countless times back to him.

"That's right, and that's what I did with the policemen. And that's why we were able to get this situation straightened out so we can put it behind us and not worry about it anymore."

He breathed out another sigh of relief as they turned back onto their own street.

Thank god the cops were willing to listen to him, because a situation like that could have been ugly.

—

The incident with Levi's mom marinated in Craig's brain as he tossed and turned that night, her words replaying like highlights on a stadium Jumbotron above him. The rage in her voice kept poking him in the back of the brain. No matter what he'd said, she wouldn't listen. It was like she was purposely ignoring facts—looking for a problem. A fight.

Craig rolled over and saw the glowing **1:58** on his bedside table. He took a deep breath and blew it out slowly, fighting against the tide of negative thoughts that easily invaded his mind under the cover of darkness.

The cops had said to pull back, to press pause on the kids playing together, but that wasn't fair. Levi made a mistake.

But had he?

Maybe he hadn't been able to find his mom when he'd gone home to ask. She'd probably been on the phone, bitching at some contractor who hadn't built their third media room up to her standards. He could imagine her waving Levi off as he approached, unwilling to take a second for her own kid.

That's probably why Levi played down in their yard so often. Why he stuck around when Craig came out back in the afternoon, because he didn't have a parent at home who gave a damn. And now, because Cassandra Ryan refused to listen—to accept that she had been wrong about the situation—Alice was going to lose her only friend.

Fine, he'd admit it. It wasn't fair to him either. MinnLit was coming up fast, and while he'd made some progress the last week, his manuscript still needed a lot of work. Work that required a quiet house.

And he didn't want to give that up. He couldn't.

She called the cops because she thought you kidnapped her kid.

There it was. At some point he'd have to admit the life preserver he'd clung to had a hole in it. Preferably before it pulled him and his future writing career down with it.

Ugh.

No. There had to be a way to patch it. He couldn't give up yet. Cassandra Ryan might be mad, but she'd have to see reason eventually. Tomorrow, when emotions had calmed under the light of a new day, he would go talk to her and show her that he wasn't some monster, some creep—just a good dad who could be trusted.

Hell, she'd probably be happy to have the kid out of her hair.

And if she couldn't see that, then maybe Levi couldn't come down to their place anymore.

Once again turn your back on the weird kid who needs help.

Craig pushed the thought out of his head. This was a completely different situation than the thing with Jacob. It wasn't his job to be there for every ignored boy on the planet.

He rolled over and tried to push the echoes of guilt out of his head so he could sleep.

Chapter Eleven

"Let's take a walk."

Alice had barely finished her breakfast, but he couldn't leave her home alone and wanted to get this situation settled before Levi showed up at their door again.

If he was honest, he was mostly just anxious to get this over with. It was easy for an idea to sound good in the middle of the night, but when faced with actually talking to Cassandra again, he felt a serpent of nerves coil around his stomach.

This is a bad idea.

But what else could he do? There was no way he could let Levi play down at their house if his mother was going to call the cops every time there was some sort of misunderstanding. Besides, he couldn't hide from her unreasonableness and allow her to bully him into accepting the role of a neighborhood villain. A new day would allow them to have a civil conversation in which he could explain the series of misunderstandings that had tainted everything.

And if not, at the very least he could say he calmly and transparently did everything he could to straighten things out. Nobody could objectively look at the situation and say he had been anything but forthright.

Craig stifled a yawn that made him consider a second cup of coffee. He'd never really drunk the stuff before he'd started on his book, so he was still getting used to the caffeine boost. When he was at the computer, he thought of it as writing fuel, but figured being too jittery wouldn't help the awkward conversation to come.

The morning air was fresh and crisp, and a sheen of dew still coated the grass as they started up the block. Alice skipped beside him, pointing out the birds and bunnies that populated their neighborhood.

Taking the sidewalk around the block and up to Deer Ridge took longer than Craig had expected, but Alice seemed to be enjoying herself, so it was worth it. Had they taken the path Levi used through the woods, they'd have been there five minutes ago.

He stared at the huge houses that lined Levi's street. Their own was the nicest place he'd lived in, and easily the most expensive, but the places up here were on another level. Resentment and judgment threatened to emerge from his gut, but he pushed them back. A little piece of the small town Craig had grown up in always sat on his shoulder, no matter how many times he'd tried to brush it off. He watched Alice peer up at a squirrel in one of the boulevard trees and reminded himself to be glad his daughter got to grow up in a nice, big house in a good neighborhood.

Even if it wasn't Deer Ridge.

They turned up the driveway to Levi's house in time to see him come out the front door. He saw them and stopped on the front steps.

"Hi, Levi," Craig said. "I stopped by to talk to your mom. Could you run in and get her for me?"

"She's not home."

"Really?" The boy couldn't be older than nine, and Craig was under the impression that he had no brothers or sisters.

"Yeah," Levi often avoided eye contact with Craig, but now held his gaze the whole time. Craig glanced over to the three-stall garage to his right. The center door was open, and he could see a white Lexus SUV parked inside.

"I just want to talk to her quickly." After what happened when they'd brought him home yesterday, maybe Levi was afraid of a repeat. "To apologize again and smooth things out a little, so if she's home, I'd really like to talk to her. Is it okay if I just ring the doorbell?"

Levi came down the steps and stood directly in front of him, eyes hard and his voice dripping with defiance. "She's not here."

Craig stared down at him, trying to figure out what to do. He could easily get past him—the kid was *maybe* fifty pounds soaking wet—but who knew how he'd react. And assuming his mom was home, it would be just Craig's luck she'd look out in time to see him pushing past her son to get at the doorbell.

Definitely not worth it.

He dug out a piece of paper he'd written his name and cell phone number on and handed it to Levi.

"Okay, then, could you give her this when she gets home and ask her to call me?"

He took it without saying anything, and the three of them stood in an awkward silence. Craig looked past him at the window, half hoping Cassandra Ryan would see them and come out to talk, half hoping she wouldn't.

"Well, all right. Don't forget to give that to your mom, okay?" The kid didn't seem to be listening at all. "Hey, Levi . . . make sure you do it, because until I talk to her and get some things straightened out, I don't think you should come down to play."

The kid's head snapped up, and Craig flinched as if he had taken a swing at him. It took a second for him to remember he was the adult in the conversation. "Make sure you give it to her, okay?"

Craig grabbed Alice's hand and walked down the driveway. He looked back as they hit the sidewalk and saw Levi's eyes practically burning a hole in the back of his head.

"Can we walk to the park, Daddy?"

He broke away from Levi's gaze and shook the unease away. "Not today, kiddo."

He looked at his watch. If they went home now, he'd still be able to get some writing in before lunch. But would he be able to get anything done without Levi down there keeping Alice busy?

For now he'd have to find out.

Chapter Twelve

Craig stepped out of the shower and reached for the towel he'd left on the counter as the Saturday afternoon sun streamed in through the skylight above him. Courtney had taken Alice out to the mall while he'd stayed home and finally mowed the lawn.

He should have gotten some writing in. They hadn't seen Levi all week, so Craig was falling behind the schedule he'd set for himself. But he'd made an extra effort to spend whatever time he wasn't sitting at his desk with their daughter. Lots of trips to the pool and going to the park and playing whatever games they could think of in the backyard, which put his normal chores—like mowing the lawn—on the back burner.

He could feel himself wearing thin.

Craig stretched out his sore back and furiously rubbed the towel over his hair. The fluffy terry cloth enveloped his head, but he thought he heard a thump from the bedroom. Courtney had mentioned about four stops she'd wanted to make, so he'd expected them to be gone most of the afternoon.

Another thud.

"Courtney?"

He wrapped the towel around his waist just in case Alice was out there with her, and stepped through the door to their bedroom.

Levi was standing by their bed, rifling through the bedside table.

"Levi?"

The kid didn't even turn around, and Craig's brain struggled to comprehend the input it was getting. He just stood dripping on the carpet, staring at the back of the kid's head until he found his voice again.

"What are you doing?"

"I wanted to play with Alice." The boy turned to face him and stared at him with the same blank, unreadable face he always had. It was like the kid didn't process things the way most did. Or chose not to react. "Why are you naked?"

The question hit Craig between the eyes with the reality of the situation. He was wet, naked, and alone in his bedroom with someone else's kid, and before Craig could think of anything to say, Levi turned back to the bedside table and resumed digging through the drawer.

A warning flare shot up from the back of his head, reminding Craig they kept a few things in that drawer he wasn't about to explain to a nine-year-old boy. He shot across the room, barely remembering to hold his towel together, and pushed the drawer closed—narrowly missing Levi's fingers as it snapped shut. The kid snatched his hand back, and his calm mask fell away, giving Craig a fleeting glance at something that looked like anger.

He stepped back and grasped at the front of his towel before it fell. The bedroom door stood open across the room, as did the blinds over the window to their left.

"Jesus . . ." Craig muttered as he frantically looked around for something to put on. "Levi, you can't . . ." He spotted Courtney's robe draped on top of the dresser, threw it on over the towel, and tied the belt. It was fluffy, pink, and barely went to his knees, but at least it covered him up. "You can't be here."

Whatever Craig thought he'd seen on Levi's face was gone, and the calm, almost disconcertingly robotic voice was back. "I can go where I want."

"No, you . . . you can't just come in someone else's house like this. I mean, I was in the shower." Craig's head buzzed with fear and, for some reason, embarrassment. It was like one of those dreams where you showed up to school naked combined with having to dismantle a bomb.

The boy showed none of the awkwardness that coursed through Craig's veins. Like they were just hanging out in the backyard.

"You've got to go. Now."

When he didn't move, Craig stepped toward the kid as if to usher him out to the steps, but Levi jumped back like he'd charged him with a knife.

"Don't touch me!"

Craig jolted back like he'd touched an electric fence. "Sorry . . . sorry, Levi, I wasn't going to touch you . . . you . . . you just have to leave, okay?"

He ran his fingers through his still-wet hair. It felt like he was tumbling down a spiral staircase. He could hear the phone ring, Cassandra Ryan's voice wanting to know why the hell her son was alone with Craig in his bedroom.

And why the hell he hadn't been wearing any clothes.

No, it wouldn't be the Ryans that called—it would be the fucking police, and they certainly wouldn't be as inclined to take his side this time.

Levi stood next to Craig's bed, defiantly not moving.

"Please, just go outside." The freak-out was still amassing on the horizon, just begging to invade, but he fought to control his breathing. Did he hear something downstairs? Courtney could be home any minute, and then he'd have a whole other front to the battle. But she'd at least believe him, right? He tugged the robe's fuzzy belt tighter for no reason and tried another deep breath. Good god, he had to get that kid out of there.

"If you just go outside now, I won't tell anyone that you were in here, okay? I mean, technically it's illegal, like . . . breaking and entering. You don't want to get in trouble, do you?"

Craig knew his rationale was lame the minute it left his mouth, but it was all his jumbled brain could come up with in the moment. Besides, he was dealing with a kid. Kids would believe anything.

"I don't get in trouble." The confidence and matter-of-factness of his voice were striking. Another kid would be embarrassed and scared, but Levi stood there fully composed.

"Right, but remember how mad your mom was the other day? If she finds out about this, she'll probably get mad, and you won't be allowed to come back and play with Alice ever again."

"I can do what I want." It was like the kid was sharpening his voice with a honing steel. Levi held Craig's gaze for a while, almost as if he was purposely making him sweat. If he was, it was working.

"You have to leave now, okay? Go home, and we can . . . we can forget all about this, okay?"

After what felt like an eternity, the kid turned and walked out of the bedroom. Craig's knees gave out as the door closed, and he dropped on the bed. He sat there, head buzzing, trying to figure out what to do. He thought about calling Levi's parents right away, laying out what had happened. Honest, up front, because he'd done nothing wrong. But Cassandra's voice still echoed in his skull, and if she couldn't see his side about what happened the other day, there was no way she'd listen to him about this. He didn't even have her phone number, which meant he'd have to go up there in person, hair still wet, trying to explain why he'd been naked and alone with their kid.

The sight of Levi smirking on the sidelines, not saying a word to back him up, came back to him.

I don't get in trouble.

A fresh spurt of acid roiled around in Craig's gut just before the rumble of their garage door came up from below.

Courtney and Alice were home.

Craig threw on jeans and a clean T-shirt as fast as he could. How long had it been since Levi left? Had Craig heard the front door? The kid wasn't sitting down in their living room, was he?

He looked around the bedroom but didn't notice anything out of place, so he went downstairs. He made it as far as the kitchen when the back door opened and Courtney walked in with a couple of bags.

"Hey, babe." She spoke with a weekend smile. "How's it going?"

"Ah . . . good." Craig tried to dump as much normal into his voice as he could, but he still sounded weird to his own ear. "Good."

"You just get out of the shower?"

He stared at her for a second before remembering his wet hair. "Yeah." The damp combination of water and sweat soaked through the back of his shirt. "I mowed the lawn and was kind of grimy."

Courtney plopped her shopping bags on the kitchen table. "Thanks."

"Did you guys get . . . get what you were looking for?" Craig asked, fighting for normalcy as he got further from the bedroom. Levi was gone; no reason to explain anything to Courtney. It would be fine.

"Yep. Got Alice some shorts and then stopped at the greenhouse on the way back." She continued detailing their shopping adventure, but Craig was still too muddled with seeping adrenaline to pay much attention. It took a minute to realize their daughter wasn't buzzing around, regaling him with every aspect of their shopping trip. "Where is she?"

"Alice?" Courtney gave him a funny look and nodded toward the backyard. "Out playing with Levi. He was sitting on the front step when we pulled up. You were probably in the shower and didn't hear the doorbell or something."

She grabbed one of the bags and headed toward the stairwell. He wanted to tell her—knew he should. They didn't keep secrets from each other. If nothing else, she'd be able to back up his story if Levi ever mentioned anything to his parents.

She'd believe him. He was sure.

Craig looked out back and watched the two kids swinging and laughing together.

Courtney returned to the kitchen. "Anything exciting happen when we were gone?"

He looked away from the backyard.

"Nope."

Chapter Thirteen

Rain slapped against the window with the enthusiastic but slightly disjointed cadence of a fill-in drummer desperately trying to make a good impression. Craig stared out the window, laptop ignored on his desk, the birch tree out front nothing more than a shadowy smear through the curtain of water dripping down the glass.

He turned back to the blinking cursor and braced himself to take a run at the brick wall that had formed between him and the page.

Things had been flowing slower lately but had now devolved into full-on writer's block.

Lighting flashed a split second before thunder rattled the windowpane and snapped his attention away from the task at hand. He pushed back from the desk and wheeled over for a pointless look outside.

It was a summer storm, nothing more, and Craig had no idea what he expected to see, but looked anyway.

Maybe he should quit for the day. If baseball teams take rainouts, why can't writers?

Because the Twins don't have a deadline.

Craig scooted back to his computer and reached for his water bottle just as another clap of thunder boomed outside. His hand jumped and knocked the bottle onto the desk. Water poured from the mouth, and Craig scrambled to pick his laptop up before the tide hit.

He stood the bottle back up and examined his computer for any signs of moisture.

Whew.

Craig set it aside and pulled a handful of tissues from the box on the corner of the desk. He offered thanks to the gods of good fortune as he wiped the water from his desk. He'd been lazy about backing up his manuscript on a USB drive, so hopefully this near disaster would be the reminder he needed.

The wind howled outside as he shook his book's near-death experience out of his head and gave himself a few mental slaps.

Time to work.

Alice was somewhere on the other side of the office door, playing happily and quietly. Even with the storm raging outside, she hadn't disturbed him all morning, yet he could still feel her out there. The anticipation of an interruption was as bad as the interruption itself. An empty house had become as much a part of his writing routine as the turntable spinning behind him. Like it was more of a talisman than a necessary environment. It was an effective drug, and the withdrawal was real.

Or maybe he was just in his own head about it.

Another, more distant, roll of thunder called out to him, but Craig ignored it.

At least he tried to.

He glanced over at the orchid on the corner of his desk. The leaves were a little less than perky, so he unscrewed the top of his water bottle and poured what was left into the white ceramic pot, where a wick would suck up the right amount and deliver it to the roots above. Courtney had bought it for him back when he first set up the office. It was idiotproof, she'd said with a smile, and therefore perfect for him.

It sat on his desk just below the calendar he'd hung on the wall, where MinnLit loomed large in red Sharpie, creeping steadily closer.

Twenty-four days.

Those letters had been so motivational when he'd written them down, fingers crackling with anticipation. But now, with the writing faucet shut off, they were intimidating. A door to the Authors' Club that could just as easily slam shut in his face if he wasn't ready to push it open.

Quiet footsteps on the stairs outside the office grabbed his attention and snapped his head around. Alice was bounding up to her room, and Craig felt a surge of annoyance that shocked him with its potency.

Jesus, calm down.

He took a deep breath and reminded himself that no matter how much work he needed to get done, footsteps were not a crime. Alice was allowed to go up to her room.

He blew the frustration out and turned back to his book, doing his best to ignore the red letters looming over him from the future. Tomorrow was supposed to be a beautiful day. Alice would be able to play outside, and he'd get back on track.

Hopefully.

Craig wanted to blame his blockage on the rain keeping Alice inside, but if he was honest, it wasn't the only thing. Finding Levi in their bedroom had shaken him, and while he told himself all he needed to get back in a groove was a quiet house, deep down he worried that might not be enough anymore.

He should have said something. To Courtney. To Levi's parents. Hell, to the police. The kid had let himself into their house while Craig was in the shower, then started digging around in their personal things. He'd been afraid of how it might look, but the further away he got from it, the worse it would look that he didn't tell anyone. At this point, if the story got out, all anyone would want to know was why he tried to hide it. Being anything but up front about a situation like that was begging for people to make their own interpretations.

And they sure as hell would.

Craig leaned back and ran his hand through his hair.

Footsteps came through the door again, and he looked back to see Alice give a tentative wave through the glass door. He forced a smile.

Even though he'd done nothing wrong, holding that secret was like swallowing a smoldering chunk of coal. He just had to hope it petered out before burning a hole through his gut.

CHAPTER FOURTEEN

Craig had been in the office for barely fifteen minutes before the doorbell rang.

He didn't need to answer it to know who it was, and Craig was more than willing to ignore him. But Alice saw his diminutive shadow through the beveled glass of the front door and opened it wide.

"Hey, Levi!"

Her voice was full of joy at finally seeing her friend again, and Craig didn't have the strength to fight it. It was a beautiful day, the kind made for kids and friends and backyards.

But, somehow, after all the days of asking and coaxing and outright bribing Alice to play in the backyard, Craig hesitated.

"I'm gonna go play with Levi, okay, Daddy?"

He wanted to say no, *knew* he should say no, but his defenses had been worn down. He'd hardly written anything in the last week, and that deadline wasn't going anywhere.

"Fine. Just . . . be careful."

Alice bounded out the door and left the house quiet. A perfect writing sanctum.

It didn't matter.

The brick wall Craig had written himself into was proving taller and stronger than he'd anticipated. He stared at his laptop, waiting for something to come. Some flash of insight, a spark of literary genius.

Heck, he'd take mediocrity.

Anything.

The quiet that he'd fought so hard for before was now almost suffocating. It was one thing to feel Alice's presence in the house, but now he could feel Levi out back. The same look the kid had given him in the bedroom, now all around him, at all times, refusing to go away. He did what he could to ignore it—cranked the music into house party range and threw himself at his book—but the kid's presence wormed his way past whatever safeguards he put up.

He could feel panic seeping in, reinforcing the wall of writer's block that surrounded his book.

No.

He got up from his desk and shut the music down. Panic was ridiculous. He just needed a break. A hard reset. Pull the plug, wait thirty seconds, and plug it back in.

A faint shriek of delight filtered in from the backyard, and it brought with it a pang of guilt. While he was inside freaking out over an awkward kid, Alice was out back having fun. Kids were good judges of character, able to take people at face value without all the prejudices and baggage that adults bring, and Alice loved playing with Levi.

Craig sighed into his empty office, and the red letters from his calendar whispered at him.

Twenty-three days.

A morning off would help get himself out of his head. He'd get some extra quality time with Alice and maybe show Levi that he was ready to move past what happened the other day, making it less likely he'd mention it to anyone.

He went out on the deck and saw the kids messing around with the croquet set Craig had bought a while back. He'd gone a little nuts on lawn games, also picking up ladder ball, a bag-toss set, and boccie in hopes of keeping them occupied and having fun while he wrote.

Alice noticed him first and waved like she was trying to land a plane.

"Daddy! Are you done? Want to play croquet with us?"

Her enthusiasm blew away his anxiety and pulled a smile across his face. Maybe this would be good for all of them.

Levi mostly ignored him, his attention fixated on the ball he was knocking around the yard.

"You guys want me to show you how to play for real?" Craig pulled the wire wickets from the rack and pointed out where they needed to go. The lawn was a little hilly for croquet, but it wasn't like they needed a regulation field to have fun.

Craig went over the basic rules of the game, and they started practicing. Like most boys his age, Levi seemed more interested in just smacking around the wooden balls as hard as he could, while Alice showed some natural talent for getting her ball through the wickets.

They were about five minutes into their first game when Levi's ball knocked into Craig's.

"Have you seen this move?" With his ball nestled up against Levi's, Craig put his foot down on it and gave a mighty thwack, sending the boy's ball flying toward the woods.

"HEY!" Levi dropped his mallet and ran after the ball. Craig laughed until he noticed the look of betrayal on the boy's face as he carried his red ball back toward the field of play. The last thing he wanted was Levi holding a grudge against him.

"Sorry, bud. That's called a foot shot, and you can do it when somebody hits your ball. Send 'em flying!" Craig tried to pump as much fun into his voice as he could, but Levi still wasn't impressed with the new move. It was an extended look at what he'd only glimpsed in the bedroom. The kid's blue eyes darkened. Cold. More offended than angry, but *definitely* angry. "I tell you what, we don't have to play that way, okay? Just put your ball back where it was. No problem. Maybe when you all get a little more practice or something."

It didn't seem to blunt the kid's anger, but they kept playing. Craig dialed back his effort, hoping if he let Levi win, it would smooth things over a bit, but eventually it was Alice who strung together a series of good shots and took the lead.

"WOO-HOO!" she cheered as her green ball knocked against the final stake.

Craig gave her a hug of congratulations, but took the hint as Levi smoldered over the loss. "All right, I'm going to head inside and start lunch."

"Can Alice keep playing until you're done?" Levi asked.

Craig looked over toward his daughter, who was still riding the high of victory. As pissed as Levi had been over the foot shot, Craig figured the kid would have been halfway through the woods by now. But the storm that had crossed his face minutes earlier had apparently blown through. "Do you want to stay and play, Alice, or come inside and help with lunch?"

"I want to stay!" she said. Craig nodded and left them out back. Something tugged at the back of his brain, but he forced himself to ignore it. Levi probably just wanted to win one before he took off. They wouldn't have time for a full game, but he could at least get some shots in before they sent him home. Hopefully that would satisfy him.

Having recently introduced Alice to the glory that was the Fluffernutter, Craig pulled out the bread and headed over to the pantry for peanut butter and marshmallow crème. He noticed a half-empty bag of potato chips on the shelf and grabbed those as well. Not to munch on, but the salty goodness might kick their sandwich game up a notch if nestled between the bread.

He was trying to come up with a clever name for his new recipe when he heard crying in the backyard. Craig ran to the window and saw Alice lying on the ground, howling and cradling her foot.

The chips scattered across the hardwood as he flew out onto the deck and took the steps about four at a time. Alice was still sobbing when he got to her, while Levi stood nearby, croquet mallet in hand, like he was waiting for her to finish up and take her turn.

Craig knelt down and put his arms around her. "What did you do, sweetie? Are you okay?"

Tears were smeared across her bright-red cheeks, and she couldn't stop crying long enough to answer, so Craig looked over at Levi. "What happened?"

The boy stared down at her with an odd curiosity on his face and didn't say anything.

Craig turned back to Alice, wiped the tears from her face, and smoothed the hair off her forehead. "What's wrong, kiddo?"

Alice choked out a few more sobs and finally pulled in enough breath to answer.

"Levi hit me with the hammer."

She immediately started wailing again as Craig looked over at Levi. He hadn't moved. Hadn't reacted. Didn't seem interested in confirming or defending himself, but it sparked the tinder of rage piled up in Craig's gut.

"What did you do?"

The kid shrugged, and it was like a gust of wind across the fire inside.

"Did you hit her with the mallet?" Smoke rose up and engulfed his brain, making clear thinking a challenge. "Levi? Did you hit her?"

Levi held his gaze for a second, still no reaction to his friend crying on the ground. "I did the foot shot you showed me." His tone held no contrition, but instead insinuated that it was *Craig's* fault.

He could have smacked the kid. Part of him wanted to. Grab that mallet out of his hands and go full *Misery* on Levi's ankles.

Luckily for both of them, that red-hot urge dissipated quickly. Craig tossed a bucket of cold water on his anger and turned back to Alice, who was still crying. "Can you show me where it hurts?"

She pointed to the side of her right foot, but since she had shoes and socks on, he couldn't see any swelling. There was no blood or anything, so that was good. The breaks between sobs got longer as Craig ignored Levi and poured his attention on her.

"Let's go inside, okay? Can you stand up?"

Craig pulled Alice to her feet, but she collapsed immediately upon putting weight on it.

"Oh, kiddo . . ." Real worry that this could be more than just a bruise crept in. If she couldn't walk on it, they might need a trip to the emergency room. A fresh wave of anger rolled out toward the kid still looming behind them.

Deep breath.

"Want me to carry you in?"

Alice nodded, and Craig scooped her up into his arms. He hadn't carried her like that since she was a toddler. She'd grown a lot, but still felt so little in his arms. He couldn't comprehend how someone could hurt her.

Craig took a few steps toward the house before glancing back. Levi was still there, watching them like it was a TV show.

He didn't want to say anything, worried he wouldn't be able to hold back if he started, but couldn't take the kid's eyes on them anymore.

"You're gonna need to go home, Levi."

He looked back at them with a look that harbored a bit of confusion. "Can Alice come out after lunch?"

The question was almost too absurd to answer. "No, Levi, you hit my daughter with a freaking croquet mallet." The fact that he'd censored himself enough to just say *freaking* was a miracle. "She's done playing. Go home."

Levi didn't move.

"It was an accident."

The words ignited a back draft from the rage that smoldered inside him, and he practically dropped his daughter spinning back around toward the little punk.

"Bullshit." Craig was well past censoring himself. He was pissed, more at himself than anyone. He'd ignored plenty of red flags and common sense, even let misplaced guilt from his childhood convince him to offer that kid more rope than could be expected, and now here he was, carrying his injured daughter inside.

"It was an accident." Levi didn't look mad; he looked offended and spoke in the slow cadence of a frustrated teacher.

Alice had gone quiet but squirmed in his arms. Craig turned his back on Levi and carried her up the stairs. His daughter—not some bratty little rich kid from through the woods—needed his attention. Levi might be a messed-up boy from a bad situation, but Craig had stopped caring when his daughter started crying.

Levi kept calling after them as Craig carried Alice inside, but they ignored him.

"It was an *accident*."

When Alice couldn't put any weight on her foot an hour later, Craig took her to the doctor. X-rays showed no break, and they diagnosed Alice with periosteal bruising of the fifth metatarsal—a bone bruise. They had no recommendation other than kids' ibuprofen and rest, and sent Alice home with a stiff-soled boot to help keep the pressure off for the next week or so.

Even with the boot on, Alice said it hurt too much to walk and asked Craig to carry her inside from the car. He took her downstairs and put her on the couch with her stuffed bunny, Pete; the remote control; and a squeezer pouch of applesauce. She scrolled through the Disney library as Craig built a little hill of pillows where she could prop up her injured foot.

He glanced out the window and noticed the croquet equipment was still scattered around the backyard. He'd suppressed his anger by concentrating on Alice while they were at the hospital, but seeing those mallets brought it right back.

Deep breath. Calm comes in, anger goes out.

"You comfy for a bit?" Craig had to ask a second time for Alice to tear enough attention away from her movie options for a nod. "Okay, then. I'm going to go put away the croquet stuff. I'll be back in just a little bit if you need anything, okay?"

She'd already started *Moana*, so he kissed the top of her head and walked toward the basement's sliding glass door. His hand was on the handle when Alice called after him.

"Can you pick a lily for me?"

A huge row of daylilies lined the back of their house, and after weeks of anticipation, they'd finally started blooming that week. Alice picked an entire bouquet that first morning, so Courtney had to put a one-bloom-per-day limit on her. She'd dug up an old crystal vase so they could keep it on the table while they ate dinner, and Alice took her selection *very* seriously.

Maybe he'd pick two that day. One for the table and one to keep downstairs with her.

"Sure, kiddo."

"One of the yellow ones, please."

Craig couldn't hold back a smile. "No problem."

He reached for the door handle and saw it was unlocked. With all that had happened that afternoon, it wasn't surprising they'd forgotten to lock it again before heading to the hospital. Unfortunately, that was hardly the first time it had happened. He'd repeatedly reminded Alice to lock the door behind herself, but she'd often come back inside through the patio door above and forget about the one down here. There had been times Craig found it unlocked and suspected it had been that way for days, unnoticed. He tried to check it every night before heading up to bed, but sometimes forgot.

Someone could easily clean out their entire basement while they slept upstairs, oblivious.

He didn't bother reminding Alice—he'd do it later. The poor kid had enough going on with her foot in a boot.

Craig headed outside and pulled the rack alongside himself as he pulled the wire wickets from the ground and scooped up the croquet balls. Four of the six mallets were lined up in the rack, and another lay in the middle of the yard. He slid it into its spot and looked around for the last one.

The yard was empty.

He looked around the swing set, around the trees: nothing. He headed back under the deck and checked the plastic box that held their backyard stuff, but didn't see it. It wasn't nestled in the flowers and bushes that lined the back of their house, or under the deck steps.

Craig looked toward the woods, trying and failing to keep his suspicions from creeping in.

—

Craig had texted Courtney from the doctor's office, letting her know what had happened and keeping her up to date on the prognosis. When she got home from work just before dinner, she had a pint of cookie-dough ice cream with her.

"They say ice cream is good for bone bruises."

Alice told her mom all about her hospital visit during dinner, from the nice nurse with the Dory pin on her ID badge to the games she got to play on Dad's phone while they waited for the x-ray tech to come back with pictures where you could see her *real bones*!

When they finished up, Courtney took Alice upstairs to help her navigate a bath with only one good leg while Craig stayed down and cleaned the kitchen.

After the bath, Courtney helped her into pajamas, and they dosed her with ibuprofen and ice cream before taking her back upstairs for books and bedtime.

Craig was topping off the cat's water bowl when Courtney came back down.

"What the hell happened?" The light tone she'd used with Alice all evening was gone.

"We were playing—the three of us—and I showed them that foot-shot thing where you step on the ball and send the one next to it flying, right? Anyway, we finish the game and I go inside to make lunch, but they wanted to keep playing. So I'm in the kitchen, and all of a sudden Alice is screaming. I run out, and she says Levi hit her with the mallet. He *said* he was just trying the foot-shot thing."

Courtney thought it through, but he could tell she was dubious. "You believe him?"

Craig paused, the sound of Levi yelling that it had been an accident echoing through his head.

"Ugh . . . I mean . . ." He'd asked Alice about it while they were waiting at the hospital, and she said she'd had her foot on the ball when Levi took a swing. Was it possible? Sure. But Craig didn't believe him. Didn't want to. "I guess it could be, but . . . I don't know."

Courtney looked at him for more, but he didn't have any answers. Eventually she shrugged and picked up a stack of bills from the counter. "Either way, that puts an end to mornings with Levi of the Forest."

"Yeah . . . I mean . . ." As pissed as he'd been, Craig hadn't really thought of the ramifications this would have on his writing time. For all his creepy faults, Levi had been the key to getting work done.

Courtney jumped on his hesitation. "You can't let her be out there with him after this. You know that, right?"

"Of course I know that . . . I'm just thinking about how I'm going to finish this book." He gave the counter a wipe and threw the rag into the sink. "That little *fucker*."

"What are you going to do?" Courtney's voice was softer. She might not be able to read Craig's mind, but she knew his body language.

"I don't know." He counted the days on his mental calendar and let out a long breath. He hadn't done anything that day, and barely anything the day before. Days wasted, his meeting that much closer, and now his quiet mornings were gone. "I'll figure something out."

"Like I said, if you want to use the office—"

"I told you I can't work at night." His voice was quick and tart, and Craig tried to pull it back. She was offering help in a shitty situation and didn't deserve to get snapped at.

Besides, it wasn't Courtney he was mad at.

"Sorry."

"What if we hired a babysitter?" Courtney offered. "Someone to come a couple times a week and give you some time to write?"

"Who are we gonna get?" Craig's tone was still more dismissive than he'd wanted. "Kaitlin is working at the coffee shop, and we don't know anyone else."

"I could ask around at work."

"No, I just . . ." He wasn't sure where he was going or why he was even resisting at this point. "I'm not going to be a stay-at-home dad who has to hire a nanny. How would that look?"

She shrugged. "I'm just trying to help you out here."

"I know, but . . ."

"But what?" Courtney said.

Craig didn't know what to say. There was too much fear and frustration bubbling through him to take her thoughts for what they were. He was so close to grabbing his dream, but it was like trying to hold on to a fistful of sand.

He exhaled again, trying to expel whatever emotions had led to his current predicament.

"Nothing."

Chapter Fifteen

Alice's foot was pretty sore the next morning, but she was able to walk on her own. Craig gave it a thorough once-over when he helped strap her boot on. The angry red swelling had doubled from the day before, and massive splotches of purple had bloomed overnight.

"You want to hang out downstairs this morning?"

Alice nodded around a mouthful of cereal. "Can I watch TV?"

"Sure," he said. "Maybe you can bring your art box down and do some stuff on the coffee table while you watch? You could make Mom something really cool for her office? I bet she'd like that a lot."

The idea was a bit of an apology, but also a way to show Courtney their daughter wasn't just sitting around all day watching movies. With everything that had been going on in their lives lately, Craig knew he had some serious making up to do. If Alice's foot allowed it, maybe they'd go to the grocery store that afternoon so he could make something halfway decent for dinner.

After Alice polished off her Rice Krispies and they split a banana, Craig got her set up downstairs with everything she'd need for a quiet—and, more importantly, self-sufficient—morning. Construction paper, glue, glitter, markers, and a couple of sheets of newspaper to cover the Pottery Barn coffee table Courtney had picked out right after they'd moved in.

"Here's the remote," Craig said. She was snuggled into the corner of the couch and had an old water bottle with apple juice in it to prevent any potential spills. "Anything else you think you will need?"

Alice shook her head, already scrolling through her movie options.

"Okay, I'm going to go upstairs and work on my book. If you need anything, just holler."

She nodded, and Craig almost made it to the stairs before she spoke. "Can you get Pete?"

He chuckled to himself and ran up to the kitchen. Pete was sitting in his usual breakfast spot on the corner buffet. Craig snatched him up and carried him downstairs.

He tossed the bunny to Alice, who gave the old toy a hug and snuggled farther back into the couch. Her injured foot stuck out from her blanket, propped up on one of the couch's throw pillows.

"You have everything you need now?" Craig asked, but her attention had already been commandeered by the television. "I'll come check on you when I'm done writing, and we'll have lunch. Sound good?"

He went back to the kitchen to make himself a second cup of coffee. If his writing time was going to be less frequent and less quiet, he needed to take total advantage of Alice being laid up for the next few days. Hopefully a little extra caffeine would be like a nitro boost for him.

Craig grabbed the mug he'd used earlier and was turning toward the coffee machine when something snagged the corner of his eye through the sliding patio door.

Levi was standing there, hands shading his eyes with his face pressed against the glass. The kid wore jeans even though it was summertime, and clumps of burrs he'd picked up traipsing through the woods were scattered across the denim.

The embers of yesterday's anger glowed with fresh oxygen, threatening to ignite again. Craig took a couple of deep breaths before he opened the door.

"Alice can't play, Levi."

The boy looked up at him like he'd said nothing and made no move to leave. "Tell her I want to play out back."

Craig tossed a handful of dirt on the anger that sparked in his gut.

"Her foot is hurt pretty bad, so it will probably be a while before she can play outside." The little shit hadn't shown any remorse for what he'd done, so Craig felt the need to make him understand the consequences of his carelessness. Somebody had to. "I had to take her to the doctor yesterday, and they had to do some x-rays because they thought her foot was broken. Now she has to wear a big boot on her leg until it gets better. Unfortunately—because of that—she won't be able to play for a while."

Craig laid it on thick because subtlety was usually wasted on children. And if he was honest, the kid was lucky a guilt trip was all he was getting.

"But I didn't do it on purpose."

Craig didn't know what kind of response he'd expected, but that wasn't it. It was like he thought Craig was holding Alice back as some sort of punishment. "Well, she still can't come outside and play."

Levi's eyes darkened. "I didn't do it on purpose."

His voice dripped with frustration born of privilege. The kind that comes from kids who say *I don't get in trouble* when you find them in your house uninvited. Craig felt the pressure build inside and took a deep breath in hopes of releasing it before something regrettable happened.

"You almost broke her foot, Levi, so it honestly doesn't matter if you did it on purpose or not." Craig had to remind himself he was the adult in this situation, and under no obligation to explain himself to some punk kid from Deer Ridge. He slid the door closed, but Levi didn't move when it passed just inches from his nose. Craig looked down at him through the glass, and the kid met his eyes. He held his gaze for a second, then turned back into the kitchen with a half shrug.

He returned to the coffee machine and hit the button. Second coffee of the morning in hand, Craig headed to the office.

Levi was still on their deck, nose an inch from the glass, staring into their kitchen.

He didn't want to engage, to escalate, so Craig waved his hand like he was shooing away a fly and raised his voice so it would make it through the glass across the kitchen. "Go home, Levi."

The kid stared daggers into their house and didn't move.

"What did you say, Daddy?" Alice's voice floated up from downstairs.

Craig turned away from the sliding glass door and leaned down the stairway. "Nothing, honey. Just . . ." He looked back at Levi. "Just talking to myself."

He didn't react to what Craig had said, but he'd certainly heard him.

Craig had wanted to be a good example for the kid, but maybe that meant being the only person to show him consequences. At some point Levi needed to learn that he couldn't bully his way into their lives whenever he wanted.

He turned his back on the deck and headed to the office without another acknowledgment.

If Levi wanted to stand out there all day, that was his problem.

Craig's leg was bouncing under the desk in time with the blinking cursor. He'd sat there for the last ten minutes, waiting for inspiration, but his focus was all over the place. His brain was like a streetlight that had attracted a swarm of moths, flittering around his head in a haphazard cloud, bouncing off each other, obscuring any light with random shadows.

He wanted to blame the caffeine, and certainly that second cup of coffee wasn't helping, but the real problem was probably still standing out on their deck.

The urge to check was there. Had been there since he'd sat down to write, but Craig fought it. Didn't want to give the kid the attention he obviously craved.

Don't play his game. Ignore him, and he will go away. Besides, he didn't need to poke his head into the kitchen to look out onto the deck. He knew Levi was still there. He could feel it, like a dark cloud creeping over the horizon, promising a storm.

Craig ran his hand through his hair and squeezed the back of his neck.

Get. To. Work.

He shook those festering thoughts out of his head and put his fingers on the keys. Words didn't come, but he wouldn't let Levi cost him another day of writing. He jammed a finger down his literary gullet and typed whatever he vomited up. It wasn't good—none of it would survive the first round of edits—but at some point he just had to prove to himself he could do it. Roll that boulder up the hill.

So he typed. Enough that he finally stopped thinking about the kid on his deck.

Eventually he stopped. He didn't check his word count—he needed to be satisfied with the fact that he'd gotten something down—and pushed away from the desk. The turntable stood still on its pedestal, and Craig realized he hadn't put any music on when he'd sat down.

That was probably the problem.

He chuckled at his own delusional joke and headed to the basement stairs. The sound of a *Toy Story* movie murmured in the background as he snuck down to peek at Alice.

She was cozied up to the coffee table, diligently working on an elaborate poster while humming what sounded like "I Am the Walrus." He could picture the tip of her tongue sneaking out the corner of her mouth as she concentrated, and it temporarily filled him with warmth.

At least somebody was getting some quality work done.

Craig snuck back up to the kitchen, not wanting to disturb his little artist. He glanced at the clock and saw it was already 11:00 a.m. Alice had done her part. Stuck inside, she hadn't made a peep for two and a half hours.

A glimmer of optimism popped up as he grabbed a glass out of the cupboard, but was immediately snuffed out when he saw Levi sitting on one of the swings in the backyard. He wasn't pumping his legs or actually swinging back and forth; he just sat, with whatever slight sway the breeze gave him, staring at the house.

So much for ignoring him.

Craig looked out at the boy and tried to shake away the similarities his subconscious kept trying to push on him. Even with that light, shaggy hair and scrawny build, he was nothing like Jacob.

He does look like him, though.

Appearance aside, Levi was proving himself to be much more than a lonely kid who just wanted someone to spend time with. Intentionally or not, he'd almost broken Alice's foot, and Craig wasn't going to be guilted into letting a kid like that hang around his daughter.

Maybe Levi needed some help, but Alice needed to be his priority.

He abandoned the glass on the counter and headed out onto the deck. Levi heard the sliding glass door open and tracked Craig down the wooden stairway to the backyard.

Craig spoke as soon as he hit the grass. "What are you doing here, Levi?"

He didn't answer. Craig continued across the backyard.

"You need to head home, okay? You can't be back here by yourself."

"Why?" Levi's voice was flat but defiant. As if Craig needed a reason to keep someone else's kid off his property.

"Because I said you can't."

"You're not the boss of me."

The kid spoke with the immature assumption of impunity, and it drove a needle into the back of Craig's brain. It wasn't like his own parents had been super strict in raising him, but he couldn't imagine copping that kind of attitude with an adult when he was a kid.

He waited two full breaths before responding. "Maybe not, but this is my property, and I am the boss of *it*, so I get to say who is allowed to be here. Go home, Levi."

The boy didn't move, just let his gaze slide back to the house. Craig glanced back and saw Alice still at the coffee table inside, working on her picture—oblivious to the fact that her friend was sitting out back, refusing to leave. He suddenly remembered his conversation with Dan.

Had Levi been out here watching Alice all morning?

The thought evaporated whatever patience he had left. "All right, I'm serious. Time to go." Craig reached over and grabbed the chain to stop the swing's gentle sway, but Levi jolted like he'd been tased.

"Don't fucking touch me!"

The outburst echoed off the trees behind them and around the yard. Craig instinctively jerked his hand back like he'd touched the stove.

"I didn't . . ." Adrenaline poured into his veins. He lurched away and banged the back of his head into the play set. Jagged stars danced before his eyes as he pressed them shut against the pain.

He pried them open to see Levi hop from the swing and stand defiantly in front of him. The kid's voice seemed to keep bouncing around the woods, and Craig scanned the neighboring houses, praying nobody had heard. He hadn't laid a finger on the kid, but if it came down to his word against Levi's, there was little doubt where the belief would lie.

Levi looked up at him as he rubbed the back of his head, then turned away before Craig got his words together. One step into the woods, Levi turned back toward the yard and stared.

Craig waited for whatever obnoxious last word Levi wanted to get in, but the kid just stood there until he broke the silence.

"Go on, now." Craig waved his hand like he was shooing a dog, but got nothing but a smarmy smirk in return.

"You don't own the woods."

Another wave of frustration replaced the pain in the back of his head, and Craig snapped his mouth shut before he responded. Levi was obviously trying to provoke him at this point, and he refused to take the bait.

Besides, the kid was right. Their property ended at the tree line. If Levi wanted to stand out in the woods all day, there wasn't much Craig could do to stop him, so he let out a breath of frustration and turned back toward his house.

He climbed the deck steps and took one last look over his shoulder before opening the patio door, and Levi was still there.

Craig walked back in and went straight downstairs. Alice looked up from her project with a smile made of sunshine and sprinkles. "Hi, Daddy! Want to see the picture I made?"

He smiled back and walked behind the couch toward the big picture window. Craig gave the cord a quick yank and lowered the blinds on Levi, who was still staring from the woods.

"You bet I do, kiddo."

Chapter Sixteen

Alice was more comfortable getting around with her boot the next day, but Craig still set her up in the basement after breakfast. Some juice and a snack so she wouldn't need to navigate the stairs, the remote and some pillows if she wanted to relax, a card table set up by the couch in case she wanted to put together a puzzle, and Pete the Bunny to keep her company.

"Why are you closing the windows?"

There were three windows on that side of the basement, and those blinds had been closed since the day before, so Alice hadn't noticed anything different there. But they never pulled the blinds across the sliding glass door, so Craig couldn't be shocked when Alice asked.

"It helps with the glare on the TV." It was a lame excuse, but he couldn't tell her he was creeped out about her friend potentially spying on them. Luckily she was still at the age where her father's word was gospel.

He pushed one of the hanging strips of plastic aside and peered into the backyard. The swings were empty, and nobody was lurking in the trees.

Maybe Levi had taken the hint yesterday.

Craig let the blind swing back into place and turned his attention to his daughter. "You good if I go upstairs and get some work done?"

"Uh-huh." She'd already queued up *Moana*.

"Didn't you just watch that one?"

"Yeah, but I like it."

Craig shrugged and kissed the top of her head.

"Okay, I'll be in the office."

His eyes swept over the windows as he turned toward the stairs. The horizontal slats let just a little bit of the morning sun bleed through.

Was there enough space to peek through? With the blinds shut like that, someone could sneak right up to the window without being seen.

Craig fought the urge to check the backyard again. He'd just looked, and nobody was there, but still . . . it wouldn't go away.

He forced himself up the stairs, only to have his growing paranoia follow him into the kitchen. He'd already had his cup of coffee for the day, and a second one would certainly not help his nerves.

But he could use a cup of water. The window over the sink looked out on the backyard, so he took a quick glance while he was filling his glass—just to put his mind at ease before sitting down for a much-needed productive morning.

The yard was empty.

Craig laughed at himself, not sure what he'd expected. Levi had talked tough yesterday, but what else did he expect the kid to do? He was saving face, but certainly wouldn't be coming down again today after that.

No, they wouldn't be seeing him for a while.

He left the backyard behind and went straight to the office, embarrassed at his paranoia but determined to get his head right and get some writing done.

Just as Craig rolled up to the desk, the doorbell rang. He froze, telling himself the nerves that bloomed at the sound were simply annoyance. He waited at the desk, not wanting to leave the sanctity of his office. He dreaded the sound of the second ring. Levi would probably stand out there ringing that bell all day if he didn't do something. The notion annoyed Craig and turned those initial nerves to anger. He could go answer the door and take care of it right then, but he sat and stewed.

The house remained silent.

Eventually the grumble of an engine he hadn't noticed before kicked up. Craig peeked out the window and saw the UPS truck pull away from the curb out front.

He shook his head in embarrassment and watched the brown delivery truck rumble down the street, where it led his eyes to a kid scootering down the sidewalk.

Levi kicked his way down their cul-de-sac, then glided around the circle. But instead of heading back up the block, the kid cut across the street and circled back in front of their house.

Craig ducked back from the window as Levi cruised by, then looped around again.

He watched him make a third lap around the cul-de-sac.

Levi's face was serene and balanced. He just rolled along the sidewalk, occasionally kicking to keep up his speed. Never looked at the house.

Craig wanted to ignore him, to get back to work.

Fourth loop.

What was he even doing on their street? If the kid wanted to scooter, he had a giant neighborhood with better sidewalks and plenty of room.

Because he'd come down here for a reason. To mess with them.

Craig wanted to go out and tell him off, but that would just make things worse. Levi had already pulled the I'm-not-on-your-property card the day before, and sidewalks were public. As long as he stayed off the grass, there wasn't anything Craig could do.

Lap five.

He yanked the cord much harder than necessary and sent the blinds crashing down over the window. Craig slumped into his chair and stared at the screen in front of him, mind still tracking the circles Levi was making out front. He forced himself to type something.

—

I hate that little fucker.

—

Not exactly constructive.

Craig backspaced over his childish frustration and tried to clear his head for something worthwhile. After a minute, he scooted back to the window and raised the blinds.

Still scootering. Still not looking at the house.

If the kid wanted to mess with him, mission accomplished.

Craig didn't tell Courtney about Levi scootering around out front all morning, because he didn't want to seem like a paranoid nutjob. Hell, if somebody told him they couldn't do their work because a kid was hanging outside their house, he'd have told them to just ignore it too. So, when asked how his day went, he said "fine" and moved on.

Whether she believed him or not was hard to tell. She'd quit asking him about his book, instead concentrating on how Alice was doing. She was still in the walking boot, but her limp was almost gone. Craig figured she'd be back to her normal routine soon enough.

Which meant he had to get his ass in gear, even if the pressure was keeping him up at night. He'd toss and turn, spending the stretching hours in the dark kicking around ideas to get his book back on track. He didn't come up with much, partly because Levi was on his scooter, circling his thoughts the entire time.

Craig eventually faded off, but not before his bedside clock had left 2:00 a.m. well behind.

He woke up exhausted and downed two cups of coffee in short order.

Craig stifled a yawn. As he picked up Alice's plate from the table, something caught his eye out back. Craig flipped the lock on the patio door and opened it only about six inches before he stopped. Felix rubbed past his leg, and Craig pulled the door closed before the cat could escape.

He stood there, hand on the door, and gave himself a mental slap across the face. Today was a workday, and he'd piddled around long enough.

There were a million things he could have seen back there. And even if it was Levi, who gave a shit? What the hell was Craig afraid the kid was going to do?

A slow thudding came from the deck stairs. Craig stood frozen as Levi's head peeked over the railing, a determined smirk on his face as he dragged a worn croquet mallet behind himself. He picked it up as he got to the deck, old blood stained maroon on the rounded ends.

"I don't get in trouble."

Craig snapped out of his daydream hard enough his forehead banged against the sliding glass door. His heart was pounding out a drum solo on his ribs as he tried to get control of his breathing.

"You okay, Daddy?"

Alice's voice sent another jolt through him, but brought him back to the real world. "Yeah, fine."

"What are you looking at?"

He forced something he hoped was a smile. "Thought I saw something, that's all. A deer."

She accepted his lie and hobbled over to the craft drawer to get some markers. Craig rubbed his temples as Alice found what she was looking for and headed back downstairs.

He had to pull himself together. This stuff with Levi had thrown him off course, and he was running out of time to grab the reins and yank himself back on track.

If he really wanted to be a writer, he had to have the ability to buckle down and get shit done. To that end, he turned away from the door and grabbed a third cup of coffee before heading to the office.

He needed some rocket fuel.

Shades drawn, Wi-Fi shut off, and music loud, Craig got to work.

Progress was slow but relatively steady for the first hour. And the stuff he was getting down wasn't half bad. Or at least it wasn't in comparison with the crap he'd been generating lately.

The extra caffeine seemed to sharpen his thoughts, allowing words to flow faster, and he felt himself getting that tunnel vision that came when he really got going.

At some point the sound of footsteps from somewhere outside that tunnel filtered in through the music around him.

Ignore it. Don't stop.

Craig shook the distraction out of his head and kept typing.

A few minutes later something rattled in the kitchen.

Keep going.

Alice was probably digging through the pantry for a snack, without asking him first—exactly what he'd told her to do if she got hungry.

He pictured her standing with her one good leg on one of the kitchen chairs, straining for something on the top shelf of the pantry. With the luck they'd been having, she'd end up toppling off and getting hurt again.

Shit.

He pushed away from the desk and lifted the needle from his record. It was fine. He could go help her reach whatever she needed and get right back to it.

"Watcha looking for, Alice?"

The words echoed around the first floor of their house and came back without a response. Craig made his way to the kitchen, which was empty. All the chairs were around the table, and the pantry door stood open, showing no kid inside digging for fruit snacks.

He poked his head down the stairs and heard the faint Scottish murmur of *Brave*. "Alice?"

"Yeah, Dad?"

He went down the stairs and saw Alice propped up in the corner of the couch, playing a math game on Courtney's tablet.

"Were you looking for something in the kitchen?"

"No."

She looked pretty well settled on the couch, and Craig noticed her injured foot sticking out the end of her blanket. "You take your boot off?"

"Just while I'm on the couch," Alice said. "You said that was okay, remember?"

"No, yeah . . . it's fine."

Craig started back up the stairs, trying to make sense of the sounds he'd heard. He stopped halfway up. "Is Felix down here?"

"He's napping."

Craig craned his neck back and saw their cat curled up in his bed in front of the fireplace.

Must have just been hearing things.

He got to the top of the stairs when Alice called up again. "Can you get Pete for me?"

Craig looked over at the buffet but didn't see her bunny in his usual spot and called down the steps. "Where's he at?"

Alice's tablet-distracted voice floated up from the basement.

"On the table."

Craig walked around the kitchen table to the corner buffet. Pete wasn't among the piles of coloring books and junk mail that had yet to find its way to the recycling bin. He looked back between the buffet and the wall, then got on his hands and knees to peek underneath.

No bunny.

Ugh.

Craig scanned around the kitchen, but didn't see the threadbare stuffie anywhere, so he hollered down the steps again.

"You sure you didn't bring him down there? Maybe he's mixed up in your blanket or something?"

"No, he's on the buffet."

"Sorry, kiddo, he isn't there." Craig didn't want to waste time yelling back and forth down the stairs. "If he isn't with you, maybe you didn't bring him down this morning."

"Will you go up and check? I don't have my boot on."

Craig felt the flow he'd been typing in slipping away. He couldn't waste his time tearing the house apart for a stuffed bunny. If she needed him that badly, she could look herself. At some point she needed to walk on her foot anyway. "Sorry, but I've got to get back to work. If you want to put your boot back on and go check, you can do that. If not, we can look for Pete later."

She started to protest, but Craig was already halfway to the office. If she couldn't find him herself, it wouldn't kill her to be without her favorite stuffed animal for an hour or so.

"It's gonna be a loooong night."

Courtney had been in Alice's room for the last half hour, lying with her and trying to calm her down. Their daughter hadn't slept without her bunny since she'd graduated from her crib years ago. There had been plenty of nights, mostly when she was a toddler, when they'd spent what felt like hours before bedtime searching for that bunny. Alice would wait patiently in her bed while Craig and Courtney tore the house apart, only to find him mixed in with random couch cushions or down in some basement corner.

But that night, no matter how much they looked, Pete was nowhere to be found.

"She *is* seven years old." Craig spit toothpaste foam into the sink. "Maybe it's time she figures out how to get to sleep without a stuffed bunny."

"You want to explain that to her?"

"No, I know, it's just . . . if we had a nickel for every minute we've spent looking for that bunny."

"We'd be able to buy a million bunnies," Courtney said. "You know what we should have done . . . once we realized how important Pete was? We should've gone out and bought half a dozen more. We could have rotated them every night so they all got 'loved in' at the same rate. We'd have never had to tear the house up again. Can't find him? Go to the Pete box and grab another."

Craig chuckled at the idea. "Until she finds our stash of Petes and is traumatized for life."

"She'll be talking to her therapist in twenty years . . . *and I opened my parents' drawer, and there were six identical bunnies. I didn't know what was real anymore.*" Courtney pulled her hair back and started rubbing a glop of cream on her forehead. "But, seriously, I hope she gets to sleep sometime soon. Can you think of anywhere you may have seen Pete today?"

Craig had already wrung his brain out, searching for any fleeting memory of Pete stuck in a strange place that morning, but found nothing. "Nope. I thought she had him at breakfast, but who knows. You know tomorrow morning we're going to go downstairs and she'll find him right away in some obvious place we missed."

"She asked me if somebody stole it."

"Yeah. They broke in *Ocean's Eleven*–style, left all the money and computers and phones, but took the rattiest stuffed bunny on the planet."

They both finished their bedtime routines and moved to the bed.

"How was writing today?" Courtney asked.

"I got some stuff down."

"Well, I've got to go in to work for a while tomorrow, so you'll have a nice, quiet Saturday morning if you want to write." Courtney pulled back the covers and sat down. She grabbed a two-week-old copy of the *New Yorker* from the nightstand. "Have you seen anything of Levi since the croquet incident?"

Craig didn't know why he hadn't told Courtney about the backyard. The cul-de-sac.

The vision of him climbing up their deck with a bloody mallet.

He hadn't told her because he didn't want her to think her husband was cracking.

But he also didn't want to lie to her. Luckily, a voice came in from the hall.

"Mommy . . ."

Courtney dropped her head in defeat and swung her legs out of bed.

Chapter Seventeen

Courtney was right. It was a long night, but not because of the missing bunny. She'd been able to calm Alice down enough she eventually fell asleep.

Craig, however, didn't.

He tried counting sheep backward from one hundred, imagining himself sinking into sand, and slowing his breathing, but the harder he tried, the further out of reach sleep seemed to be. His book kept creeping into his thoughts, reminding him of the lack of progress he'd had the last few days and promising that futility would continue in perpetuity.

Insomnia fed his anxiety and welcomed thoughts from the most paranoid corners of his brain.

And on those conspiratorial edges of reason, he found Levi.

Spying on him from the woods.

Telling his parents that Craig had kicked him out of their yard.

Hitting Alice with that mallet.

Craig tossed and turned long enough to see midnight turn to one, then felt the dark stretch into two before eventually turning his clock toward the wall. He might have drifted off once or twice for a minute, but time blurred so much it was hard to tell if he'd gotten any real sleep. Finally, Courtney's alarm went off and started their day.

The day went about as well as the night had.

Craig's insistence that Pete would magically appear in the morning had been an optimistic fantasy, and Alice was adamant they restart the search for him the second she woke.

They rechecked all the obvious places—behind the kitchen buffet, around the couch in the basement, under her bed—and came up as empty as the night before, so Craig started expanding his search. Maybe she'd taken him into the bathroom. Maybe she'd plopped him on a shelf in the pantry when she grabbed her breakfast cereal. Maybe she'd gotten him mixed up with the laundry.

But the bunny didn't show up no matter how many random places they looked, and after an hour Craig had used up the little patience he'd been given for that day.

"It's almost nine," Craig said. "We need to go have breakfast."

"Not until we find Pete."

"No, Alice, you've got to get something to eat." Craig stifled a yawn. He needed caffeine. "He'll turn up eventually, but we can't just keep looking in the same places all day. Eventually we need to move on."

"But I need Pete."

"You don't *need* Pete." It was louder and snappier than he'd wanted, and he could feel the hot spring of frustration bubbling much closer to the surface than he liked. Alice heard it, too, because tears lined the bottoms of her eyes.

Guilt poured over him, and Craig knelt down to give her a hug. The poor kid had already limped around every square inch of their house on a bad foot, trying to find the most important thing in the world to her, and come up empty. Having a dad tell her it wasn't important probably didn't help. "Sorry, Alice. I know Pete is super important, but we've looked everywhere we can think of and haven't found him yet, so let's take a break and get something to eat. If you want to keep looking after that, fine. Maybe if we take a step back for breakfast, you'll remember where he is?"

He purposely didn't promise to help her look. Whether she'd noticed that or not, Alice started up toward the kitchen.

Breakfast was mostly silent because Alice wasn't talking and barely touched her cereal. Craig drank a cup of coffee, then made a second without debate.

"Can we keep looking for Pete?"

"I've got to do some writing," Craig said. "But if you want to keep looking, go ahead. But maybe it would be good to take a break—for a bit at least. If you want to watch a movie or something, that's okay."

Craig eventually retreated to his office, even though he knew it would be fruitless. Another wasted day, staring at a blank page. He could hear Alice thumping around the house in her boot, unwilling to admit defeat, and it brought back memories of the footsteps he'd dismissed yesterday.

She asked if somebody stole it.

Craig shook his irrational accusations of Levi out of his head. The kid wasn't responsible for everything bad that happened. Pete would turn up eventually, like he always did.

Alice's footsteps came back and headed up the staircase. Soon they filtered down through the ceiling above him.

He's been in the house before.

Craig slammed his laptop shut and pushed away from the desk. The lack of sleep was messing with his head. He got up to leave and realized that, once again, he hadn't even put on a record. His subconscious must have known there would be no writing that day.

The calendar caught his eye as he sulked out of the office.

Nineteen days.

CHAPTER EIGHTEEN

By the end of the next week, Alice was begging to take off her boot. There was no structural damage, so Craig figured if she felt good enough to walk around without it, he wasn't going to stop her. Hanging out on the couch had apparently gotten old, and she was itching to play outside again.

He wanted to spend time with her, but hadn't taken advantage of the relative quiet of the last few days, and his lack of productivity was backing him into a corner. MinnLit was thirteen days away. Craig still couldn't concentrate, but it wasn't just when he was staring at his computer. His anxiety was creeping up into the red zone, and it was shortening his temper.

The lack of sleep certainly wasn't helping.

Pete had been missing for a week, and their inability to find him was a sliver in his skin that he couldn't dig out. Bedtime was a challenge because it always reminded Alice of his absence, but once they calmed her down, she'd fall asleep without him.

Craig was a different story. He had spent hours staring at the ceiling, intermittently checking his alarm clock to figure how much sleep he could get if he fell asleep right then.

It was never enough, and it shortened every time he looked.

In the morning, he'd down a second cup of coffee, then a third, in an attempt to function, not thinking about how the extra caffeine would affect him that night. He'd become a hamster stuck in his wheel, seemingly powerless to get off. Every second he sat in front of a blank screen just added to his anxiety.

His meeting with Jennifer DiAmato loomed on the calendar, lumbering toward him with the determined walk of a masked slasher. Any hope of finishing up the first draft and doing a full editing pass had already been tracked down and gutted, left to bleed out on the ground. He was in survival mode, desperately hoping to cobble *something* together to show her.

Yet every time he sat down, he was paralyzed. And his anxiety was putting on as many different hats as it could find. Little things annoyed him more. Minor infractions fed his anger, and he had increasing trouble letting them go. Molehills became mountains that derailed his day.

And often the one standing at the summit was Levi.

He hadn't returned to their door or peered through their window—that Craig knew about anyway—but he was becoming a fixture on their block, riding that damn scooter around their cul-de-sac, seemingly begging for a reaction Craig was determined not to give him.

He'd close the office blinds, but that only made him wonder if he was still out there. Better to keep them open so he could see. But even when Levi wasn't out there, Craig would roll over to the window so he could see down the street, waiting for him to coast around the corner.

Sometimes he did, sometimes he didn't. That's when Craig assumed he was out back, creeping around the edge of the woods. Just like when he stayed on the sidewalk, the kid would be sure to not be on their property.

Nothing Craig could do about it.

Something inside him knew it was nothing but paranoia, but that voice was being increasingly drowned out. Logic had no place at the table, and he'd walk back to look out the living room window again.

Craig stared out at the backyard until the logical part of his brain kicked in.

Knock this the fuck off.

He shook his head like it would clear the decks inside his mind. He was stuck in a rut and needed to break the cycle. It was Friday, the start of the weekend. Time to relax, have some fun, and reset his head. As of Monday he'd have ten days to finish his draft. He didn't need a rewrite. He'd explain it was a rough draft, and hopefully she'd be able to get a good feel for where it was going.

That would be enough.

Deep breath. Everything would be fine.

He headed down the basement stairs to Alice's recuperation HQ. "Hey, kiddo . . . want to play outside?"

Her brown eyes sparkled with excitement. Unlimited movie access notwithstanding, she'd been laid up all week and was probably itching to get out in the fresh air and do something fun. It would do them both a lot of good. "Do I have to wear my boot?"

"Not if you don't want to," Craig said. "As long as it doesn't hurt too much."

"Barely at all!" Alice lifted her left knee and balanced on her injured foot. "See?"

Craig smiled, flipped the lock on the basement's sliding glass door, and held it open like a Victorian butler. Alice giggled and ducked under his extended arm. She still had a slight limp in her gait, but it didn't seem to bother her too much as she jogged over to the swing set.

He'd given her a few big pushes before she stopped giggling.

"Where are all the lilies?"

Craig looked over and saw nothing but bunches of skinny leaves and empty stalks along the back of the house. The daylilies that had added a late-summer explosion of color to the backyard—and their dinner table—were nothing but a row of green.

"I don't know, kid. Something must have come and eaten all the flowers." They had plenty of bunnies around their yard, and they were known to nip off the blooms from time to time, but they'd never gone hog wild like this. Maybe a deer had come through?

He and Alice crossed the yard to examine the flowerless plants. Each one was popped off at the top of the stem, not chewed halfway down like a rabbit would do. Craig felt his suspicion gurgle down low.

"Will they grow back?"

"I don't know." That wasn't true. It was too late in the year for new buds to grow, but he didn't have the heart to tell Alice that. She'd been asking about that row of plants since the spring, and once they started to bloom, she'd been in heaven.

Now they were all ruined. Craig wanted to believe it was some backyard critter that had passed through, but couldn't. Wrecking those plants was petty and juvenile—exactly what a nine-year-old would do.

Alice drifted back toward the swings.

"Come push me, Daddy!"

Craig stared at the plants, throwing water on the anger growing inside him.

"Daddy!"

"Coming, kiddo."

He swallowed what he could and turned back toward his daughter, one eye on the woods behind her.

Craig tilted his head back and drained the last drops of beer. His head remained on the back of the couch as he dropped the can to his lap. The bitter bite had been smoothed over, and his head was encased in a nice, warm glow.

Maybe he'd actually get some sleep that night. Heck, if he had another beer, he might pass out right there on the couch.

Craig leaned forward and plopped the can on the coffee table next to its two empty siblings, then flopped back next to Courtney. She'd picked the movie, which was fine because he hadn't been paying much attention anyway. He was just happy to hang out with his wife on the couch, have a drink or three, and get out of his own head.

But even three tallboy pilsners couldn't completely dull the dark thoughts that fed off his lack of sleep and a creepy neighborhood kid.

Craig glanced over at the big picture window again. The blinds were open. He'd made sure to close them, but Alice must have opened them that afternoon. He felt exposed and wanted to close them but didn't. No reason to draw attention to it. Not a big deal.

The backyard was completely black, no movement, innocent or otherwise. Not even vague shapes at that time of night. He couldn't even see the headless daylilies lined up in the flower bed just below the window.

But Felix was on the edge of the couch, staring out the window.

Craig watched him for a minute, waiting for the cat to stretch his back and curl up to sleep. But Felix just sat there, back legs crouched under him, staring out into the blackness with eyes that shone in the night.

It's nothing. Probably. There's just a squirrel out there or maybe a deer like the one that ate all the lilies because THAT'S what happened to them. Or maybe he doesn't see anything—he's just a stupid cat spacing out, staring out the window. It's nothing. It's nothing. It's nothing. It's nothing. It's—

Craig got up and reached for the blinds.

"What are you doing?" Courtney asked.

"Closing the blinds."

"Why?"

Craig stared out into the backyard as he twisted the rod that brought the blinds together. "I don't know."

Courtney chuffed out a laugh. "You afraid someone's peeping in?"

He looked back without saying anything. Craig had hidden his suspicions from Courtney so far. Which was good, because they were probably crazy.

Were they, though?

Dan had said he'd caught Levi peeping in on Kaylene.

And Craig hadn't told Courtney that either.

He stood there for a second, staring through the slats to find whatever had caught Felix's eye. He was still looking when Courtney changed topics.

"Alice told me about the daylilies. That's a bummer. Stupid rabbits."

Craig pulled himself away and stared at her like she'd read his mind. "Yeah . . . maybe."

"What, do you think it was a deer or something?" She was still watching the movie as much as she was having a conversation.

He eased back onto the couch and stared blankly at the screen, inner monologue having a debate-team-worthy performance about how much he actually wanted to say. Maybe articulating what he'd been feeling would help him straighten his head out a bit.

Or maybe it was the three beers he'd had.

"No, I think Levi did it."

"What?" Her voice had equal amounts of confusion and disbelief.

"I think he tore off the blooms. Every single one, gone."

"Why would he do that?"

"Because he's fucking with me. He's pissed that I won't let him play down here anymore." Craig's voice was louder than he wanted, so he mentally shushed himself.

Courtney grabbed the remote and hit pause on the movie guy's heartfelt speech and left him frozen with his eyes closed like a simp. "Are you serious? You think he'd do that just to fuck with you?"

Yes, but he didn't want to tell her that because he knew how it would sound. She'd think he'd lost it. Unfortunately, his internal clearinghouse had closed for the night, and it was all coming out. "I don't know, but ever since I told him he can't come down anymore, he's been, like, everywhere."

Courtney's eyebrows arched and told him exactly what she thought about that idea. "Then tell him to go home."

"I *did.* But now he's not in the yard but always in the woods or riding that stupid fucking scooter around the cul-de-sac, and I'm afraid if—" The gates holding back all the paranoia he hadn't realized he'd been storing in the back of his head flew open and unleashed a torrent of thoughts he'd hidden away. It wasn't just the peeping and the lilies, but every sound and creepy feeling he'd had. It was Alice's foot and Pete disappearing and the croquet mallet all rolling downhill into a massive ball. He wanted to get it all out and tell her everything, but something in his head pulled him back. A voice of reason, shouting through a haze of alcohol and frustration, telling him to shut the hell up before his wife decided he had completely lost his marbles.

"What?" Courtney sat up and leaned toward him.

"Nothing. Never mind." Craig had never told her about what had happened in sixth grade. He'd buried it deep and paved it over, but ever since Levi had shown up, cracks had formed, and long-repressed emotions had been seeping to the surface. He wanted to tell her, to get it out, yet he was still afraid to open that box and risk all those memories flying out unchecked.

"Don't do that." Courtney reached over and put her hand on his. "Tell me."

Before he realized it, he was telling her about Jacob Westerholt, the weird boy who had lived down the street from him as a kid, product of a dysfunctional and, if the rumors were true, abusive home.

"Mom asked me if I would watch him one afternoon. It wasn't really babysitting, but he was a few years younger than me and not quite old enough to stay home alone. I think Mom felt sorry for him, because I remember her saying I could be a *good influence*, whatever that meant." Craig snatched one of his empties from the table and tried to coax whatever remaining drops were there down his throat. "It wasn't even that bad—we pretty much just played video games for a few hours—but when Andy and Todd heard about it, they kinda let me have it. I don't even know why they cared. He was just an awkward kid, but . . . you know. Then, a few days later, Jacob showed up at my house while the guys were there, so I . . . I kinda told him to get lost."

Guilt bubbled up inside Craig. Even if he couldn't tell Courtney exactly what he'd said to the kid, *he* knew, and there was no taking it back.

"I didn't even mean it, which kinda made it worse. It was just for show, you know? But the look on the kid's face always stuck with me. It wasn't betrayal, really, more acceptance. Like he felt he should have known better. That he deserved it."

Craig kept his eyes straight ahead, afraid to see his wife's reaction.

"Yeah, that's rough, but the fact that you recognize the impact of what you did shows growth and maturity," Courtney said. "Have you ever thought of apologizing?"

"I can't."

"I bet you could find him on Facebook or—"

"He killed himself about a month later."

The movie remained frozen in front of them as the rest of the room came to a screeching halt. He could hear Courtney breathing beside him as she tried to process what he'd said.

"I remember the guidance counselor went class to class to tell everyone. Kid was ten years old." Craig turned back toward Courtney. "I know it wasn't all my fault, but it always felt like it was. All he wanted was a friend, but I was too worried about what everyone else would think to do it. Instead, I piled on."

He felt her hand on his back.

"You ever talk to anybody about it?"

"Nobody did. Kids were joking about it by the end of the week. I think back on it and . . . ugh." Craig dropped his face into his hands and rubbed his eyes until purple swirls came. "It bothered me for a long time. Nightmares, insomnia, all that. Eventually, I buried it. Hadn't thought about him for years, but then Levi showed up and it all came back. Weird skinny kid, shitty parents, same scraggly blond hair . . ."

Courtney reached forward and pulled him back next to her. "You're projecting a lot onto this Levi kid, you know? He isn't Jacob. Besides, you've got an amazing girl of your own who loves you and needs everything you can give her, right?"

Craig nodded, even as he thought of every day he'd kicked her outside to play with Levi so he could write.

"I know you've got a lot of other stress with your deadline and everything, but try not to let it worry you too much." Courtney played with his hair. "Maybe you need to take a break for a bit."

Craig took a deep breath and ground his molars together. He knew what she meant—and she was probably right—but in his fragile state, it came off like a dismissal of all he'd worked on. He'd invested so much mental energy and identity in writing his book, any suggestion that it was nothing more than a glorified hobby cut him deep—intentionally or not.

Courtney kept her arm around him and clicked the movie back on. Craig closed his eyes and tried to let her good intentions push away his petty resentments, but they got lost somewhere in the swirl of alcohol and paranoia sloshing inside his head.

Chapter Nineteen

Craig broke through the surface of sleep into the middle-of-the-night black of their bedroom, gobbling air as if he'd been drowning. His sheets were damp with the sweat of restlessness and alcohol, and his heart thudded out a panicked beat against his sternum.

He tried to blink the darkness away, but a glowing red blob was all he could see. Craig rubbed his fists across his eyes, and the numbers on his alarm clock slowly pulled themselves into focus. He rolled over and propped himself up on his elbow, head still swimming in a fog of sleep and beer. A crust of drool had dried in the corner of his mouth. He wiped it away with the back of his hand.

A drumming hum pounded his ears, blotting out the quiet of the house and sending early notice of the headache that would certainly follow that morning. He tried to listen through the ringing to find whatever had yanked him from the first real sleep he'd had in days, but he couldn't pick up anything.

Something had made a noise, though. A thud or a clatter, Craig couldn't remember. It had drifted into his unconsciousness as an alarm, blaring through whatever boozy dream had been playing inside his mind, shaking him awake with a warning.

Someone was in their house.

Craig focused on listening, searching for any sign of what had kicked the beehive of fear inside him. The silence that came back merely turned up the thrumming in his eardrums.

Courtney's soft, regular breathing beside him indicated she'd heard nothing. The room around them slowly went from pitch black to a dark navy blue as his eyes adjusted. The dresser along the far wall showed its edges and a few blurry lumps of clothes he'd tossed on top of it. The bathroom door across the room was partially open; the edges glowed with the faint bit of moonlight that came down from the skylight inside.

His breath caught when a dark silhouette emerged against the wall behind their bedroom door. Every nerve in his body fired and sent pins and needles down his extremities. Craig stared, afraid to move, afraid to wake Courtney—as if she remained safe as long as she was asleep.

The silhouette didn't move. It loomed, waiting for him to close his eyes again to strike.

It took a few moments for the adrenaline to clear his head and Craig's eyes to adjust enough that he recognized the shape staring at him. It wasn't an intruder intent on harm, waiting for the opportune moment to slash them through their sheets.

It was Courtney's steamer, a blouse hanging from the top.

Craig fell back on his pillow and resumed breathing. Fear seeped from his veins and made room for relief.

And then he definitely heard something.

It could have been one of the dozen random noises that popped up during the night from the furnace or the refrigerator's ice maker or the house settling. Just like the steamer, something completely normal that only seemed sinister in the middle of the night.

He swung his legs out of the bed as quietly as possible. If he didn't check it out—prove to himself it was nothing—he'd obsess about it until dawn.

And maybe it isn't nothing.

Courtney rolled over on her side but remained asleep. He stood up and crept away from the bed. His tongue felt big and sticky in his mouth, but his head was clear. He grabbed a pair of old gym shorts from their laundry basket and pulled them on over his boxer shorts. He still had on the T-shirt he'd worn to bed—the same one he'd worn all day.

The hinge on their bedroom door had a small squeak that sounded like a record scratch with nothing but silence to hide it. He waited, listening back at his sleeping wife and into the hallway beyond before slipping out the door.

The stairway was empty ahead of him, and the hallway night-light cast a small halo along the open walkway that separated their room from Alice's. Craig listened for any noise from the first floor, then slowly snuck toward their daughter's room, doing all he could to keep his footsteps from echoing down through the floor below.

He pressed his ear against the wood of her door and couldn't hear anything over the silence. Craig debated opening it to check on her, but was afraid the knob would make too much noise. Not that he'd wake her up. Like her mother, Alice slept like a fallen log, but he didn't want to scare off Levi before he could catch him red handed.

Did he really think the kid had come into his house in the middle of the night? The thought had hidden out in the back of his brain since he'd woken and was probably the reason he felt brave enough to explore the house. Levi had already shown he had no problem breaking in.

But at 2:00 a.m.?

Craig turned away from the door and looked down over their entryway. A bit of the night-light caught the glass on the chandelier that was suspended in front of him. He listened and scanned the room below but caught no sign of movement.

Had he blown it? Should he have gone straight down to look for him without checking on Alice?

He crept along the rail toward the top of the stairs, where he waited and listened again.

Nothing.

Craig started down the steps, taking them one at a time and stopping on each to listen. He stayed along the side, then peered into the living room. The huge upstairs picture window above the couch let moonlight stream in from the backyard, but it also created a lot of shadows to hide in. The dining room on the other side wasn't as bright, but Craig couldn't find any movement over there either. He stayed low, practically crawling down to the hardwood floor at the bottom of the steps.

He slid around the end of the banister and poked his head behind the love seat.

Nobody there.

He crept to look under the couch across the room, but nothing was back there either.

A thudding clatter from the basement stairs broke the stillness of the house and sent Craig scrambling away until the wall stopped him.

He was staring into the kitchen—frozen against the wall—when Felix flew around the corner into the living room. The cat trotted over to him and offered a glad-to-see-you headbutt, and Craig ran his hand over the fur on its back as a way to calm them both down. He didn't want to admit that for a brief second, he'd thought Levi had broken into their house and was thundering up the stairs toward him.

He listened for anything else in the house, then pushed himself up and padded over toward the stairs.

The stairway extended down into blackness, no sounds or signs of movement, so Craig eased his bare foot onto the top step and waited. He gripped the handrail and kept his footfalls as light as possible on the carpet. The stairway scene from *Pet Sematary* sliced its way into his consciousness—a little boy's hand silently drawing a razor blade across his Achilles tendon. But it wouldn't be a razor here. It would be a croquet mallet. Smashing into his ankle, pulverizing bone, and sending him careening down into the dark below, where he would hit the ground hard only to look up—

I don't get in trouble.

He shook the thoughts from his head, but the stain they left remained.

The blinds on all the windows downstairs were still shut, so the sliding glass door under the deck was the only thing allowing light to slip in. Their television stood dormant in the far corner, surrounded by the sectional couch. The empty beer cans he'd neglected to take upstairs earlier stood on the coffee table.

Craig stood on the last step and waited for Levi to reveal himself. The water softener kicked on back in the utility room around the corner, its rattling drone providing cover to anyone slinking around.

He stepped down into the basement and slipped along the wall. Craig tried to will his pupils wider so he could see into the dark corners of the room and find the kid before he bolted away.

Or jumped out at him, croquet mallet whistling through the air between them.

The water softener stopped, leaving the room in silence again. Craig held his breath, afraid the sound would betray his position. He pushed back into the wall, trying to blend in as he waited.

Nothing happened.

Sweat beaded on his forehead while he stood, pressed against the wall, brain feeding on the fear to produce more fear.

Something brushed against his leg, and Craig leaped away from the wall with a yelp.

Felix jumped back with his spine arched. Even in the dark, Craig could see how puffed up the cat's tail was.

If he'd had any cover, it was now blown. Craig snapped his head around the room, waiting for Levi to burst out from whatever shadow he'd buried himself in.

Nothing happened.

Craig headed toward the opposite end of the basement, where some shelves and a few baskets held a plethora of Alice's toys. A herd of stuffed animals lay piled in a corner. The plastic keys of a toy piano seemed to glow in the dark.

He was heading over to check the utility room when suddenly the recessed bulbs above him snapped on and flooded the basement with light. His eyes clamped shut against the sudden onslaught, and his hands instinctively shot out in front, ready to ward off whatever came for him.

"Craig?"

He spun around toward Courtney's voice, but still couldn't see anything in the torrent of light. Craig put a hand above his eyes and forced them open as much as he could, but his wife wasn't much more than a blur near the light switch on the other side of the room.

"What the hell are you doing down here?"

He tried to blink some clarity into his sight as his eyes slowly adjusted. His wife came into focus near the base of the stairs in striped pajama bottoms and a faded purple T-shirt, her dark hair draped around the sides of her face in an unkempt tousle.

"I . . ." The light also brought a new wave of clarity to his thoughts as he looked around the basement and saw nothing out of the ordinary because of course there wasn't.

What *was* he doing down there?

"I thought I heard someone down here."

The water softener kicked on again as if to provide an answer, and his eyes cleared enough he could see the concern on Courtney's face as she glanced around the room. "Well, I don't see anybody. Let's go back to bed."

She either was too tired to keep the disdain from her voice or figured the middle of the night wasn't the time to hide it.

"Hold on . . ."

Courtney spun back to him. "What?"

The door to the utility room was ajar. Aside from the furnace and water heater, they'd piled all kinds of things back there. Old toys, holiday decorations, boxes they hadn't even opened from the move.

There were a million places to hide. If he *had* heard something, and wasn't just a paranoid lunatic, Levi could have easily slipped back there and nestled himself between Alice's old baby clothes and the water heater, waiting for them to go back to bed so he could slip out the patio door.

Or worse.

"Come on." Courtney turned toward the stairs.

Craig stared at the utility room, telling himself to forget it and go upstairs. Who knew what Courtney thought, finding him down here in the dark? He stepped toward the door.

"What are you doing?"

He didn't want to answer, mostly because he didn't have an answer that made him sound like anything but a paranoid whack job.

"Come on," Courtney said.

"I just . . ." He couldn't resist the pull anymore. Craig pushed open the door and snapped the light on.

Nothing but boxes and heating equipment. He looked in every corner, behind whatever he saw, but found nothing that didn't belong.

Craig turned back to the living room and jumped when he saw Courtney standing in the doorway.

"What the hell is going on?" The sleep was scrubbed from her voice and replaced with the annoyance of someone pulled out of bed in the middle of the night.

"I just wanted to check the water heater. If it's making weird noises, we may need to call someone."

The annoyance on Courtney's face faded into genuine concern. "Are you okay?"

"I just thought I heard something. I'm sorry I woke you up."

"I'm serious. I'm starting to worry about you. You're not sleeping, and you seem really stressed lately. I don't know if it's your book or staying home with Alice or the move or me working so much or what, but if you are having troubles, maybe you need to talk to somebody about it."

Craig could feel his defensiveness rise and tried his best to keep a lid on it. "I'm fine. I just thought I heard something, and it freaked me out a bit. You know how things are in the middle of the night—the imagination runs wild and every little thing becomes way more than it is. I'm sorry."

She looked at him in a way that left no doubt she didn't believe him, but let out an exasperated breath and turned to head up the stairs. "I'm going back to bed."

He watched for a second before following her up. Doubt had invaded his own mind and was chastising him for overreacting. Courtney was right. He was stressed, sleep deprived, and becoming more and more paranoid every day.

Halfway across the basement, Craig felt something tug at him. He tried to ignore it, because he wanted to go back to bed and chalk all this up to stress or whatever, but he couldn't, because it would eat at him the rest of the night.

"Are you coming?"

He turned back toward the sliding glass door and could see it from across the room.

The lock was closed.

Chapter Twenty

The sun beat down on the barely contained chaos that was the Southeast Minnesota Athletic Club pool. Kids in every conceivable color of swimsuit, who appeared to outnumber parents at least ten to one, splashed in the water like hooked sailfish and ran around the cement deck, completely ignoring the whistles of the teenage lifeguards imploring them to walk.

By the time Craig and Alice arrived, most of the lounge chairs around the pool were either occupied or claimed by a draped towel and giant beach tote full of goggles and snacks. A single lounger was available over by the deep end, one row removed from the water.

Craig had barely been able to keep Alice from the slide long enough to get sunscreen on her back, and he thought she would explode waiting for him to get some on himself.

"You can go ahead, you know?" he said. "You don't have to wait for me."

Alice looked at him like he was putting her on. "But who's going to catch me at the bottom?"

Craig chuckled. He'd waited in the water at the bottom of the slide the last time they were there, but it was more out of an abundance of caution than anything.

"You're a good swimmer, right? Can you make it to the ladder?" He could see her face light up as the realization she could do it herself hit her. "Or do you still need me to help?"

Alice barely finished shaking her head before she was halfway to the base of the waterslide. It wasn't just the parents who couldn't believe how quickly kids grew up; sometimes kids needed to be reminded.

A line of dripping children snaked about halfway down the stairs leading up to the summit of the waterslide. Alice joined the back of the line and turned to wave down at her dad. Even from his lounge chair, he could see the combination of excitement and pride on her face that her first solo adventure on the slide brought. He waved back, then sprayed more sunscreen over his arms and squinted up into the piercing blue sky above.

He'd have to make sure to keep his baseball cap on and remember to reapply his sunscreen every half hour or so.

Craig looked up to the top of the waterslide in time to see Alice disappear into the mouth of the giant blue tube. He stood up and mentally counted the seconds as she spiraled down. Right as he was starting to wonder what was taking so long, Alice was dumped out into the pool on a wave of chlorinated water. Her head popped up among the white foamy bubbles, and she immediately kicked over to the ladder on the side.

She pulled herself out of the pool and waved back at him before heading off to join the line again.

Craig was secretly glad Alice was comfortable going on the waterslide by herself, because—honestly—an afternoon of watching and catching and encouraging was exhausting. Sleep had been a struggle and only gotten worse since the incident on Friday night. He'd expected Courtney to bring it up the next morning, when he'd get a chance to explain himself in the logical light of day, but she'd never mentioned it. Now every night he'd lie in bed, where every creak and bump grabbed him by the scalp, but he didn't dare check them out, for fear of drawing more attention from his wife. So he'd just lie there, imagination running wild in the dark, paranoia growing inside his skull like mold, then get up with Courtney's alarm and act as natural as possible while examining everything in their house.

Was the pantry door open last night?

Weren't my keys on the counter?

I swear I closed those drapes.

He needed to find a way to relax, to get out of his own head, because right now if felt like he was standing in a hurricane, getting battered from every angle. There were just ten days left until MinnLit, but he hadn't even attempted to write since last week. Too scared the words wouldn't come. Scared that he was blowing the only opportunity he would get. Scared he'd embarrass himself and embarrass the friend who'd stuck her neck out for him. Confirm to his wife that he was a failure and prove right everyone who thought he was nothing but a leech.

Craig took a deep breath and tried to blow out the negativity.

If you quit now, they win.

Maybe tomorrow, if today's sun burned off the top layer of stress inside him, he could try again. Squeeze something out, anything, just to prove he could.

Craig leaned back on the pool lounger and pulled out the same Nick Cutter book he'd been reading for the past month. With everything going on, he hadn't picked it up in weeks and had forgotten so much of the plot he seriously considered just starting back on page one. He glanced up from the paperback and spotted Alice once again on the upper platform of the waterslide, third in line. She had her back to him, talking to the kid behind her. Craig put his book down and sat up for a better look that he absolutely didn't need.

She was talking to Levi.

A chill cut through the eighty-eight-degree air as he watched the lifeguard tap Alice on the shoulder and motion that it was her turn. She had a big smile on her face as she disappeared down the tube, leaving Levi waiting at the top. She'd barely disappeared when he jumped in after, ignoring the lifeguard's attempt at traffic control.

Craig leaped from his lounger and stared at the bottom of the slide, waiting for Alice to pop out. Time slowed as his body tensed; the sweat on the back of his neck had nothing to do with the sun.

Alice finally flew out and landed with a splash. Her head had just broken the surface when Levi barreled out behind and hit the water just inches away. Alice disappeared in the chlorinated foam, and Craig's feet took him to her without being asked.

He was practically hurdling an empty lounge chair when her head popped up at the ladder, a smile plastered across her face. Craig pulled back on the reins and watched. She climbed out and waited on the deck for the kid who'd almost landed on her to pull himself out of the pool. The two of them dripped their way to the stairs again, talking and laughing, indistinguishable from any other pair of friends having a fun day at the pool. Alice looked thrilled to have someone to slide with, and no matter what Craig tried to put on Levi, he looked like he was having fun too.

He wanted to stop it. To pull her off the slide and take her home, away from him, but the look of joy on her face was one he hadn't seen in a while and he couldn't bring himself to kill that.

Even if it meant allowing her to spend time with Levi.

They were at the pool, in public. What could the kid do?

A woman lying out in a nearby lounger noticed him standing and staring, so he stretched out his back and twisted from side to side in the most obviously casual way possible. He realized his book was still in his hand and folded over the page he'd been reading, then tossed it back on his chair.

Craig forced a smile at the woman and weaved through the row of chairs in front of them toward the pool. It was a hot day, and dipping his feet in would cool him down. As a parent, he would obviously do that from a spot where he could keep an eye on his daughter. A spot he could offer help if needed.

A little girl who couldn't have been much more than four years old cut in front of him as Craig made his way to the water's edge. With his focus on Alice and Levi, he barely avoided knocking the poor kid down. She ran across the wet cement to a group of women who'd commandeered a handful of chairs and umbrellas into a pod filled with beach towels, fruit snacks, and gossip.

The kid pulled on her mom's swimsuit, and the woman instinctively started digging around a large beach bag alongside her chair without leaving her conversation. The little one grabbed a treat from her mom's hand and ran right through Craig's parental judgment back to the shallow end. When Alice had been that age, he wouldn't dare let her out of his sight when they were at the pool and she couldn't go near the water unless she had her arm floaties on. The little girl in the pink-and-yellow swimsuit made her way into the shallow end and carried her snack in the general direction of a group of kids via the zero-depth entry.

He shook his head and sat down at the edge of the pool just as Alice came rocketing out of the slide once again. She saw him as soon as she resurfaced and stopped to wave. Craig waved her out of the landing zone just in time for Levi to splash down behind her.

"You can't hang out under the slide, kiddo," Craig said as Alice floated over toward him. "You've got to get out of the way so the kids behind don't land on you."

She put her face in the water and kicked hard toward the side, stopping just before she rammed into his knees.

"Levi's here!" Alice said as she blinked the droplets from her eyes.

Craig watched him climb the ladder out of the pool, convinced he saw a smirk among the dripping water.

"Yes, he is." He didn't hold back the disdain he had for the kid, but Alice was having too much fun to notice.

"Are you going to slide too?" She floated in front of him, one hand on his knee and one pushing the wet hair from her face.

"Not now. I just came down to dip my toes in and cool off."

"Okay. Levi wants to play in the shallow end for a bit, so we're going to go swim down there."

Alice grabbed the edge of the pool and tried to hoist herself out. Craig scooted over so she had room to swing her leg up and boost out. "That's fine. Just . . ." He had no idea what he wanted to say. "Be careful."

"It's only the shallow end," Alice said. "I can touch the whole place."

"I know, I'm just sayin'."

"Let's go!" It took a second for him to realize she was talking to Levi, who was still hovering over by the ladder. He met Craig's eyes before running off after Alice. A whistle bleated but didn't slow him down.

Craig stayed where he was, feet dangling in the cool water and eyes on the two kids as they splashed their way into the shallow end. They ran through knee-deep water under a waterspout, Alice screaming with delight as the golf ball–size droplets rained down on her.

Craig didn't dare take his eyes off them. Alice was only a few days removed from wearing a protective boot after Levi had slammed her foot with a croquet mallet. Her cries still echoed inside his brain when he thought about it, the sight of her tears rolling down her red cheeks still fresh.

Alice sat down in water no more than a foot deep, then lay back until her head floated. Levi reached over and pushed her forehead down. Bubbles erupted, and Craig leaped up from the side of the pool.

Before he could start his sprint over, Alice burst from the water, laughing.

Levi then lay back, and Alice pushed down on his forehead in the same way, holding him under for a few seconds before letting go.

Craig told himself they were just playing but had a hard time flushing the panic from his system. When Alice leaned back to do it again, he was already walking across the deck. He hopped into the water and wove through a dozen kids splashing around.

"Hey, Alice . . ." She didn't hear him in the chaos of swimmers. *"Alice!"*

It was louder than he wanted, but it got both's attention. A few other kids' too.

"Maybe don't play that game here?"

She looked at him, confused. "Why? It's fun."

Because I don't trust Levi to let you up.

But he couldn't say that. Craig could feel the nervous looks from the kids around them. He was a stranger in their party. Someone looking to kill the fun.

"You're not supposed to hold anyone's head under," Craig said. "If the lifeguards see you, you may get in trouble."

Alice never wanted to run afoul of the lifeguards, as she was not old enough to understand they were bored teenagers who probably paid as much attention here as they did in world history, so she agreed.

Craig ignored Levi as he turned to leave, but the kid's words rattled around his head.

I don't get in trouble.

As Craig headed back to his chair, he scanned the others camped out around the pool. They'd never seen Levi there before, and based on his limited interactions with her, Cassandra Ryan didn't seem like the type who took her kid out to do things. Craig didn't see her anywhere, but his self-consciously subtle peeking wasn't the most efficient way to find someone. She'd probably off-loaded her parenting duties on a nanny, because running the Deer Ridge rumor mill was a full-time job.

He stewed and pulled his lounger forward about six inches so he had an unobstructed view of the shallow end. Craig held his book up in front of himself, but his eyes stayed on Alice.

But mostly on Levi.

The two kids splashed around for another five minutes or so before Alice marched back up the gradual slope out of the pool. Craig watched Levi's eyes follow her along the deck, then settle on him.

"Getting tired?" It was a long shot, but Craig hoped he could convince her it was time to leave.

She shook her head hard enough that her wet hair slapped the sides of her face and sent water flying in all directions. "Levi still wanted to play the dunking game, but I said we couldn't because you said not to, but that's all he wanted to do, so I said I was going to go down the waterslide some more."

Her last words trailed behind her as she headed off to the slide, her bare feet slapping the wet cement as fast as possible without breaking into a rule-breaching run. The line of waterlogged kids had grown as the afternoon stretched on, almost to the bottom of the stairs.

Craig watched her slide in behind a group of older kids, practically bouncing with anticipation. He leaned back into his chair but could still feel Levi's gaze on him like a laser guiding an incoming missile strike.

The kid hadn't moved from where Alice had left him. He stood in waist-deep water, pale skin already taking on the angry red tint of sunburn, eyes locked on Craig with a confidence he'd never seen in a kid that age. The kind normally reserved for con men and politicians. Craig wanted to look away, but he couldn't. It was a challenge, and he could do little but stare back at the kid.

A huge pack of kids had formed up near Levi, dominating that side of the pool with shouts and splashes. They were older kids—too old to be in the shallow end—and Craig watched as their roughhousing started to feed off itself. He was glad Alice had left, but Levi seemed unfazed by the chaos.

He just kept staring at Craig.

One of the gang suplexed a kid into the water right next to Levi. It brought up a huge splash and drew a halfhearted whistle from the lifeguard, but the kid kept staring.

Craig shook his eyes away just as that little girl in the pink-and-yellow swimsuit bobbed between them. She'd been hanging around the periphery of the older kids, one of whom was probably her brother, but was now drifting away from the pack like a wounded gazelle.

Levi never took his eyes off Craig as he reached out and pushed her head underwater.

Craig sat frozen, his brain refusing to believe what he'd just seen. The girl's hands broke through the surface, but her thrashing blended in with the bedlam around her. A kid body-slammed his friend not five feet from where Levi held her, but no one noticed.

A smirk grew on Levi's face, almost daring Craig to do something.

He looked over at the group of mothers he'd seen the girl go to before, but they were too engrossed in conversation to bother checking on their kids.

Levi's other arm was underwater now, the effort he was using evident on his face.

Two of the lifeguards were over by their elevated chair, talking to each other during a shift change, ignoring the water.

Craig waited for Levi to let her up, end this sick game of chicken, but seconds kept ticking by. The thrashing in front of Levi had stopped. Either she was too far under, or she had quit fighting.

How long has she been underwater?

Craig swung his head around, desperate for someone to step in. Anyone.

Why is nobody else seeing this?

The boys continued to wrestle behind them, and the moms kept gossiping, and the lifeguards weren't even looking, and Levi kept fucking smiling, and it finally hit Craig that he wasn't going to let her up.

He bolted out of his chair, slipping on the wet cement and almost going flat on his back as he scrambled to a stop at the edge of the water. His heart pounded all the way up to his temples as his veins pumped nothing but adrenaline. The girl was little more than a blurry blob under the surface, and he leaped into the pool, legs churning through the water as he desperately tried to high-step across the shallow end.

Levi held his gaze the whole way as kids dove away from the grown man plowing through their fun.

He was about ten feet away when Levi released his grip and the little girl burst through the surface. Blonde hair was plastered down the front of her face as she coughed and tried to gulp air at the same time.

Craig came to a stop and felt the wake his run had created roll out through a pool full of kids all looking at him like a crazy person. The girl found her brother, who pulled her over with a confused look.

Levi still hadn't moved, while Craig's body shook with anxiety and effort.

For a second the pool was quiet; then the little girl let out a racking cough.

Levi laughed, and Craig felt something snap loose inside himself.

He pushed through the water, but Levi didn't shrink at all from the look of fury on his face. The smug expression didn't even go away when Craig grabbed the kid's wiry bicep and screamed in his face.

"What the fuck is wrong with you?"

Levi pulled out a little grin, and it was gas on a fire that was already well out of control. Craig tightened his grip and very nearly pulled the boy off his feet.

"I fucking saw what you did." He was mad enough he couldn't hear his f-bombs echo over the now silent crowd of parents and kids, and wasn't aware of anyone behind him until a hand clamped down onto his trapezius muscle and jerked him back.

"Good god, man. Take it easy."

Craig kept ahold of Levi and turned to see that a dad with wrap-around sunglasses and board shorts had followed him in. Before he could say anything, a wail started up behind them. He looked back and saw Levi's face grow red as tears streamed down his face. The man pushed past and slapped Craig's hand away, putting himself between him and Levi. He knelt down in the water and tried to comfort the boy before turning back on Craig.

"What the hell is wrong with you?"

Craig couldn't believe this dipshit was coming after him, not Levi. "He was holding that little girl underwater."

The guy completely ignored what Craig had said. What Levi had done.

"He's just a boy. You can't talk like that to a kid, man."

"He was *drowning* her!" Craig could barely process what was happening. Levi had just held a four-year-old underwater for a dangerous amount of time, and this guy was more worried that he'd said the f-word in front of them? Levi could have *killed* her—he'd seen it plain as day. And just in case his intent wasn't obvious—fucking *laughed* about it.

Levi increased his wailing, putting whatever he could into his performance. And, of course, Sunglasses Dad was eating it up.

"It's all right, buddy." The guy knelt down in front of Levi and put a hand on his shoulder. "I'm sure it was just an accident."

Levi kept the tears streaming down his face and wiped his nose on his wrist. It was too much.

"Oh, come on," Craig said.

The guy's head snapped up with righteous fury; then he turned his attention back to Levi. "Is your mom or dad around?"

Craig stared down at Levi, waiting for the kid to break character and prove him right, but he kept the act going.

"We'll find them," the guy said, scanning the still-gathered crowd for someone willing to claim the crying kid.

About two dozen people were hanging around the deck, all gawking at the scene in the pool like they were creeping past a three-car accident along the side of the road. One of the lifeguards stood by the edge of the crowd with the terrified look of someone whose sunny summer job had just gotten very serious. Craig needed a supportive face—someone who had seen what went down. Someone who could back him up.

But that person wasn't there. There was nothing but a sea of weak, scared eyes, all willing to go along with whatever easy narrative was presented to them.

He saw the little girl and her brother heading over to the cluster of chairs the supermoms had formed—none of whom had stopped talking to notice what had gone down. They should have been over here defending him. Thanking him for looking out for one of their daughters. But they were content with ignoring everything, letting him twist in the wind as the boy who'd attacked a little girl turned a judgmental mob against him with his pathetic performance.

"What's going on?"

Cassandra Ryan's raspy voice cut through the tension of the crowd and heralded her arrival on the scene. The crowd stepped back and parted for her, some pretending to look away and the rest too invested in the forthcoming drama to bother. Levi's mom was dressed in black-and-pink spandex, with her phone strapped to her bicep. She held a single white earbud in her right hand, the other still stuck in her ear.

Levi resumed crying at the sight of his mother, while his champion led him over to the side of the pool as if he were presenting the boy to her. They climbed out. "Just a little mix-up, but he's gonna be fine."

Craig's eyes rolled so far back into his head he thought they'd snap and never come back. If he hadn't witnessed the entire thing with his own eyes, he'd think Levi had almost drowned.

Cassandra looked up from her boy and found Craig. Her eyes frosted over with accusation, and Levi's white knight noticed. He leaned in and muttered something in the ear Cassandra had bothered to pull the earbud from. Craig wasn't about to wait for this guy to twist the story around when he hadn't even seen what happened. He waded over to the side and pushed himself out of the pool.

"Did you touch my kid?" She didn't wait for Craig to get upright and spoke as if her next sentence would be a demand to speak with his manager.

"Your kid was holding a little girl underwater." He almost said *just ask him*, as if Levi would ever confess to wrongdoing or his mom would believe him if he did.

True to form, she completely ignored what her son had done. "Did you touch my kid?"

Craig turned to the crowd, the ones who'd tried to be subtle earlier having completely dropped the act. It was now a movie to them, one they would recount to their friends later, and one in which they had already cast the villain. Their faces told Craig he'd put himself on an island, and none of them were prepared to contribute to a rescue mission. The anger inside him burned up and evaporated into fear at the realization. He'd made a leap no one was willing to take with him, and now he stood alone while they quickly pulled the net from underneath.

"Listen—" Craig took a step forward, and Cassandra recoiled as if he were brandishing a bloody knife. She bumped into a young man in a black fitted SEMAC polo shirt with "Caleb" stitched below the logo.

"What's going on here?" Craig vaguely recognized the guy, who had the physique of one of the dozens of trainers that crisscrossed the exercise floor inside, but who spoke with the concerned authority of one whose job was more than assisting with proper dead lift form.

Cassandra, who'd still barely looked at the boy she was so adamant in defending, jabbed a finger at Craig.

"This guy's out here harassing my son."

"Jesus, I'm not *harassing* your son." It was loud and defensive and definitely not helpful. He needed to calm down and explain what the hell had happened.

Deep breath.

"Okay, things are getting way too mixed up here. I was sitting right over there when Levi pushed that little girl underwater." Craig flailed his arm back in the direction of the mom group but didn't see them. He frantically scanned the deck and saw the girl following her mom and brother out to the parking lot. Fleeing the scene when they should be here defending him. "I watched and waited for a long time, but nobody else noticed. Not her mom, not the lifeguards . . . nobody was doing anything. The poor kid was going to drown."

A glimmer of belief shone behind Caleb's face. If he'd worked at the club for any amount of time, he was probably familiar with the Ryan family. This couldn't be the first time Levi had pulled something like this, and there was no way Cassandra hadn't kicked up a fuss about some perceived injustice or blown something way out of proportion. They probably had the kid's face on a wanted poster in the break room, whereas he and his kid had never caused a bit of trouble.

Craig hoped he'd found his lifeline, but Levi's little voice derailed all that.

"We were just playing." Levi stood behind them, tiny and scared, stripped of the fearless arrogance he usually drizzled over his speech like syrup. He let his eyes well up before pointing a finger at Craig. "But he ran in and grabbed my arm and yelled at me."

"Call the police right now." Cassandra Ryan's voice was cold with rage.

Caleb's face looked about five years younger as he watched the situation escalate above his job description. "I don't know . . . let's just—"

Cassandra was having none of it and swung her anger like a cudgel. "This man has been harassing my boy for weeks, and I want you to call the police *immediately*."

Craig watched whatever sympathy Caleb might have held for him being chased away and realized the situation was in real danger of spiraling out of control, so he put his hands up and softened his tone as much as possible. "Okay, look . . . I admit I used some words I shouldn't have, and I apologize for that. But that little girl . . . they were *not* playing. If I hadn't been here, she would have drowned, okay?"

"Oh, please." Cassandra jumped in before Caleb could react. "You need to do something right now. I don't know what this guy's problem is, but he's obviously unbalanced or something, and I'm not comfortable at all with him around us."

Caleb looked back and forth between Levi's mom and Craig, painfully out of his depth.

"I wasn't holding her under." Levi looked pathetic in his wet swimsuit and fake tears. "We were just playing, and he hurt my arm." The kid made sure to get that last part out before crying again.

"Did you grab his arm?" Caleb asked.

Craig was thrashing around in a pit of quicksand, inching lower the harder he fought to free himself. He tried to pull in a calming breath and find a dangling branch he could grab on to. "Look, I held on to his arm while talking, because I didn't know if he was going to run away or what. He could've killed that little girl . . ."

"I didn't try to hurt anybody." Levi obviously knew when to pipe up for maximum effect, because his words bolstered his mother's rage and erased any understanding the SEMAC staff member could have had.

"You can't physically confront other people's kids," Caleb said. "We have a code of conduct here, and this goes way over the line."

Growing exasperation overruled Craig's good judgment and raised the temperature of his voice. Nobody seemed willing to listen. It felt like he was using a colander to bail water from a sinking ship. "He tried to drown that little girl! Where does that fit in your code of conduct?"

He spun back, searching for anyone who could back him up, but saw his own daughter instead. Alice stood ten feet away, still dripping from her last time down the slide, eyes the size of silver dollars. She looked as scared as he'd ever seen her, and Craig wondered how long she had been there.

It didn't matter. What she saw was her father accused of assaulting her friend, and it drained all the fight out of Craig.

"Sir, I think we should go inside and speak with our general manager about this."

Chapter Twenty-One

They allowed him to check Alice into the kids' club before his meeting with the general manager, and the look on her face as he signed her in was quite possibly the worst thing he'd experienced. Even if she didn't necessarily understand what was going on, she had to know something big was happening. The guilt was a backpack full of sand hanging on Craig's shoulders. He wanted to reassure her—and he said something with a forced smile before he left—but they both knew it was bullshit.

The general manager's office was in a spacious cluster just off the main fitness floor, the door always open to be accessible to members.

When Craig got there, the door was closed, but Cassandra Ryan's voice came through clear as day from the other side. He didn't know whether he should knock and go in so he could defend himself instead of letting her weave whatever tale she wanted. Instead, he slumped into one of the chairs arranged out front, like a kid summoned to the principal's office. He'd have his turn, without Cassandra in there pouring gasoline all over the place. He'd wait.

A young woman working the activities desk nearby almost snapped her neck not looking over at him while keeping her ear cocked toward the door. Random members weren't as subtle as they rubbernecked their way past toward the locker room.

He wondered how many times Levi had been in his exact situation, waiting outside an office while his mom berated and bullied someone on the other side of the door.

The only difference was this time she was advocating *for* punishment.

Craig's knee bounced up and down as he sat, waiting for the door to open and thinking about what he was going to say.

The word *expulsion* filtered through the door, but it wasn't in Cassandra Ryan's voice, and Craig suddenly realized how high the plank he stood on was. He couldn't imagine telling Alice that the pool was no longer an option, and telling Courtney would be worse. He wanted to believe she would take his side, understand why he'd reacted the way he had, but part of him was terrified she wouldn't.

The office door flew open and jerked him out of his worries. Cassandra blew past, either too harried or too pissed to notice him, which was probably a good thing.

Levi trailed behind her and looked back as if he could sense Craig there. There was no emotion in his face, just a nonchalance that burned Craig more than a smirk would have. It was as if the drama he'd started had no effect on him. Kick the hornet's nest and move on.

No thought as to who got stung.

A fresh wave of anger bloomed in Craig's stomach, and he had to quash it before it pushed him over the edge again. Aggression wasn't his friend. He needed to be calm. Contrite. Part of a situation that had been blown way out of proportion.

Unfortunately, the general manager didn't buy it.

Their meeting was short, and Craig was barely given a chance to defend himself.

The club's code of conduct was painfully clear and had a well-defined zero tolerance policy for aggression between members. Add in the fact that one of the parties was a nine-year-old boy, and Craig never stood a chance.

He still tried to explain what Levi had done. Begged him to talk to the little girl. To recognize *why* he'd reacted the way he did, but the GM refused to consider it. As far as the club was concerned, nothing that had happened before he made contact with Levi mattered.

He repeated the phrase *zero tolerance* multiple times.

Nothing Craig said was heard, and he was dismissed with a three-month suspension.

It could have been worse, Craig figured, and it explained why Cassandra had seemed so upset when she'd left, but it was still a punch in the gut. Three months would last until autumn and erase the remainder of the pool season for Alice.

He broke the news to her on the drive home, and she burst into tears. Craig tried to explain it was just temporary, but she was inconsolable. She loved the pool, had just learned to go down the waterslide by herself. Alice didn't say it outright, but he could hear the anger in her cries.

Craig tightened his hands on the wheel, trying to figure a way to make this right. He couldn't, because nothing about this situation was right. Just because nobody else saw what Levi had done didn't mean it hadn't happened. His reaction might have been a little over the top, but should be understandable when faced with a situation like that.

This was a shit situation from the top down, and it was Levi's fault.

When Alice stopped crying, Craig asked if she wanted to go for ice cream. He knew it was a lame way to make amends, but it was all he came up with.

Alice probably thought the same, because she said no.

"Are you sure? It's just right up ahead."

"No." It was as curt an answer as he'd ever heard from her.

"Levi was hurting that girl, honey." He never thought he'd have to defend himself to his daughter. He'd always been her hero, and the blame in her voice was more than he could handle. He expected it from Cassandra Ryan, and honestly wasn't that surprised to get it from the club, but he couldn't have his daughter think it was his fault. "On purpose. And she almost drowned. She *would* have if I hadn't jumped in and gotten Levi to let her up. And then he laughed about it. That's why I yelled at him, and because he didn't want to get into trouble, he pretended to cry. He lied to the workers there and said it was an accident, that they were just playing, even though we know that wasn't true. So if you want to blame somebody for the fact that you can't go to the pool, blame Levi."

He looked at Alice through the rearview mirror. She wasn't even listening to him, just staring out the window with a face that suddenly looked much older than it ever had. She only cared about not being able to go to the pool for the rest of the summer because her dad had gotten suspended.

"For god's sake, he already practically broke your foot. Remember that?"

Craig mumbled it more to himself than to Alice, but she still answered. "He said it was an accident."

He practically had to bite his tongue to keep from yelling back at her.

"He said the same thing about the girl today, but I saw him with my own eyes, Alice. Some people are liars. They do whatever they want and then lie about it when they get in trouble. Unfortunately for Levi, his mom and dad don't seem to care that he does it, so that's how he's going to grow up, and when he's an adult, he's going to have some real problems when they aren't around to bail him out anymore."

He'd driven on autopilot, barely noticing they'd pulled into their neighborhood. As if on cue, Levi's house appeared a half-block away on the left. Their garage door was open, and Levi was doing something on the front porch. The sight of him roiled Craig's guts enough, he actually thought he might throw up across the dashboard. Luckily, the kid didn't look up as they rolled past.

—

Alice retreated to her room as soon as they got home, and Craig let her go. She'd often do that when upset, curl up on top of her bed and page through some books with Pete tucked under her arm.

But since Pete had never resurfaced, she had to read by herself.

Craig paced around the main floor, the events at the pool playing inside his head on a loop. He watched, desperate for some way to hit pause right before his hand clamped down on Levi's arm, a way to rewind and choose different words. It was ridiculous that people were more concerned with a nine-year-old boy hearing the f-word than him almost drowning a four-year-old girl in their pool, but Craig should have expected it. He'd played right into Levi's hands. For whatever reason, the kid kept messing with him.

And Craig had to stop playing his games.

But what was done was done. There was no edit button. He'd done what he'd done, and he would have to live with the consequences, however unfair he thought them to be.

Some of those consequences would be coming home relatively soon, and Craig still had no idea how he was going to tell Courtney.

His stomach ached at the thought. He knew things had not been good between them lately, and that it was mostly his fault. This would make things a lot worse.

No, she'd listen to him. She was smart and emotionally stable, and she loved him. She wouldn't be happy about it, but she'd see past the bullshit to what this really was.

She had to.

He looked out over the backyard. The swings hung still, the trees behind them motionless in the breezeless air. He could see the tramped-down spot behind the play set where Levi had first emerged, and he let it convert a little of his stress into anger.

The first time that kid had shown up, Craig had been convinced he was the solution to all his problems. He ignored the red flag behaviors and the casual warning from his neighbor because he was desperate to be an author and arrogant enough he thought he could help the kid.

He'd welcomed him into their lives, played with him, tried to be the only adult willing to show him a bit of attention.

And what thanks did he get? Levi threatened to derail his entire life.

The rumble of the garage door heralded Courtney's return from work.

Craig was glad. There was no point in trying to sugarcoat anything. Rip it off like a Band-Aid; it would hurt but fade quickly. He'd had a bad reaction to a bad situation. The consequences were overly harsh, but there was nothing he could do about that.

The door to the garage opened and shut, and Courtney's leather messenger bag hit the floor in the back hall. Craig stayed in the kitchen, staring out the sliding glass door to the backyard.

"Hey." Courtney's voice hadn't shed the weight of the last few days, and his confidence in her understanding evaporated. She looked across the kitchen at him, the concern she'd had about him arched in her brow. "How's it going?"

His mouth dried up as if doing whatever it could to forestall the inevitable. Craig no longer thought she would understand. She'd be pissed. She'd blame him just like Cassandra had. She'd storm up to Alice's room, snatch her off the bed, and load up the car.

He knew that was overly dramatic—Courtney wasn't going to leave him—but it didn't calm his guts any. The silence stretched well past awkward before he found his voice.

"There was an incident at the pool this afternoon."

"What happened? Is Alice okay?" She instinctively looked up toward their daughter's room.

"Yeah, she's fine." He walked over and plucked the glass he'd been drinking from earlier off the counter. His mouth was still dry, but getting a drink felt more like a way to delay the inevitable. "Levi was there."

Craig filled the glass and felt her breath change behind him. He took a long drink before continuing. "He pushed a little girl under the water. Held her there. The kid's mom wasn't watching her, and nobody else noticed. And he was, like, staring me down the whole time. Daring me to do something, you know?"

He turned to Courtney and leaned back against the sink. She looked concerned. Not about what had happened, but about whatever was next.

"So what happened?"

"I kept waiting for somebody to notice. To do something. But nobody did. The kid's mom was off with her friends, and the lifeguards were fucking oblivious, and he's got her underwater . . . fucking smiling at me." Craig took another sip. Courtney waited. Stalling was pointless. "So nobody's doing anything, and he's still holding her underwater. I don't know how long it was, but it was a *long* time. Finally I ran over and jumped in, and he let her up. It was like he was goddamn baiting me the whole time."

Courtney was calm, but Craig could see the trepidation in her face. Waiting to hear the first big crack from the ice they were on. "Was the girl okay?"

"Yeah, her brother was there dicking off with his friends, and she went to him, and he took her over to their mom."

"The mom didn't come talk to you?"

"No, they just left. Didn't say a word to anybody about what happened."

"Okay, so nobody saw what he did, but the girl was okay?"

He took a breath and made the leap. "Well, that's where the problems start."

Whatever goodwill and understanding she'd brought to the table were wiped away. If Courtney had been waiting to find out how this was all his fault, he might as well give her what she wanted.

"So Levi lets the girl up, and I'm just standing there in the middle of the pool, and he just starts laughing."

"He was laughing?"

"It's like he was fucking with me. Drowning a little girl and daring me to do something about it, then when I jump in to help her, he lets her go and acts like nothing happened. So I grabbed him by the arm and am like *what the fuck is wrong with you*."

Courtney looked with disbelief. "Jesus . . . you didn't actually touch him, did you?"

"I didn't *hurt* him. I held his arm so he wouldn't swim away or anything. But he starts crying and—"

"Oh god . . ." Courtney's face was pale.

"He was one hundred percent faking. I barely even touched him."

"Did anyone see you?"

Craig tried a steadying breath, but it was useless. The pulse in his temple thudded an erratic beat that spread through his skull. "His mom showed up and threw an absolute fit and got one of the staff there. I explained what happened, but they wouldn't hear any of it, and all the staff guy cared about was the guest code of conduct. I mean, I yelled at a kid who almost drowned a little girl, and *that's* the problem."

"You can't grab someone else's kid!"

"He tried to drown her!" Craig's voice echoed through the kitchen and certainly made its way up to Alice's room. If she hadn't heard them fighting before, that certainly did it. "Yes, I grabbed him. I yelled at him. But that kid looked at me, fucking smiled, and pushed a four-year-old underwater. Held her there while staring me down like it was a fucking dare."

Craig stared at Courtney, waiting for a response, but she looked too exasperated to offer one. The silence hung in the kitchen like a heavy fog. He needed someone on his side, someone to understand, even if she didn't agree with his reaction.

"So, anyway, we had to go to the general manager's office and talk. Levi's mom was yelling about how *I've* been bothering her kid and she wants me kicked out and everything."

Apparently the thought of suspension hadn't caught up to Courtney, because her eyes widened at the suggestion. "You didn't get us kicked out, did you?"

"I explained what happened to the GM and told him to talk to the little girl's mom, but apparently there is a zero tolerance policy for 'guest-to-guest aggression' in the code of conduct."

Courtney let out a long breath and shook her head. "Jesus."

She abandoned the conversation and headed upstairs to their bedroom.

Craig followed her up the steps. Alice's door was still closed at the end of the hall.

"It's only three months." Craig closed their bedroom door behind him. "And I've already thought about appealing to the board of directors. I mean, even if they don't change my suspension, they can suspend Levi. The kid almost drowned a little girl. If that isn't 'guest-to-guest aggression,' I don't know what is."

Courtney still faced away from him and had the shirt she'd worn to work half off. Her head was down, and she'd stopped fumbling with the buttons. It took a second for Craig to notice the shake in her shoulders.

"Just stop." The words were quiet between her tears. "I don't give a shit about the pool, okay? Jesus, Craig, you haven't been yourself all summer. You aren't sleeping, you're paranoid, you're paying more attention to goddamn Levi than your own daughter. It's like you're fucking obsessed. Where was Alice during all of this? Did you even know? I don't know what's happening, but you have to talk to somebody."

She turned around, and Craig could see the tears streaming down her face. They scared him. They had disagreements like any married couple, but they were always over minor annoyances, and they were easily mended by a stupid joke and a promise to try harder.

This felt different.

"Because I've done everything I can to help you, but you've been fighting me every step of the way."

He stared at her from across the bedroom, shirt half off her shoulder and cheeks wet with tears. She was hurting, that he could tell, and she cared about him.

But good intentions didn't stop her from hurting him.

"Maybe you could start by believing me."

Chapter Twenty-Two

Courtney didn't talk to him the rest of the night. She spoke to him—more *at* him than anything—but that was probably just to keep Alice from thinking anything was wrong. But their daughter was equally upset. For the first time in her life, Alice concentrated more on eating dinner than telling stories.

After dinner Courtney left the dishes to Craig and hung out with Alice up in her room. When their girl went to bed, she retreated into the office.

Craig ended up downstairs, staring at a baseball game on TV. His stomach was a hollow vortex, churning around nothing as guilt and betrayal pummeled each other in a quest for dominance. He could still feel Levi's skinny bicep in his grip, see the smirk on his face as he strained to hold that girl underwater, hear the righteous indignation in Cassandra Ryan's voice echo through the gawking club members who'd gathered around.

At some point footsteps above told him Courtney was heading upstairs to bed. He wanted to go up and talk to her. Even if she wouldn't forgive him yet, he wanted to try to make her understand why things had gone so wrong.

Maybe she already did.

Craig took a deep breath. It did nothing. His insides were a mess. His anxiety had been festering for a while, but that afternoon had brought it all to the surface.

She thought he needed help.

She wasn't wrong.

Her footsteps faded as she went upstairs, but Craig didn't move. Best to give her space. Let her process what had happened. Hopefully in the clear light of morning, she'd understand.

He stayed on the couch through the end of the game, the post-game wrap-up show, and half of a behind-the-scenes-meet-the-players-they're-just-like-you special to give his wife plenty of time to get to sleep before he went upstairs.

If she wasn't sleeping when Craig crept into their dark bedroom, she faked it well. He didn't bother brushing his teeth, telling himself he didn't want to wake her. He dropped his shorts and slipped into his side of the bed with the boxers and T-shirt he'd worn all day, knowing any attempt at sleep was pointless. He was awake to hear every creak and moan the dark house could offer. He might have drifted off once or twice for an indeterminate amount of time, but was wide awake when Courtney's alarm went off at 5:30 a.m. He watched as she rolled out of bed in the dark, wanting to talk to her but not knowing what to say.

"You sleep at all last night?" The room was nothing but blue-gray shapes, but she'd noticed.

"Some." His lie felt loud in the morning stillness.

Courtney sat back on the bed, and her hand found his forehead. She brushed his hair back and scratched the top of his head. Her touch felt so good. A reminder that she hadn't forsaken him.

"I really think you need to talk to someone."

The serenity of the early morning kept him from rejecting the idea right away.

"Yeah . . . maybe."

He could tell that noncommittal answer hadn't satisfied her, but she trod lightly. "I think it would help a lot. We've gone through a lot of changes this year, and you've taken the brunt of them. I've had my job, which helps a lot because it gives me something to focus on. But you've got Alice and a new house and your book . . . I know it's a lot, and I want you to have the support you need."

She played with his hair for a minute before heading to the bathroom. Craig stayed in bed, staring at the glowing yellow frame leaking around the bathroom door as he heard the shower come on.

She was right. Craig knew he was struggling, but he didn't need a therapist to know why. Shit had been piling up all summer, and he'd simply hit a breaking point.

But things would get better. All he had to do was get through the summer. Alice would start school and find a bunch of new kids to play with—ones who weren't budding psychopaths—and he wouldn't have to worry about finding writing time.

His book.

Craig's meeting was in nine days, and he'd barely done anything over the last week because of goddamn Levi.

He lay back on his pillow and closed his eyes. It was pointless. There was no way he'd have a completed manuscript done in time, much less a fully edited one.

But maybe he didn't need to. Most agents started by looking at the first few chapters, just to get a feel for the writing. It was pure arrogance on his part to think Jennifer DiAmato was looking to read the full thing right away anyway. If he polished up the first three or four chapters, he could give those to her at MinnLit and have the rest finished by the time she was ready to see the whole thing.

Something bordering on relief flooded through him. He could salvage this.

For the first time in a long while, he felt optimistic about something.

He'd tell Courtney when she got out of the shower. She'd see that as a positive step, that he was taking this seriously and actually doing something. And if it didn't work—if things didn't get better—they could talk about a therapist later.

—

Craig rolled over and cracked his eyelids. The bedroom was quiet and full of sunlight. He pushed himself up and looked through the open bathroom door. The room was empty, which made sense because the bedside clock said 8:41. Courtney would have left almost two hours ago.

He stretched and swung his feet to the floor. That extra bit of sleep he'd stolen that morning had done little to erase the exhaustion that plagued him, and it had cost him a chance to tell Courtney about his new plan.

No big deal; there would be plenty of time down the road to get into it. Or, instead of talking it over, he could let his actions speak for themselves. If he could show her he was doing well, there would be no need to see a therapist.

No need to fix what didn't need fixing. Or, more accurately, what he could fix himself.

Craig showered and headed downstairs. To his surprise, Alice wasn't there waiting for him. He checked the living room and poked his head down the stairs—nothing. He walked around to the foyer and looked up at her bedroom, where the door was still closed.

"You up there, kiddo?"

No answer, so he trudged up the stairs. It was almost nine, and Alice was usually up and bouncing around way before this. He tapped on her door and pushed it open. "Alice?"

She was sitting on her bed, fully dressed, reading a Rainbow Fairies book. Two others of different colors lay abandoned on her bed, implying that she had been reading in there for a while. She barely glanced up at him and kept reading.

"Have you had breakfast yet?" He flipped through his mental Rolodex for a recipe that would bring a smile to her face, something special to start them on a new path. "I think we have chocolate chips, marshmallows, and graham crackers, so what if we made s'mores pancakes?"

It was bribery, and she looked up just enough for Craig to know it would work. She took a second to finish her page or show her dad she was still mad at him, then closed her bright-green book and slid off the bed.

It was still strange seeing her climb out of bed without her bunny Pete, and even stranger that he hadn't resurfaced yet. Alice never took him out of the house, so by the laws of physics and the universe, the thing *had* to be around somewhere, but it had been more than a week, and eventually she'd stopped looking. Craig had wondered if another of her dozens of stuffed animals would get promoted to the top spot at some point, but she was stubborn. It was Pete or nothing—at least so far.

She didn't say much as Craig cooked, but the combination of chocolate, marshmallows, and crushed-up graham crackers nestled between pancakes did a lot to lighten Alice's mood. By the time she'd soaked up the remaining maple syrup with her last bite, she was seemingly back to normal.

As Craig cleaned up the debris, a feline headbutt against his leg reminded him that the cat was still waiting on his breakfast.

It gave him an idea.

"How about we take Felix for a walk around the block this morning?"

"Really?" Alice had wanted to take him for a legitimate walk since the day they'd gotten the leash, but Craig had always been too busy. They'd only taken him into the backyard and hadn't even done that since the day Levi hoisted him up on the swing set.

Man, the red flags had been obvious early, but he'd been too preoccupied with his book to see them. Not a mistake he'd make again.

Now he was focused, committed to being a good dad who could handle whatever shit was thrown his way.

Even when it was a lot.

"Why don't you give him his breakfast while I clean up a bit, and then we can go?"

Alice bounced off her chair with enthusiasm that had seemed impossible just a half hour ago, and Craig's chest swelled.

Yes, this would work. Things could get better. Sometimes it took a tough moment to force a badly needed course correction, and he felt like they were starting on a fresh path.

Felix wasn't too keen on wearing his harness. Whether it was traumatic memories of the last time or just general feline obstinance, the white-and-orange tabby ran and hid when Alice approached him before their walk. Craig had to step in to help coax him out from under the couch. After a few minutes of pets and chin scratches, they were able to slip the harness around his shoulders.

Alice was itching to go, but Craig convinced her to hold off and allow Felix to get used to wearing the harness again. While Alice played with him, Craig went to the pantry and put a handful of cat treats in his pocket, figuring they might need something to motivate their stubborn cat while out and about in the neighborhood.

By the time he got back to the living room, Felix was stretched out on his back, accepting all the belly rubs Alice could give.

"Think he's ready to go on an adventure?" Craig asked.

"Yes." Alice moved her hand up through the white fur on his tummy and scratched the spot under his ear. "He's really excited."

"Good." Felix rolled over, and Craig clipped the leash to his harness. "We'll see how it goes."

Alice reached her hand out. "Can I hold the leash?"

Craig handed it over and went to the front door. Felix remained on the floor, legs tucked under himself, with a wary eye cast up toward both of them.

"Take it really slow to start." He unlocked the front door and held it open to the outside world.

"Come on, buddy." Alice took a step and gave the slightest tug on the leash. Felix wasn't going anywhere.

Craig dug a treat out of his pocket and dropped it in front of the door. Felix jumped up and almost pulled the leash from Alice's grip as he pounced on it. She giggled, and it was the most beautiful sound Craig had ever heard. He winked down at her and tossed another treat farther out onto the front step. Felix jumped outside to snarf it up.

He locked the door behind them and started down toward the sidewalk.

"Go slow," Craig said. "He'll probably want to sniff everything out here."

He handed a couple of treats to Alice, but she was staring up the street.

Levi glided around the corner on his scooter and made it to the second house before he recognized them and skidded to a halt. The three of them stood there, four houses apart, deer in headlights with no real determination as to who was the car. Craig could feel Alice tense up, but before he could say something, Levi hauled his scooter around and took off the way he'd come.

The sight of that little shit turning tail and bolting was sweeter than the frosting on a cinnamon roll. Craig tossed a treat up the sidewalk to get Felix moving again.

"Let's keep boogying." Craig didn't even acknowledge seeing Levi. The kid was a tumor he was more than happy to excise from their lives. "Think we can make it to the park?"

It was farther than he'd planned on going, but Alice could barely contain her excitement at the thought. He watched the final remains of her resentment from the pool melt away, and it felt good. They both needed this.

They made their way down the block in fits and starts as Felix slowly meandered along the sidewalk, sniffing whatever he could find and randomly freezing to stare off into the distance. Whenever they stalled too much, Craig threw a treat to spur them along.

Eventually Alice started getting impatient, so Craig scooped up the cat and carried him the final block. A couple of other families were already at the park, and a cat on a leash was quite the attention grabber for his little girl. She led Felix over to the wooden climbing structures and let him hop from platform to platform while the other kids gathered in awe.

Craig smiled and waved at the two mothers hanging out with a pair of strollers and got bemused nods back as Alice held court with their kids. They all looked roughly the same age, and the ease with which Alice seemed to make friends wrapped a comforting blanket around his heart. If they lived nearby, maybe they could be new playmates?

The kids burst into laughter as Felix chased a treat.

Brighter days on the horizon.

—

They stayed at the park for a half hour. Alice wanted to stay longer—and things were going so well, Craig wanted to, too—but he could tell their cat was wearing thin. The bounding and frolicking after treats had stopped, and Felix lay down. The kids tried hard to goad him into more antics, but Craig recognized a cat that'd had his fill. Best to get him home before the claws came out.

He carried him most of the way back to their neighborhood, only letting him down when he started getting squirmy. The three of them were a half block from home when their neighbor's dark Subaru Forester pulled up in front of them.

Craig put Felix down and handed the leash to Alice as the window slid down and Dan appeared. "Out for a walk, eh?"

"Just coming back from the park."

Dan stuck his head out the driver's side window and looked down at Felix. "So you've got a leash . . ." He looked back at Craig with a friendly smirk. ". . . for your cat."

Alice didn't register anything other than an honest question. "He loves it."

"I'm sure he does," Dan said. "Nothing better than taking your cat out for a morning walk around the neighborhood, I'd say."

"We took him to the park, and he climbed all up by the monkey bars." Alice relished telling someone new about her pet.

"So how're things going?" The jovial ribbing was gone from Dan's voice. He glanced down at Alice and waited until her focus had moved back to the cat. "I heard about the pool. What happened there?"

Craig took a second, then handed Alice the remaining treats. "Hey, kiddo, why don't you take Felix home, okay? I'm gonna talk to Dan for a minute."

She tossed a treat and tried to get Felix to chase it, but he'd lain down. His walking day was done. After a few gentle tugs of the leash, Alice picked him up and started toward the house.

Craig turned back to Dan and shook his head. He knew people would talk; there was no stopping that. Gossip spread like COVID around town, and places like the club were hot spots. But he was still surprised it had gotten all the way back to his block that fast. It felt like a blade between the ribs, and Craig didn't know how to react. He should have been ready with a reply. Some talking points to explain himself, to get his own version of the story out there, because if Cassandra Ryan was the only one talking, he'd be crucified. Luckily, Dan and Kay knew a lot of people around town too. Maybe they could be a conduit for his side of the story.

"Bad reaction to a bad situation." Craig explained what happened. Watching Alice play with Levi. The dunking game he'd stopped. Levi holding that girl under the water. He left out the looks Levi had given him—not sure how to explain that to Dan without sounding paranoid—and could hear himself downplaying his reaction once Levi had let her up.

"So, yeah . . . they have a zero tolerance policy, and I got suspended for three months. And, well . . . I get it, I guess. I'm the adult, and I need to keep my head . . . but, man, it's frustrating. It's like nobody gave a shit what *happened*. Just that I swore at a kid. I mean, that little girl could have drowned, right? My adrenaline was going and . . . uh."

Dan looked sympathetic, but doubt lingered in his eyes. "Yeah, but kids, man . . . especially when you're dealing with Deer Ridge folk. They aren't going to listen to shit when it comes to their kids."

"I know, it's just . . ." Craig trailed off because he didn't know how to finish that sentence. Dan was right, and that's what burned him.

"Only reason I brought it up was because I saw that kid in your backyard again this morning."

That snapped Craig out of his one-man pity party. "What?"

"Yeah, that's why I was surprised to see you out walking. I assumed you were home."

Craig pulled out his phone and checked the time. It had been about an hour since they'd seen Levi at the end of the block. "When did you see him?"

"I don't know, not that long ago."

Alice had made it to their driveway, where she'd put Felix down and was trying to coax him toward the door. Craig fought the instinct to run down there and scurry her into the house. "What was he doing?" He didn't take his eyes off his daughter as he spoke.

"I don't know. I just saw him there for a second—then he disappeared into the woods."

He thought back to when Levi peeled around the corner at the beginning of their walk. The kid hadn't been running scared—he'd known their house was empty.

Craig didn't even mumble a goodbye before he took off down the street.

Chapter Twenty-Three

Craig tried to slow down before Alice saw him, but a grown man sprinting down the sidewalk made more noise than he'd expected.

"What's the matter, Daddy?" He wanted to smile and wipe away the worry in her eyes, but he didn't have it in him anymore. Instead he waved her behind him as he glanced around the garage.

Nobody there.

"Nothing." He looked back around the cul-de-sac, the neighbors' yards. Levi wasn't there, which made sense since Dan said he'd seen him take off into the woods. Craig tried to slow his heart down, release the sudden burst of paranoia that had flooded him. "Let's head inside, okay?"

The front door was still locked, which was a relief, and Craig pulled his keys out to let them in. The house was quiet, the jingle of his key ring and their footsteps echoing up through their open foyer. Alice unclipped Felix's leash, and he trotted into the living room for a well-deserved nap under the couch.

Craig stood in the entryway, listening as hard as he could for something off in the house. Alice followed the cat, and he scanned the living room behind her. Everything seemed normal. The kitchen was fine, and nothing seemed off in the basement.

He came back upstairs but didn't see his daughter anywhere.

"Alice?"

No response, so he tried again. After a few increasingly tense seconds, her voice floated down from above.

"Up here, Daddy."

Craig headed up the staircase to her bedroom. Alice had her back to him and was digging through her drawers. "I was kinda hot, so I wanted to change into shorts."

He looked around her room, but like the rest of the house, nothing seemed out of place. "Yeah, that's fine."

Alice turned back toward him and stared. Craig could feel someone creeping up behind him and spun around.

Nobody was there. He turned back to see her giggling. "I just wanted some privacy so I can change."

The spike of fear dissolved into embarrassment and heated the back of his neck. Nobody was in their house. He took a deep breath before bowing out of her room and heading downstairs.

Alice came down with her shorts on and asked if she could do some crafts on the dining room table, so Craig set her up.

With her occupied and the paranoia hopefully out of his system, he figured it was a good time to start polishing those first few chapters.

Craig made himself another cup of coffee and winked at Alice as he headed into the office.

His laptop stood open on the desk where it always did, but was now in the middle of a huge puddle of water.

Craig's brain went numb, unwilling to accept the input it had received.

The white ceramic orchid pot lay on its side nearby, the flower's stem snapped in half and draped across the keyboard. He pulled the chair away from the desk and felt water squish up between his toes as more dropped to the carpet. He set his idiotproof planter back on its base and felt the tiny bit of water remaining inside slosh around the bottom. The laptop was still plugged in to a power strip below, and Craig yanked the cord out before considering what electricity and water could do to a person.

He picked up the laptop, and water dripped out of every space and seam between the keys onto the lake already on the desk. Nothing happened when he wiped his sleeve across the keyboard in a pathetic attempt to soak up at least some of the moisture, and the reality he'd been fighting off caught up to him.

Craig set the computer next to his turntable and pressed his finger against the fingerprint sensor on the top right.

Nothing.

He wiped his hand across his shirt, as if his wet finger were the problem, and tried again to an expected result.

His laptop, along with everything on it, was dead.

Craig turned back toward his desk and tried to come up with a logical, nonhysterical way this could have happened.

The desk was huge, and the orchid lived on the far corner, but it and its water had made their way over to his computer. He could have blamed it on the cat if he really tried, but Felix had been with them at the park. Besides, there was no water in the corner.

The front door had been locked—he distinctly remembered unlocking it when they'd gotten home. Dan said he'd seen Levi in their backyard, so Craig went out to the kitchen and checked the patio door.

Also locked.

"What's the matter, Daddy?"

Craig had forgotten about his little girl working on her crafts at the table. "Something happened to my computer, and it got spilled on. You didn't forget to lock the basement door again, did you?"

She shook her head hard enough that her ponytail slapped each side of her face. "No way. Promise. I check it every time like you told me to."

He wanted to believe her but headed into the basement to check it anyway. She was right. From the bottom of the stairs, he could see the latch on the door handle was in place—just like it had been that night Courtney had found him down there, convinced Levi had gotten into their house.

Craig let the doubts swirl around his mind as he headed back upstairs.

He thought about calling the police, but what did he have besides suspicion? Dan had seen Levi out back, but that was a far cry from catching him in the act. He considered talking to Levi's parents, but that would be even more pointless. They'd twist it around that he was somehow bullying their innocent little boy again.

He grabbed a towel from the kitchen and headed back to the office. His computer sat dead where he'd left it, and as frustrated as he was, Craig thanked the universe for that close call he'd had a few weeks back. Seeing his book's life flash before his eyes like that had reminded him to save it to a backup file on a USB drive every day, so at least all his work wasn't gone.

For whatever that's worth.

There was an old computer around on a shelf somewhere that he'd kept to let Alice play some games, but she'd always been more interested in what was on the iPad. He should be able to limp along with that until he could buy a new laptop.

Craig plopped the towel on the desk and soaked up as much water as he could. The adapter he used to plug in his USB drive lay off to the side, empty. Craig scanned the desk around it, picked up a notebook and some random papers, but the little silver drive wasn't there. He looked under the desk—nothing but wet carpet. He yanked the drawer open, even though he never put the thing away. He wasn't surprised it wasn't there.

Panic surged through his veins as Craig tore apart the office, looking for his old flash drive. Losing a $1,000 laptop was bad, but that drive was the backup. With his computer dead, it was the only copy of his book left in the world.

Losing it was not an option.

When he finished in the office, he expanded his search through the rest of the house, even though his USB drive had never been more than five feet from his desk.

Alice asked him what was wrong as he went back to sweep the office again.

"My flash drive is gone, and it's got my book on it, so I really need to find it." Craig looked under the dining room table, muttering to himself and praying for a miracle. "It's gotta be here somewhere."

Alice spoke as he stood back up. "That's what you said about Pete."

Craig stared at her, pieces fitting together in his paranoid brain.

Before he thought better of it, Craig headed to the backyard.

A trickle of sweat dripped down Craig's neck as he stood in the middle of their backyard, scanning the trees in front of him for any sign of Levi. Dan had seen him take off into the woods not that long ago, but the little shit was like a constant tickle in the back of your throat. A persistent cough that wouldn't go away.

The shade from the trees was a welcome respite from the sun, and a breeze blew through strong enough to give him a quick chill when it hit the sweat that had beaded up on his skin. Craig looked back at the house before getting too far into the woods, half expecting to see Levi sliding through their patio door. He thought of Alice in there, working on her crafts alone. He should be with her, making sure she was safe.

But that's what he was doing out here. If Levi was getting in their place, this went well beyond juvenile harassment. Who knew what a kid like that would do?

Craig pushed through the underbrush and headed farther into the woods.

An unnatural silence settled around him. In a place full of a million things that chitter, crash, and rustle, it was like all the noisemakers had stopped to watch the interloper invading their wooded sanctum. Did this happen when Levi traipsed through, or had they accepted him as one of their own? Maybe this was where he belonged, a perfect fit among the shadows and rotting foliage.

The wispy branches of brush and saplings, skinny from the shade, grabbed at his legs as he made his way up the makeshift path Levi had beaten to their backyard over the last month. Craig stepped over a log onto the thin ribbon of packed dirt he'd discovered the last time he'd been back here. It twisted up toward the Ryan house to the left. The right-hand path led deeper into the woods.

Craig headed right.

Alice and Levi had come from that direction the day he'd taken them out for lunch. They'd been at his fort. If the kid was hiding out anywhere, that would be a good place to start looking.

But what happened if Craig found him?

He'd get his flash drive back, then go show Levi's parents. They wouldn't be able to deny that. They'd pay for a new computer; they'd keep their kid away from his family; and—possibly most satisfying—they'd eat their goddamn words. Craig imagined how many people Cassandra Ryan had told about him, the awful man who blamed their innocent son for everything.

He smiled to himself at the thought.

The path narrowed the farther he went, and more fallen branches crunched under his feet and lashed at his ankles. He stopped and strained his eyes through the trees. He'd never been this way and tried to picture where he was in relation to the neighborhoods. The woods were thick but didn't go on forever. At some point he would break through into someone else's backyard, but it was impossible to tell if he was twenty feet away or if he was separated by fifty yards of dense trees.

After another dozen steps, a gap in the underbrush popped up to his right. Craig pushed aside a branch and stepped over a fallen log. Long dead sticks snapped under his feet as he left the path, arms held in front to keep the foliage from slapping him in the face. Ahead, he could see a mass of branches piled around a tree. He headed that way.

His nose picked up the earthy smell of decay as he got closer, and he remembered why Alice never went inside Levi's fort.

It smells bad.

As he got closer, Craig saw the tree had caught a fallen trunk in its branches and held it at a rough forty-five-degree angle. A row of branches were lined up along each side to form a primitive lean-to. Some still had leaves attached, while some looked like they'd been on the forest floor for years before Levi had picked them up to make his headquarters.

Alice hadn't been exaggerating about the smell. It was like rotten cabbage—a warning to stay away—but he had to look.

Craig circled around toward the open end in the back. The fallen tree Levi had used as a ceiling beam couldn't have been more than four feet off the ground at the entrance, so even a nine-year-old would have to duck inside. A dark, dirty piece of tarp hung down as a makeshift door. Its edges were torn instead of cut, and it had mud caked over most of it. Like the branches and sticks he'd used for walls, it was definitely something scavenged from the woods as opposed to taken from his family's garage.

A little hidey-hole to squirrel away his treasures.

He pushed the soiled tarp aside and was punched in the face by the rancid air that spilled out. Craig stumbled back, and something snagged his heel. The impact with the forest floor knocked the wind out of him, forcing him to suck in more of that tainted oxygen than he'd ever wanted. He could taste the molecules of whatever made the stench, and the thought made him retch.

He rolled over onto all fours as the sounds of his dry heaves echoed through the trees, but the more he tried to hold back, the more they forced their way out his throat and broke the still of the woods. Tears burned in his eyes as Craig held on to the ground in front of him, desperately trying to wrest control of his chest.

Only one thing smelled like that, and the thought made Craig want to run. Fear and morbid curiosity kept him there.

The tarp had fallen back over the entrance to the fort, and Craig approached it like a member of the bomb squad. He pulled his shirt up over his nose and eased the tarp aside. The smell rolled out again, battering his senses. He closed his eyes against it, then cracked them open slowly as his body tried to adjust to the putrid assault.

Little light seeped into the fort from between the haphazard branches that formed the walls, and his vision was still foggy. Blurry blobs slowly condensed into shapes he could recognize—an old shoebox, a white five-gallon bucket, a foot-long metal cylinder he'd seen in the woods before.

Hanging above a squirrel trap was a tiny white skull, a piece of yarn threaded through the hole once occupied by an eye and tied to a branch above. It slowly rotated in whatever breeze he'd let in, yellow teeth at the end of a pointed snout that looked terrifyingly alien when not covered by fluffy gray fur.

The bucket in the back was covered by a ratty slab of plywood. Craig knew it was the source of the smell. A rusty ball-peen hammer leaned up against the side.

He was too repulsed to shiver, and part of him screamed *run*, to get out of the woods and call someone about this, anyone, and if they didn't listen, call someone else because this wasn't anywhere close to normal kid behavior.

The shoebox was only about six feet in, but Craig couldn't force himself under that makeshift roof, where he'd have to breathe that air, get near that bucket. Something was tucked in with the branches that Levi had used to make the walls. Craig reached in and pulled it out.

The croquet mallet.

Craig could hear the echoes of Alice's cry in the silence of the woods, and the thought of Levi keeping the mallet back here like some sort of perverted trophy ate at him.

Or is he . . . using it?

Craig looked at the little squirrel skull dangling from the roof and pushed that thought away.

He tucked the tarp back around a branch and reached in with the mallet. Craig snuck the head behind the shoebox and pulled it toward him. Just putting his arm inside the fort made him feel dirty, but his curiosity had taken over. The box slid fairly easily, its few contents jostling around inside as Craig maneuvered it closer. When it got within arm's reach, he dropped the mallet and pulled the box out.

It couldn't have been out there long. The glossy cardboard looked relatively new, but the top felt a little wilty when he pulled it off.

No flash drive.

Craig stared into the box with confused disappointment. There was only a handful of change, a roll of duct tape, and a multicolored plastic bag with Japanese writing on it. He reached in to grab it before realizing it was bonito flakes and jerking his hand away. It was more instinct than anything. Handling the bag wouldn't be enough to trigger his fish allergy, but he was on edge.

It was probably what Levi used for bait in the squirrel trap.

His eyes went to the bucket again. Pins and needles danced through his skull.

A ball of fur was tucked in the corner where the shoebox had been. Craig shuddered but couldn't resist a closer look. He grabbed the mallet and poked it. Whatever it was didn't move. He stretched farther into the fort to get at it. Unlike the shoebox, it didn't slide easily. He prodded it back toward himself as best he could, until the thing was within arm's reach and he could pull it out.

Pete the Bunny.

Craig couldn't believe it, but the dark parts of him certainly could. He turned the stuffed rabbit over and over. It was a little dirty, but there wasn't any damage that hadn't been done by seven years of hugs and love.

His missing flash drive was pushed aside at the thought of presenting Alice with her favorite thing in the world, presumed gone forever. He could see the look on her face and that of his wife when he told her where he'd found it.

Proof that he wasn't paranoid after all.

Craig brushed some dirt off Pete's ears, and his knees popped as he stood up from the fort, missing croquet mallet at his feet.

Levi stood just ten feet away, hands clenched at his sides, voice practically a growl.

"Get out of there."

CHAPTER TWENTY-FOUR

Craig stood frozen, towering over the scrawny, barely four-foot-tall boy in front of him, yet still scared even though he was the adult in this situation. No matter what had happened between them, his age gave him authority.

But it sure didn't feel like it.

Levi held his gaze with an entitled mandate. The kid had much more confidence than when Craig had kicked him off his property that first time.

You don't own the woods.

Well, neither did Levi, but the look on his face said he felt otherwise.

"Did you wreck my computer?"

The kid's expression didn't change, and he offered no denial.

"I know you've been in our house, Levi."

His eyes turned dark when he saw Craig holding his daughter's stuffed bunny.

"Put that *back*."

The ferocity in the boy's voice was unsettling, and Craig had to puff up his chest to play the adult. "No. It's not yours. You stole it, and you're going to get in big trouble."

"I don't get in trouble."

"You will this time, I'll make sure of that." Craig looked for a crack in the kid's face but didn't see one. His belief was unshakable and probably well earned over his nine years. "You broke into our house, Levi. That's a *crime*. You poured water on my computer and stole Alice's bunny."

He held Pete up for effect but got no reaction.

"Did you take my flash drive too?"

Levi's voice was low and steely. "Fuck you."

"Those are big words, kid." Craig put as much condescension into his tone as he could. He needed to remind Levi of his place, reclaim his hand. "But you didn't answer my question. You took it, didn't you? You wrecked my computer and stole my flash drive. That's got my book on it, and I need it right now, you hear? This is serious, no messing around. If you don't give it back, I'm going to call the police. When it comes to real big-boy crime like that, they don't give a damn how much your mommy yells or who your daddy is. They'll come to your house and look through every place you could even think of hiding something. Your room, your little fort here." Craig hoped to scare the kid, but he seemed unmoved. "I wonder what else they'll find. Does your dad know what you're doing to those squirrels back here?"

Craig watched as the fires of hate burned behind Levi's eyes and braced himself for an outburst, but none came. He let him stew in his own juices for a minute, then continued.

"I know you took it. Give it back, and I won't call the police."

No reaction.

"You think you won't get in trouble when the cops show up? Think about it, Levi. Give me my flash drive, and you won't have to find out."

He studied Levi's face for any sign that the kid knew the offer was bullshit. Flash drive or not, the second Craig got back to the house, he was calling the police. It was time this little punk faced some consequences. If Levi could come into their house, steal or wreck their most important possessions with no ramifications whatsoever, it would never stop.

And it *had* to stop.

"Is it in there?" Craig nodded toward the fort. "Maybe I should check?"

The second he moved toward the fort, Levi's face cracked. *"NO YOU CAN'T!"* His shrill outburst reverberated out like seismic waves and shattered the still of the woods. Craig could have sworn the leaves had shuddered at the sound. He froze midstride, scared of who might have heard as well as the level of unbridled rage that could produce such a sound. It was fury with no restrictor plates to hold it back. A nuclear reactor with no safeguards—something that could feed off itself, growing stronger as it metastasized.

Any authority Craig thought he'd enjoyed evaporated. The air had changed, almost as if a winter breeze had decided to snake through the woods and find him. He fought off a shiver.

And just as quickly the rage was gone from Levi's face. He was back in control. Had his voice not still echoed in Craig's ears, he'd have thought it had been a hallucination.

He tried to press on toward the fort, but it was too late. The situation had flipped, and they both knew it.

"Stop it, please." The kid's voice was loud but stripped of the anger from before. "What are you doing? Don't . . ."

Craig could hear it bouncing around the trees, reaching toward the backyards that lined the woods. He had no clue how far sound traveled or how much underbrush it had to plow through to find receptive ears, but he couldn't afford to find out.

If somebody heard him . . .

"Shhhhh!" As if Levi would listen. As if he didn't know what he was doing. The kid knew exactly how powerful the card he'd slapped on the table was, and so did Craig.

"Please stop!" Louder than before. Desperately searching for someone to hear. Craig had the urge to run over and clamp his hand over the kid's mouth, but that idea was so bad that even in his panicked state, he shot it down instantly.

So he did the only other thing he could think of—turned and ran. The mallet caught between his feet and sent Craig crashing to the ground. He refused to let go of Pete and was unable to brace himself, so he hit hard, Levi's cries weaving through the stars in his vision.

Craig pushed himself up and tore off into the woods.

—

Craig's breathing was heavy and ragged as he lurched through their patio door. His heartbeat thundered in his ears, blocking out any noise that might still be coming from out back as sweat smeared across his forehead, as much from fear as exertion.

The yelling out back had ceased, and Craig's only hope was they'd been too far back in the woods for anyone to hear. He could see Alice through the hall, staring in from the dining room. The giant bucket of art supplies sat ignored in front of her, pipe cleaners and puff balls strewed across the table in a jumble that mirrored the little girl's eyes.

Craig forced a smile and waved at her, but it did nothing. He'd reassured her so many times over the last few weeks, smiles and hugs and *don't worry, it's okay*s, all while spilling anxiety all over their lives. How long before his affirmations were worthless to her?

And what becomes of a father who loses his daughter's trust?

"What are you working on, kiddo?" The hollow words were ignored and quickly evaporated.

"What happened to your arms?" Alice asked.

Craig looked down and saw an angry crosshatch of pink and red scratches across his forearms. Panic had driven him through the woods, forgoing paths and ignoring the branches that lashed at him on the way.

He held his arm out to show her it wasn't too bad, and it pulled a shriek from her.

"PETE!"

"Oh . . . yes!" He'd completely forgotten about the stuffed bunny in his hands. "I found him!"

Alice leaped out of her chair and sprinted toward him with a face full of joy. Both arms were outstretched, ready to give her bunny every hug it had missed since Levi stole him.

The memory of where he'd found him hit as hard as the smell from Levi's fort, and Craig instinctively jerked it out of her grasp. Alice skidded to a stop at his feet, her face slapped with betrayal as if her father had just played the cruelest prank imaginable.

"Let me wash him first. He's really dirty."

"Dirty?" Alice's voice hesitated like she didn't believe him—as if this were still a trick—and that hurt.

"I found him back in the woods, and . . ." The smell from Levi's fort wafted back through his sinuses. "He needs a good bath first."

Alice took a step back, too anxious to ask questions that Craig wasn't sure he wanted to answer anyway. "Okay . . . can you wash him right now?"

"Absolutely."

Craig turned toward the washing machine in their back hall, and Alice slotted in right behind him.

"Can I give him one hug first?"

He looked down at the bunny in his hands. The thing had been loved to death over the years and didn't look much different from when Alice had brought it downstairs every morning. But Craig couldn't make himself hand it over without washing it. Not with where it had been. He'd dip it in bleach if he could. Bring in a priest and perform an exorcism.

"Let's wash him first . . . in case there are any germs on him or something." Disappointment fell across her face like rain, but she agreed. "It'll be quick. I promise."

Craig carried Pete into the back hall and tossed him into the washer. Usually they put him in one of the laundry bags Courtney used to wash her bras, but it didn't feel right putting something so contaminated into something his wife used for her intimates. He turned the knob all the way to the rarely used "Sanitize" setting and pressed start.

Alice was waiting in the hall, so anxious to get her bunny back she could barely stand still. Given the option, Alice would have stood in front of that washer, stealing whatever glance she could through the little round window.

"Why don't we go finish your crafts?" He practically had to push her back to the dining room table.

Craig worked hard to keep Alice preoccupied as Pete sloshed through the cleaning cycle. The drama of their reunion had distracted him enough he'd been able to temporarily push what had gone down in the woods out of his head, and Alice either didn't care or knew not to ask where he'd found Pete.

Or maybe she didn't need to ask.

The computer presumably still dripped in the office. He either wanted to leave it as evidence or didn't want to face the ramifications of months of work lying dead in a puddle of water.

Maybe both.

He still planned on calling the police—that kind of stuff couldn't just be swept under the rug, and Levi's behavior had been ignored for too long—but Alice's joy had been too much to ignore.

After everything they'd gone through, he just wanted to get that bunny in her hands.

Eventually, the muffled thump of a stuffed bunny tumbling around the dryer stopped, and a melodic trill called to them from the back hall, announcing the completed drying of Alice's long-lost friend. She bolted from the table, her artistic endeavors abandoned.

"You're faster than Felix when we open up a can of food." Craig pushed back from the dining room table to follow her just as a police cruiser came into view out the front windows. He watched as it circled around the cul-de-sac and came to a stop in front of their house.

For a second he had to remind himself that in spite of his plans, he hadn't, in fact, called them yet.

Two officers got out—the same two he'd talked to when he'd brought Levi home that day. Their faces didn't betray the reason they were there, but something started eating its way through Craig's gut as his admittedly addled brain began to click pieces together.

A wave of panic swept through him.

NO! Pull your shit together.

They had listened to him last time, understood how a lack of communication led to an unfortunate incident. They'd listen again—and this time he had proof. He just had to be calm.

Be calm.

The dryer door slammed in the back hall and jolted Craig out of his own head. He ran his fingers back through his hair and looked out at the cops walking up the driveway.

He was still standing there when the doorbell rang.

Craig sucked in a deep breath and blew it out slowly before trusting himself to open the door.

"Hello, Mr. Finnigan. I'm not sure if you remember me, but I'm Lieutenant Shaw. We spoke a few weeks ago up at the Ryan house."

"Of course, how are you?" Craig thought it weird that he would imply there was a way he could have forgotten that interaction, but tried to keep that out of his tone. The cop was just being polite, and he was being paranoid.

"Fine. Do you mind if we come in and talk to you for a minute?"

He ushered them into the foyer even as a voice inside screamed at him not to. But why not? This was his chance to let them know what Levi was doing. Hell, his still-wet computer was in the office to their left. He wanted to spill out everything that had happened that day—the last few weeks—but something held him back. Lieutenant Shaw had that practiced voice of a veteran police officer. Steady. Not about to tip his hand. But there was something in the way his partner carried himself that told Craig he needed to tread lightly, to not throw his cards on the table without knowing what game they were playing.

Lieutenant Shaw wasted no time laying down their hand.

"We got a call from Stephen Ryan that you have been harassing his son, Levi."

"What? No . . ." Craig felt anger bubble over inside him and desperately tried to keep a lid on it.

Becalmbecalmbecalmbecalm.

The facts were on his side. Blowing up would only put him in the box they wanted. But his lack of sleep and constant stress had left his margins painfully thin. He took a deep breath and wrestled calm back into his voice. "Like you suggested, I've done my best to avoid him altogether."

"Did you see him this morning?" That question came from Officer Perez. Craig had to glance at his name tag to remind himself of his name.

"I see him all the time because he keeps coming down here even though I told him not to, but I ignored him. If anyone is harassing anyone, it's him."

The look on Perez's face told Craig how much of a threat he considered a nine-year-old boy.

"Were you in the woods behind your house this morning?" Shaw asked.

"Yes, I was looking for—"

"Was Levi back there too?" Perez jumped in before Craig could explain.

"Um, yes. But like I was saying, I—"

"I thought you were trying to avoid him?" Shaw asked.

"I was, but . . ." This back and forth bouncing between questions was keeping him from stringing his thoughts together. "What did they say I did?"

Craig noticed Shaw give his partner a silent glance before he spoke. "Why don't you just tell us what you were doing back in the woods."

"Like I was trying to say earlier, I was back there looking for my flash drive."

"Your flash drive? Like a USB drive? Why would that be back in the woods?"

Craig felt like he was being pulled in seven different directions, but was happy to finally get where he'd wanted to be. "Because Levi took it."

The cops exchanged another glance, much less subtle than the last time. He'd been spraying his story around scattershot and knew he needed to focus things quick, or there would be no chance of them believing him.

"I'm an author, and that thing's got my book on it. This morning, when my daughter and I were at the park, it disappeared."

"And you think Levi Ryan took it?" It must have been years of experience that allowed Lieutenant Shaw to keep the doubt out of his voice.

"I do, and that's not all." Craig stepped over and pushed the office door open. "Come look at this."

The computer was still dead on the desk; the towel he'd brought in earlier had soaked up most of the puddle. The empty orchid pot sat next to it.

"When I came home, my computer was ruined and the flash drive where I back up my manuscript every day was gone." Craig pointed to the USB adapter still hanging off his computer. "That thing is plugged into my computer at all times, and I back up the file onto it every day when I'm done. I'm religious about it. And it's gone. The kid came in, doused my computer, and took my flash drive."

"This where the water came from?" Shaw reached over and picked up the orchid pot. He couldn't keep the doubt out of his voice anymore. "Seems to me that this could have just gotten knocked over and wrecked your computer, right?"

Officer Perez jumped in as if on cue. "I thought I saw a cat out there. My wife's cat is always sniffing around plants. Maybe it got a little curious and accidentally knocked it over, ya know?"

"No, the cat was with us at the park when it happened."

"You take your cat to the park?"

"Yes. My daughter has a leash, and we took him for a walk this morning because I thought it would be a fun thing to do."

Too much annoyance in his voice. Playing into everything the Ryans said about him.

"So you and your daughter took your cat to the park this morning. Did you lock your door when you left?"

"Yes."

"Then how did Levi get in to pour water on your computer?"

Things were spiraling, mostly because Craig didn't have an answer to that. He'd been religiously locking and double-checking doors this whole time, yet Levi kept finding a way in.

Did he?

Standing in front of two cops was like opening his eyes to morning-after sunlight. Everything looked different. It was almost enough for him to entertain their doubt.

Almost.

"I don't know, but I think he's been doing it for a while now."

Perez shot a doubtful look at Shaw, who ignored him. "You think he's been in your house before?"

"Well . . ." Craig thought of getting up to check those weird sounds in the middle of the night. Creeping downstairs to find . . . locked doors and nobody when he'd been so sure. *Still* was so sure. Out in the entryway, Alice poked her head from behind the stairs to peek in at the policeman talking to her dad. "Hold on!"

Craig hustled past Shaw and Perez as Alice ducked back like a frightened rabbit. "Hey, come here for a second, kiddo."

She fled into the kitchen, and Craig tried to look as reassuring as possible when he found her standing by the table.

"Can I see Pete for a minute, honey?" She pulled her stuffed bunny in closer, reluctant to let him out of her sight. "I'll give him right back, I promise. I just have to show the policemen something."

Alice hesitantly extended her bunny toward him and flinched when Craig snatched it away. He turned and almost ran into Shaw and Perez, who had followed him out of the office and filled the little hallway like a row of hay bales. Instinct pushed Craig back a step, but he recovered and held up the bunny for them.

"This is my daughter's bunny—literally her most favorite thing in the world. Never sleeps without it. A while back, I don't know, about two weeks ago it disappeared." The cops didn't look impressed, but Craig didn't care. He was practically baiting them, like a prosecutor holding back his surprise evidence. "I found it back in the woods this morning . . . in Levi Ryan's fort."

BOOM! Craig had been rattled by the cops showing up, and for a bit it had felt like he was losing them. His lack of sleep certainly wasn't helping his coherence, but he'd pulled it together. Shaw had his cop face on again, but it didn't bother Craig. He knew a police officer couldn't yell *woo-hoo* and give him a high five. But as the seconds ticked past, he expected some kind of reaction. A question or two at least.

But they just stood there looking at him.

He held Pete over toward them. "Take a look if you want."

Shaw held up his hand as if he'd offered him a second slice of pie, but Craig was undeterred.

"I found it out there this morning. I was going to call you myself, but Alice was so excited to see him when I got back that we got distracted and put him in the wash right away." He turned to his daughter, who had backed another few steps away from him. "Isn't that right, kiddo?"

Her eyes were wide, and her lips were little more than a thin pink line where smiles usually lived. She offered only a quick nod.

Craig turned back to the officers, both of whom were still looking down at Alice before coming back to him.

"How have things been around here lately? You been doing okay? Everything all right with the family?"

The question landed with the subtlety of a falling anvil, and Craig felt his face drop. How were they not getting what was happening here? It was like they were willingly obtuse, as if nothing he said or showed them mattered. What the hell had they been told about him? Sweat popped up on the base of his neck, and Craig suddenly felt like he was under a heat lamp. He had to get control of (*himself*) the situation quickly before things spiraled further.

He was not the bad guy here.

Deep breath, and another when that didn't work.

"Things are fine." He worried it had taken him too long to say that and that it had come out too fast, but it was the best he could do. He couldn't let a question like that—which was nothing more than an accusation—hang. But Shaw looked past him at Alice.

"How about you, little lady? Everything okay with you?"

She just stood silent, obviously nervous that cops had shown up at her house and started interrogating her father. Craig didn't like the way they were roping her into this at all.

"Like I said, everything's fine." He turned and put on a reassuring smile for her. "Why don't you head downstairs while we finish talking, okay? You can watch a movie or something."

Alice headed toward the stairs, and Craig called after her. "Don't forget Pete."

She took him without a word and headed into the basement. Craig waited until she had gotten down and out of earshot before turning back to the policemen. "Why are you asking about me? About my family?"

Lieutenant Shaw's eyes narrowed slightly, as if Alice leaving allowed him to get more serious. "Because we've heard some things that are concerning beyond what happened this morning. You want to tell us about what happened at the SEMAC pool yesterday?"

"I can explain that . . ." Again, Craig fought hard to keep his voice down. He couldn't let Alice hear him yelling, and these two didn't look like the type of cops who appreciated someone taking a tone with them. "Levi Ryan was holding a little girl underwater, and I had to jump in to get him to let her up."

"Did you accost the boy after you . . . jumped in?"

"Jesus Christ, he was going to drown her, and nobody was doing anything." There was force and certainty in Craig's voice. He'd admitted his fault in what had gone down at the pool too many times and was sick of getting raked over the coals for it. At some point he had to stop letting people take free shots at him. "I saw the whole thing from start to finish, and I can one hundred percent guarantee that was no accident and they weren't *just playing*. He was staring right at me, holding her underwater, like he was daring me to do something. It's like some sick fucking game with him or something."

Lieutenant Shaw did not seem impressed, which shouldn't have been surprising since he'd undoubtedly been indoctrinated with Levi's version already. "Whether you believe it to be an accident or not, you can't go after a child like that, and this is the second time the Ryans have called the police with their concerns about you."

"That last time was a misunderstanding. You *know* that."

Or maybe it wasn't. He'd always assumed Levi had just forgotten to ask or his mom had been busy and he hadn't bothered, but maybe it had been intentional. Some way to maneuver a chess piece into trouble for his twisted amusement.

It would explain a lot.

"Maybe it was, but the Ryans are very concerned about your behavior around their son." Shaw said. "Have you ever tried to contact Levi without his parents' knowledge?"

"What are you talking about?"

"You ever try to call him? Invite him down to play or anything?" Perez jumped in with the follow-up as if he were trying to trip him up somehow.

"Call him, like on the phone?" Craig felt like he was being pulled back and forth between the two officers. "Of course not. Like I told you, that kid is not allowed down here anymore. I don't want him anywhere near us. Even before all this, I literally never invited him down here. Not once. He'd just show up every morning."

He was talking to Perez, but he noticed Lieutenant Shaw glance over at his partner while he spoke, and it spiked his nerves again. He had no idea where they were going with this.

"His mother found a scrap of paper with your phone number on it in Levi's room. Why would he have that?"

Craig was discombobulated enough it took him a second to realize what they were talking about, but then it hit him like a shot from an EpiPen. *That's* what they were worried about, and *that* had an easy explanation. "Oh no, no, no . . . I mean, yes, I gave it to him, but he was supposed to give that to his mother." He looked back at Lieutenant Shaw for validation. "It was after that lunch mix-up thing. I went up there to talk to the mom and give her my number so that wouldn't happen again. But when I went there, Levi was out front and said she wasn't home, so I left my number with him and said to give it to her."

"He ever use it?"

"No."

"And you've never called him? Texted?"

"I already told you, no. He's a nine-year-old kid, for god's sake." If they didn't want to believe him, he'd prove himself. "You know what . . . wait a sec." Craig doubled back into the kitchen and snatched his phone off the counter. He thumbed it open and pulled up his recent history. "Here."

He held out his phone and showed them the screen. "See?" Craig scrolled down through the last few weeks of calls. "Nothing."

Shaw reached out for the phone. "Do you mind?"

Every warning from every cop show he'd ever seen screamed out to say no. The cold, hard realization that he could be in serious trouble hit for the first time, and handing over his unlocked phone seemed like something that would give any decent lawyer a heart attack. But he'd walked himself out on this particular gangplank, and backtracking would only throw lighter fluid on their suspicions. Besides, there was nothing incriminating on his phone.

He handed it over and watched Shaw scroll through his call log. "See?"

Craig reached over to take his phone back, but the cop didn't offer it. Instead he closed out to the home screen and tapped on Craig's text messages.

Perez read over his partner's shoulder as he scrolled.

That was much more invasive. It wasn't just a list of numbers, but conversations he'd had laid bare. Personal things. Maybe some bad jokes that could be easily misconstrued out of context. It was like they were flipping through the files in his head, reading his thoughts.

His hands itched, dying to snatch his phone away, but he didn't dare. He kept telling himself this was the only way to prove his innocence.

Eventually Shaw handed the phone back without a word.

"I told you—nothing." Getting his phone back gave him a shot of confidence, and he was ready to go on the attack. Things had happened so fast he still hadn't processed all he'd seen back at Levi's fort—the trap, the skull, the bucket.

That smell.

The kid acted untouchable, and based on his parents' responses, probably had good reason to. He'd been in their house. Stolen their stuff.

Alice's ankle.

Craig had been so concerned about what was going on he never saw the forest for the trees. What he'd played off as kid behavior or accidents snapped together in a disturbing picture and sent a chill through him.

"You said Levi's parents are concerned with my behavior? Well, I'm concerned with his. And they need to be too." The cops didn't give a response, which made sense because Craig had kept half the conversation in his brain. "Listen . . . I know how all this looks, but I legitimately think there is something wrong about that kid. That fort where I found my daughter's bunny, he's got . . . stuff back there. And not just stuff he's taken, but, like . . . dead animals and stuff."

Perez rolled his eyes and let out a chuff of air.

"I'm serious. The smell is horrendous. You can ask my daughter about that." Craig started toward the basement stairs, but Lieutenant Shaw put up his hand.

"That's fine."

"But I'm serious. It smells like death."

"Yet you let your daughter play back there?" Perez's voice told him that if it were not for his partner, he'd have left long ago. Maybe dragging Craig in cuffs behind him.

"No . . . I didn't know what he had back there then, but she told me he wouldn't let her in and it smelled really bad. Then this morning I went back there looking for my stuff and, oh my god, the smell. He's been trapping squirrels and . . . there's this bucket." The memory of that odor smacked him in the face. "I don't know what he does, but there was a skull hanging from the ceiling in there."

Perez tapped Shaw on the shoulder and got a look of agreement. They didn't believe him and were going to leave with Craig having done nothing but make his situation worse.

"Wait, wait, wait . . ." He'd put himself out on a limb, talking about Levi like that, and couldn't let them leave while they still didn't believe him. "I'll show you. It's right back there, and you'll see what I'm saying. The kid is twisted . . . sick maybe."

Perez was halfway to the front door and didn't bother to answer.

"I don't expect to get any more calls from the Ryans about you, right, Mr. Finnigan?" Lieutenant Shaw had his right thumb looped over his belt, almost casually dismissive.

"No, please . . . let me show you. It will literally take a minute. It's right back there. You'll see what I'm talking about." Perez was at the door, but Shaw hadn't moved yet, so Craig focused on him. Calm and serious as he could manage. "I know how this sounds, okay, but please . . . just come see what I'm talking about. It will explain a *lot* of the weird stuff that's been happening. Please. All you've heard is their side of it, and I bet they don't know the half of what's going on."

Perez nodded his partner toward the door.

"I let you guys look through all my stuff 'cause I've got nothing to hide," Craig said. "All I'm asking is that you go look at his. You'll see what I'm talking about."

The exasperation rolled off Lieutenant Shaw in waves. It was obvious he still didn't believe Craig. So obvious that Craig was shocked when he said "Fine."

Chapter Twenty-Five

Craig could hear Officer Perez mumbling as he blazed them a trail back through the woods, but didn't care. They'd see the fort—or, more importantly, smell it—and realize there was a lot more to this story than the Ryans were saying. God, how great would it be to be a fly on the wall when they made a visit up to ask Stephen and Cassandra Ryan if they knew what their innocent little boy had been doing down at his little hideaway.

"Through here." Craig pushed some branches out of the way and stepped off the path. He held them aside, careful not to let them slingshot back in Lieutenant Shaw's face. No sense in being petty. "It's just up ahead."

They trudged through the underbrush in what Craig figured was the same basic approach he'd taken that morning. A few bent and broken saplings seemed to confirm it, although the brush was thick enough that it was hard to tell exactly where they were going.

They'd probably pick up the scent before they actually saw it.

"I bet my flash drive is back there. I didn't dare look too much inside. It was too disgusting." Now that he'd gotten them back here, the fear was gone. But he could feel the nerves that kept him talking.

"Honestly, if I can get that back and get a promise from his parents to keep him away from us, I don't care about pressing charges or anything."

He could practically hear Perez roll his eyes but chose to ignore it. Validation was just ahead through the trees.

Craig stepped over a fallen log and paused.

"We almost there?" Shaw's practiced cop voice was weighed down by the patience he was forcing into it.

"Should be right around here." Craig studied the foliage around himself, looking for a familiar landmark or two, but he hadn't exactly left a trail of bread crumbs the first time.

But they should definitely smell it by now.

A bush was trampled off to their left and led to a stretch of matted-down plants that looked familiar, so Craig headed that way.

He recognized the big oak that served as a tent pole for Levi's fort up ahead and picked up the pace. "Over here."

The fallen tree was still propped up against the oak, but the branches Levi had used to make the walls of his fort were strewed about the forest floor. The fort was gone. So was the bucket. The shoebox. The croquet mallet. "Where the fuck . . . ?" Craig nudged a few of the branches aside with his foot, but there was nothing underneath but dirt and decaying leaves. The smell was faint, but still there if you knew what to look for. To anyone else it would just blend in with the damp funk of the forest.

"Is this it?" Perez asked.

Panic gripped Craig's heart and squeezed. He didn't even have to look at the doubt on their faces. "It was right here—I swear to god." He kicked at the branches on the ground. "These were all lined up against that log right there. All the way down, and there was a tarp underneath . . . a black tarp."

As if details would get them to believe him. Perez had already turned back the way they had come by the time Craig looked up, but Lieutenant Shaw, as the senior officer, probably felt the responsibility to end this professionally.

"Look, Mr. Finnigan, I don't know what's going on with your life and all this, but for now, all I can say is I want you to stay away from the Ryan family, okay?"

Craig stared, mind racing to figure out how this could have happened. Perez was already out of sight on his way back to the path. "But . . . what about my computer? My book?"

"Accidents happen, right? And things get lost all the time. I'm willing to bet if you take some time and look around your house, your USB will show up somewhere." Shaw breathed out what was probably the last of his patience. "But I want to be crystal clear about this . . . you end all this nonsense right now. Leave the Ryans alone. Don't contact them. Don't talk to them. If you see the boy playing in your neighborhood or at the park or wherever, ignore him. Better yet, turn around and leave. You have a beautiful daughter of your own. Spend your time and energy on her. Are we clear?"

Shaw stared at him, waiting for an acknowledgment that Craig was psychologically incapable of giving. After a few seconds, he turned to follow his partner.

"It was right here. You've got to believe me." Craig's voice was low and beaten. The cop didn't bother turning back.

Chapter Twenty-Six

Craig drifted around in a fog the rest of the afternoon. His chores puttered to a stop every time he passed a window and stared out, expecting to see Levi. He made Alice a sandwich for lunch, but she retreated to the basement after barely eating half.

Before he knew it, the clock said six and he had to find something for dinner. Courtney would be home soon, and not only had he not figured out what they were going to eat, he had no idea how he was going to tell her about everything that had happened that morning.

He pulled a box of dried macaroni and a jar of spaghetti sauce out of the pantry and set some water to boil. The garage door opened just as the bubbles started to pop.

"Hey, sorry I'm late." Courtney plopped her bag on the corner buffet and dropped her car keys on the counter. "Where's Alice?"

"Downstairs," Craig said. "I can call her up in a second."

Courtney leaned down the basement staircase. "Hey, Allie cat, you down there?"

Alice's tiny voice hollered back and was followed by little thumps on the steps.

"How was work?" Craig asked as he dumped the jar of sauce into a pan and set it to medium. He tried to be calm, normal, but wasn't even sure what that felt like anymore. Life was a haze of anxiety. His nerves numb yet constantly firing.

Courtney glanced over with an I'll-tell-you-about-it-later look as Alice emerged into the kitchen, where she was greeted with a fierce hug. "Hello, my girl, how was your day?"

Alice offered a little shrug and said fine, but she was a terrible liar.

"What's the matter?"

Craig knew she didn't want to answer the question, and it felt like an ice pick to the heart. It was so unfair that she'd been put in this situation.

"It was just kinda boring."

Courtney threw a quick look at Craig before her follow-up. "Well, what did you do all day?"

"Mostly just watched TV."

"Why were you watching TV all afternoon?" The tone made no secret that she wasn't asking her daughter that question. "What was Dad doing?"

"Well, the police came, and he was talking with them."

Courtney stood up and looked at Craig. "Why were the police here?"

A bubble of sauce burst and splattered up on Craig's wrist. He'd had all afternoon to think of how he would break this to his wife, but still had no answer, so the question hung. Her voice was calm, but exasperation radiated from the other side of the table. "Apparently Levi has been telling his parents some more lies about me, and the police had to check them out."

Courtney dropped her head and let out a long breath.

"But, honestly, I'm glad they came because we had some things to tell them about, too, didn't we, Alice? Want to tell Mom who we found today?" He looked over at his daughter, who very obviously did not want to be part of the conversation, so he answered his own question.

"We found Pete . . . I should say I found Pete. Back in Levi's fort in the woods."

Courtney's eyebrows crinkled above her nose. "What?"

"Yep, Levi apparently came into our house and stole Pete, but that isn't all. While we were at the park today, he broke in and dumped water all over my laptop and stole the USB drive that had my book on it." Craig could hear his voice rising in tone and volume but was pretty much powerless to stop it.

"So *you* called the police?"

"Well, no, like I said, Levi has been telling his parents lies about me, so they called them, but I was able to show them all of that. I mean, I was going to call them anyway but—"

Courtney cut him off with a raised hand. "So what did they do? Did they talk to the Ryans? Get your stuff back?"

Another bubble popped and splattered against Craig's shirt. He stirred up the sauce and lowered the heat before answering. "Well . . . I took them back to Levi's fort—where I found Pete this morning—but he must have known I would take them back there, because he'd torn the whole thing down."

Courtney turned to Alice and told her to go wash her hands.

"I can explain it all later," Craig said, but Courtney ignored him and started clearing the table for dinner. Alice was back, and the pasta was done before Craig could figure out what to say, and Courtney made it painfully obvious she wasn't looking to continue the conversation during dinner. She chatted mostly with Alice, who told her all about their adventure taking Felix to the park.

Craig listened to her tell the story and could barely remember that it had happened just that morning.

Courtney kept the mood light with their daughter—even included Craig in the conversation at times, which was more disturbing than anything. She'd closed off her anger, but he knew better than to think it was gone. It was locked away somewhere, probably growing, festering.

He could feel the pressure from across the table, but knew Courtney was too good a mom to let it out in front of their little girl.

So he'd have to wait and hope it dissipated some before she got him alone.

When they were done eating, Courtney and Alice sat at the dining room table drawing various animals. Craig listened in from the kitchen as she taught Alice the finer points of drawing a cat. Even though they were right there, a hole of loneliness had torn through his stomach. All he wanted was to explain himself to her, make her understand, chase away that look of doubt from her face and earn her trust back—but the clock said Alice wouldn't go to bed for another hour, so he kept drying dishes.

He was staring out the window over the sink, towel aimlessly rubbing against a saucepan, when Levi popped out of the woods. Craig dropped the pan, and it made a ringing clatter in the sink as he headed for the sliding glass door. He pulled it open, wet dish towel still in hand, and hurried across to the deck railing.

Levi was gone.

Craig stared at the trees, looking for any sign of the kid. The shadows were long that late in the evening, providing plenty of dark spots for a creepy little kid to hide in.

Something bumped against the back of his leg and ignited all the nerves inside him. Craig jumped and banged his knee against one of the wooden spindles as Felix lurched back, tail puffed out from the scare.

"You're letting mosquitoes in." Courtney closed the door and headed back to her art project with Alice.

Craig watched her through the glass door as the adrenaline seeped from his system. He wanted to tell her what he'd seen but was afraid she wouldn't believe him, and he didn't want to make things even worse. He bent down to scoop up their cat and headed back inside, taking one last look at the woods before locking the patio door behind him.

—

"So do you want to hear about this afternoon?"

The strain had built up inside Craig all evening. He'd held it in until they'd gotten Alice to bed, expecting a chance to explain himself, but Courtney had retreated into the office and left him alone on the couch with his thoughts.

It was a really bad place to be.

He bounced between the guilt of what he'd brought to his family, anxious about how Courtney would react, and indignation at the fact that she didn't seem to care.

And then there was his book. He hadn't even thought about it since Courtney had come home. Probably pushed it aside out of self-preservation because there was only so much he could handle. The hole he found himself in had been dug in service of his precious writing, and with his computer dead and USB drive gone, it had all been for nothing.

Craig steeped in his toxic stew, blankly staring at the television until he heard footsteps on the floor above him.

By the time he'd gotten upstairs, Courtney had changed into her pajamas and moved into the bathroom. His question hung as she brushed her teeth, and she didn't say anything after spitting and rinsing.

"Can I at least explain?"

Courtney ran a washcloth under warm water to clean her face. "I thought you already did."

"Courtney . . ."

She worked the washcloth around her face, concentrating on the mirror in front of her more than the man behind. "You know, Prisha Nelson came up to me at work today and asked how things were going at home? She said her daughters were at the pool and saw the whole thing with Levi, so she wanted to know if Alice and I were okay." Courtney dried her face and started dabbing cream on her cheeks. "Didn't really know how to answer that one."

"Did you tell her what happened?"

"She *knows* what happened. Her kids saw the whole thing, and it made such an impression that they told their mom about it that night. And she felt the need to do a welfare check on me. At work. Not really the kinds of questions I want to answer at my job, you know?"

Her voice was calm, but the subtext left no ambiguity about how she felt.

"Did they see what Levi was doing to that girl?"

Courtney dropped her hand from her face and found his eyes through the mirror. "They saw you grab Stephen Ryan's kid and yell at him. It doesn't *matter* what happened before that. Do you not understand that yet? You had a public fucking meltdown on someone else's kid, and you act like everyone should just forget about it because of what you said he did."

"What do you mean, what I *said* he did?" Craig had never cared much about what random strangers thought, but Courtney *had* to believe him. To believe *in* him. She was the anchor he moored himself with, but if that connection was fraying . . .

"I'm not saying I handled it well, but you do believe me, right? What I saw him do to that little girl?"

She turned around to face him, her expression tired. "Honestly, Craig, I don't know. But I know what Prisha's kids saw. I know she asked me about it at work, which means the whole division probably knows about it. And here's the thing that you can't seem to get—they don't care what Levi was doing to a little girl right before, because they aren't going to hear about it. They're just going to hear that my husband freaked out on Stephen Ryan's boy in front of a hundred people at the pool. And if that's what Prisha's girls are saying, imagine what his wife is saying about you."

It was a ball-peen hammer between the eyes.

She was right. What actually happened didn't matter. When he put his hands on Levi, his side of the story stopped mattering. The Ryan family was a pillar of the community, while he was a nobody who had publicly assaulted a kid. He'd never thought about how this would affect Courtney's career. The stink of his actions would certainly follow her around. The medical community was big in this town, but still tight knit, and they were out-of-towners. Transplants who hadn't built up a lifetime of social capital they could use to blunt this.

"You're right," Craig said. "I'm sorry. I'll find a way to fix this."

"*You can't* fix this. You need help." She didn't yell, but her voice was hard. Her eyes told him the rope that tied them together was tight, but it was frayed more than he realized. "Will you please go talk to someone?"

Craig didn't need a therapist to know where his problems had come from. Without Levi around, things would get better. If Craig could just get the kid out of their lives, get him to just stay away, he couldn't bait him into anything. Eventually, memories would fade, and they'd all be able to move on.

He took a deep breath. "I tell you what—"

Courtney shook her head and walked past him into the bedroom.

Chapter Twenty-Seven

Craig grabbed a mug out of the cupboard and set it next to the French press. Bubbles broke loose from the bottom and floated up to the top of the murky brown water that couldn't be coffee soon enough. He stifled a yawn. Maybe he'd gotten some sleep around one or two last night, but it was so hard to tell anymore.

"We're out of cereal," Alice said.

Ugh. Okay, they'd have to make a trip to the grocery store. He'd always tried to keep Alice away from those sugar bombs that tried to pass themselves off as part of a balanced breakfast, but over the last week, she'd worn him down to the point that she'd eaten Cinnamon Toast Crunch every morning. "You can have some of mine if you want. It's got cinnamon, so it's pretty much the same."

She emerged from the pantry with his box of cinnamon oatmeal squares and a disappointed look on her face. "They aren't the same."

Craig hauled the milk over to the table. "Well, it's all we have."

Alice stared at the bowl like he was asking her to eat rotten cabbage. "We'll go to the store after breakfast."

He turned back and stared at the press next to his mug, willing the darkening liquid to infuse faster as the cascading pings of pouring cereal came from behind. Going to the grocery store would at least give them something to do that morning, which was good because finding ways to keep busy had become more and more of a challenge. The pool was off limits, and Craig didn't even want to go out back. He squeezed his eyes shut.

Scared of your own fucking backyard.

A prisoner in his own home. Under siege from a nine-year-old boy everyone, including his wife, tied themselves in knots to defend.

Unwilling to wait any longer, Craig pushed the plunger on the French press and poured the coffee into his mug.

"This tastes bad," Alice said.

Craig glanced over at the table, where his daughter's nose was wrinkled up beneath closed eyes. "Oh, come on, it's not that bad. You've eaten it before—you've just had your taste buds ruined by all that sugary stuff."

He wasn't in the mood to have a breakfast debate, but swallowed his frustration and strolled over to examine the box. He'd opened it the day before, and the "best by" date confirmed it wasn't old.

Alice took another bite and winced. "It's yucky." She put her spoon on the table, which meant she wasn't picking it up again as long as that bowl was sitting in front of her. Normally he'd let her sit there and not eat—just because it wasn't coated in neon sugar with Styrofoam marshmallows didn't mean it wasn't good—but he recognized his mental margins were pretty thin at that point, and a hangry daughter wasn't something he was equipped to deal with that day.

Sometimes it was better to cut your losses.

He went over to the cabinet next to the sink to get her a juice glass, but froze when his eyes found Levi lurking just inside the tree line. Craig put the glass down and headed toward the patio door. As evil as the Ryans thought Craig was, you'd think they'd do everything they could to keep their precious son away. But that would take actual parenting, which was evidently too much to ask.

Craig paused before opening the sliding glass door, but Levi hadn't moved. He was half behind a tree, staring up at their house like a low-rent private eye on a stakeout.

"Dah-dy?" Alice's voice was thick and scared enough to set off alarm bells. Her cheeks were splotchy, and her eyes stared at him with terror. The wheezing of air already fighting its way through her throat filled the kitchen, while her shoulders heaved with the effort. Panic spread across her face with the flush of anaphylaxis.

Craig's adrenal glands dumped into his bloodstream, setting his nerves on fire and bringing a sharp focus to his eyes. He could see the red threads of inflammation across the whites of his daughter's eyes while the skin around them swelled.

Alice had never experienced an allergic reaction before. Knowing of his own fish allergy, they'd had her tested at six months, and avoidance had been part of her entire life. He'd gone through it himself—once as a kid and once in a restaurant on the way home from their honeymoon—and it was terrifying both times.

Seeing his daughter gasping for air as her body attacked itself was much, much worse.

Craig forced calm into his voice. "It's okay, Alice. You're having a reaction, but it's going to be fine. We're going to give you a shot like we always talked about, and you will be fine, okay?"

He briefly wondered what had triggered her immune system but brushed that aside for later. They were in a race against the clock, and the how and why could wait until Alice was breathing normally. Craig slipped around the kitchen island, and a sunburst of pain erupted from his hip as it banged against the corner. He ignored it and tore open the drawer where they kept a pair of EpiPens for just this situation.

They were gone.

Craig's fingers shook as he dug around the drawer, desperately hoping a pair of eight-inch plastic tubes with bright-orange caps on both ends were somehow hidden by chip clips and a box of toothpicks.

He yanked open the next drawer over, despite having never put the lifesaving needles in there. They were always kept in the first drawer, in a white plastic tray at the front, so they'd be easy to find and readily accessible in an emergency. Everyone in the family knew where they were. Always. It was one of the first things they'd established when they moved in.

This is the EpiPen drawer.

But now, when every second was imperative, they were nowhere to be found.

Craig ran back to Alice, who had tears streaming from her rapidly swelling eyes. Every breath was a high-pitched rasp, and they were coming way too fast. He put his hand on her forehead—as if he needed to worry about a fever—and brushed her hair back. "It's going to be okay, honey, I just need to find the EpiPens . . ." He looked around the kitchen as if they'd be sitting on the counter. "Did you move them?"

The question was nothing more than desperation, and she shook her head short and fast anyway.

"Dah—" She couldn't get the word out before a whoop of breath cut her off.

"Don't talk, just breathe . . . breathe, baby . . . it's going to be fine." He needed that EpiPen, but if it wasn't lying at the ready in that drawer, he had literally no idea where it could be. Craig's brain flipped through and discarded a million ideas as desperation invaded his thoughts. There was a python coiled around Alice's neck, constricting the flow of oxygen as her lungs burned, and if he couldn't get help soon, his daughter's throat would collapse right in front of him, and he would hold her as she died.

Every doctor either of them had ever seen had been clear on what to do in this situation.

First administer epinephrine via autoinjector.

Then call 911.

But the EpiPens were gone, and the hospital wasn't far. Ten minutes, maybe. Six if he drove like his daughter's life depended on it. By the time he called 911 and an ambulance got to their house, he could already have her in the emergency room.

Alice's breathing got faster and increasingly shallow. Her hands braced against the table in front of her, knuckles stark white against the increasing redness of her skin.

They had to leave now, but Craig was afraid he'd already waited too long and she wasn't going to make it. He needed that EpiPen.

He was frozen between trying to find an EpiPen and throwing her in the car right then.

Alice forcefully sucked in a whoop of air and knocked her bowl of cereal to the floor.

The clatter spurred Craig out of his paralysis.

"Hold on, baby." He tore out of the kitchen and up the carpeted stairway in the front of their house toward the bathroom by Alice's room. Maybe there was an old EpiPen in the cabinet below the sink—even expired, it might work well enough to give them time.

He threw the cabinet door open and scanned the inside.

Nothing.

Craig saw a bottle of pink liquid and snatched it before sprinting back. He grabbed the banister and swung himself around—and almost tumbled down—the stairway.

Alice was still at the table, wheezing, which was almost a relief at that point. If she was wheezing, that meant her throat was still slightly open.

He pushed down and twisted the white cap off the bottle of Benadryl and held it to her lips. "Drink this."

She pulled back with a confused look, but Craig practically poured it into her mouth. *"Just drink."*

The thick pink liquid dribbled down her chin, and Craig literally pushed it up between her swollen lips with his finger.

"Let's go to the hospital."

He grabbed her by the hand, and she gingerly got out of her chair, but they had no time for gingerly. Craig scooped her up in his arms and ran out the back hall.

The cold cement of the garage reminded him he wasn't wearing shoes, but he was well past caring. They'd already wasted enough time that footwear was a luxury he couldn't afford.

Craig placed her in the front seat of their SUV and pulled the seat belt across her body. Alice had never ridden in the front before. At seven years old, she was still required to use a booster seat in the back, but he felt the need to have her within arm's reach as they drove. What good that would do wasn't clear to him. He was running on instinct.

He hurried around to the driver's side and threw himself behind the wheel. Alice looked at him with desperate eyes as he cranked the ignition. "You're gonna be fine." He reached over and put his hand on top of hers as they backed out of the garage. Craig shifted into drive and stomped a bare foot onto the accelerator the second they hit the street.

"You're gonna be fine."

The chairs in the emergency department were hard—all wood and vinyl. That was probably by design, to make for easy cleanup, because they never knew what fluids wouldn't wait until their owners were called.

But Alice didn't have to wait. Blue lips bump you to the front of the line every time.

He'd burst through the automatic double doors, carrying his little girl and shouting at the top of his lungs. The women behind the desk didn't flinch, and a pair of nurses appeared almost immediately. One took Alice from his arms and had her in the back before Craig answered the other's questions. He told her she was allergic to fish. She asked about any other allergies, and Craig said no. She offered a comforting pat on the shoulder and pointed Craig toward the desk with the promise they'd take care of his little girl and that she'd be back as soon as she could with an update. He'd wanted to go back with her but was told he'd just be in the way.

Stay here for now, get her checked in, let them do their job.

Craig leaned back and dropped the clipboard he'd been given to his lap. The walls were painted in cool colors, but if the purpose had been to keep those in the waiting room calm, it wasn't working. A bowl of Xanax would have been more effective.

The blanks on the form in front of him blurred, and Craig pressed the back of his hand across his eyes. It wasn't like they had to diagnose the problem. The words *allergic reaction* and Alice's face would have told them everything they needed to know, so they would have given her epinephrine immediately. There was probably a whole cabinet full of EpiPens at the ready back there.

Unlike his kitchen, apparently.

Craig could still see the empty EpiPen drawer—they *literally* called it the EpiPen drawer—and couldn't comprehend what had happened. It was the most important thing in their house, and they treated it as such.

Where the fuck were they?

The nurse came out to the waiting room, and he vaulted out of the easy-to-clean vinyl seat before she waved him back. Craig's bare feet hustled him past the people still waiting for their chance at medical care, and every question he wanted to ask piled into a logjam at his mouth.

"Alice is doing fine." She offered a practiced smile and reached for the intake form in his hand. "We gave her epinephrine, and she's already breathing normally."

"Thank god." The built-up nerves flowed out with the words as he handed her the clipboard. "I didn't get to finish . . ."

The nurse took a cursory glance and smiled again. "You can finish it back here, no problem." She turned back and held the swinging door open for him.

The emergency department was a jarring change from the waiting room. White. Stark. All business. There was no effort to calm anyone down with soft colors and comforting art—they were too busy saving lives.

"She's right down here." Craig followed the nurse's tight blonde ponytail past a few glass patient bays that looked more like office cubicles than hospital rooms. Everyone they passed wore light-blue scrubs. Some had white coats. All had game faces on.

The nurse pushed aside a curtain and motioned into a patient bay.

Alice looked tiny in the hospital bed. Her arm was laid out beside her, an IV tube taped down to the inside of her elbow snaked up to a small bag suspended on a pole above. On her other hand, a plastic oxygen meter was clamped over the tip of her middle finger. Red splotches dotted her porcelain skin, and her eyes were still puffy and bloodshot. The nurse who had taken Alice out of his arms and carried her back sat by the bed, talking to her. Just ten minutes away from anaphylactic shock, and she was already storytelling the nurse.

"Hey, kiddo."

She looked over and gave her dad a tiny smile. "I'm okay, Daddy."

Alice's small and raspy reassurance unleashed all the tears in Craig's eyes. The blonde nurse who'd brought him back left, while her partner stood up and offered him her chair. She had a kind face that could comfort scared little kids like Alice, but a stocky build that could probably hold down an unruly drunk during a midnight shift.

"She's a tough little cookie." The nurse procured a tissue from somewhere and handed it to Craig. He took it and wiped his face but needed another right away. "Alice was telling me about her cat, Felix, and how he likes to go for walks on a leash." The nurse looked down at Alice again. "I said I have never seen a cat on a leash before, but she said he loves it."

Craig held the saturated tissue in his hand and wiped his eyes with the back of his wrist. He didn't respond, but the nurse didn't seem fazed. She probably dealt with emotional parents all the time.

"Why don't you have a seat? The doctor will be by in just a little bit." She glanced down at his feet. "I'll see if I can dig up some slippers."

Craig sat down next to Alice's bed in the seat the nurse had just given up. He didn't care about his feet. All he wanted to do was hold his little girl, but he didn't dare touch her for fear she'd break. Across from the bed hung a small whiteboard, where someone had written in blue dry-erase marker:

Nurse—Abby

Doctor—Dr. Christine Russi

Craig took a deep breath and found his voice again.

"How are you feeling?"

"My throat is scratchy," Alice said.

"Yeah, I bet," Craig said. "But it'll feel better soon."

Nurse Abby looked over from one of the machines and smiled down at Alice again. "Yes, it will."

Craig realized he was still holding the clipboard the receptionist out front had given him. "I still haven't filled this out."

"Just do it whenever you can, no hurry," Abby said.

Craig set it on a little table behind him, and a tall woman came in through the door.

"So how are we doing in here?" She wore the same blue scrubs but had a long white coat and dark hair tied up in long, tight braids tucked under a navy-blue scrub cap. Her brown eyes were kind but held the confidence of someone unafraid to make saving lives her job.

Alice offered a tired smile at the sight of her. "Okay."

"Good." She looked up from Alice toward Craig and offered her hand. "I'm Dr. Russi."

Craig stood and could feel the nervous sweat on his palm as he shook her hand. "I'm Alice's dad, Craig Finnigan."

"So, Alice is doing fine right now," Dr. Russi said. "She was in anaphylactic shock when she came in, so we gave her epinephrine right away. That reduced the swelling in her throat and eased her breathing immediately. Right now we're giving her prednisone, which is a steroid that will continue to reduce the inflammation, and some antihistamines. Those should reduce the swelling and redness you can still see and hopefully hold off any more reaction. Symptoms of anaphylaxis can reoccur after the initial attack, so we'll keep Alice here for a while to keep an eye on her and make sure that doesn't happen."

She reached down and patted Alice on the arm. Her bedside manner was impressive. Not purely clinical but still clear and to the point. Good for both scared kids and nervous parents.

"According to her chart Alice has an allergy to scaled fish?"

Craig nodded. "We both do, actually."

"Do you know how she was exposed this morning?"

For the first time Craig realized he had been more worried about getting his daughter help than considering how it had happened in the first place. Being careful was second nature in their family, and nothing had seemed out of the ordinary that morning.

"No. I mean, she was just eating breakfast. Cereal. I don't know where it could have come from."

"Well, as you probably know, sometimes there can be cross contamination with foods packaged at the same plant as fish."

Of course Craig knew that. He'd been checking labels his entire life and wouldn't even consider buying something new without looking. "It was my cereal. I mean, I just had some yesterday. If it was contaminated, I would've had a reaction, right?"

"I can't say for sure, but that would make sense. What else was she exposed to before the reaction?"

Craig rewound his brain and rewatched the scene in the kitchen, looking for anything that could have slipped fish portions past his guard and into his daughter. "Nothing. We're always really careful, and I can't think of anything."

He looked across his daughter's hospital bed and studied the doctor's face for belief. Since he'd been allowed back in Alice's room and seen her breathing again, guilt had been metastasizing inside him. As the primary caregiver, his most important job was to keep Alice safe.

Craig needed to know this wasn't his fault. Courtney already thought he was slipping, and this . . .

He hadn't called Courtney yet.

In his defense, the last forty-five minutes had been pretty hectic. And he hadn't even known what was happening until a few minutes ago. He'd text her as soon as he was done talking with the doctor. When he had some more information to pass along. No sense worrying her without the full story.

"If that is indeed the case, it's possible she has developed a new allergy," Dr. Russi said. "You may want to check with her allergist about some new tests. In the meantime, keep a close eye on what she's exposed to so if she has another reaction, you can narrow down where it's coming from."

Craig nodded and looked down at his daughter. He didn't want to think about adding another allergen to the list, but he couldn't think of what else could have caused this.

"And remember if that does happen, you should always use an EpiPen before coming to the hospital. Honestly, we were lucky today. When someone's in anaphylactic shock, literally every second counts. The EpiPen needs to be the first thing you think of."

He could see the empty drawer. "I couldn't find it."

"The best thing to do is keep it in an easily accessible place that everyone in the family knows about. Preferably right there in the kitchen since that is the place she's most likely to have a reaction."

He did. Kept two in the first drawer from the first day they'd moved in. It was *always* there, but the one time they needed it, the thing wasn't where it needed to be.

The paranoid part of his brain shouted a theory from the back. It was the same one that had whispered when Pete disappeared. It was ridiculous, but nothing else made sense.

Craig glanced up at Dr. Russi, who was looking at him like an ER doc used to explaining the most basic rules of self-care to people. Often more than once. But he didn't need that. He knew how to be careful, and dammit, he *always* was.

Which meant that maybe he wasn't so paranoid.

"Yeah," Craig said, because he wasn't ready to say what he really thought out loud. "We will."

Dr. Russi said they'd have to keep Alice there at least a few more hours to monitor her for any recurrence of symptoms. Nurse Abby brought in an iPad loaded with kids' movies to help pass the time and handed him a tan pair of socks with rubber grippers on the bottom.

Craig pulled out his phone and finally texted his wife.

Alice had a reaction and I took her to the ER. She's fine now. Watching her for a few hours before we come home.

He stared at the screen after hitting send, waiting to see the three dots of response flicker into view.

A phone call came instead. Courtney's voice was immediate and panicked.

"Is she okay?"

Nurse Abby motioned that she was going to leave for a bit. Craig nodded, stood up from beside Alice's bed, and walked toward the far corner for some illusion of privacy. "She's fine."

"What the hell happened?"

"We were having breakfast, and she had a reaction, so I threw her in the car and drove her to the ER. They gave her epinephrine, and now she's recovering."

The line was silent for long enough Craig almost asked if she was still there.

"Wait . . . *they* gave her epinephrine? Didn't you use the EpiPen at home?"

It was Craig's turn to pause. "It wasn't there."

"What do you mean it wasn't there? You couldn't find it?"

"No, it wasn't *there*." Craig took a breath to gather himself and blow the defensiveness out. "I went to the EpiPen drawer, and neither one was there, so I gave her some Benadryl and brought her here."

"Benadryl?"

"It was all I could think of without an EpiPen."

"How the fuck couldn't you find an EpiPen?"

He took another breath. Craig didn't know where they were, but at that point all he could think about was Levi staring at the house from the woods. Even if Craig wouldn't admit it to his wife. Honestly, he had a hard time admitting it to himself.

"I don't know. If they were there, I would have used them, but they weren't. Did *you* move them?"

Something that was either a breath or a sigh came through. Craig could hear muffled rattling in the background.

"I'll be there soon."

"If you've got work stuff, she's going to be—"

"Our daughter is in the emergency room, Craig. I'm leaving work now, and I'll be there in a few minutes."

He was downplaying it because he didn't want it to be serious. Didn't want her to blame him for it.

Because she wouldn't believe who *he* was blaming.

Chapter Twenty-Eight

Nurse Abby brought Courtney back to their ER bay, and she flew to their daughter's bed, interrupting Alice's viewing of *Inside Out* with forehead kisses and hugs. Craig didn't even get a nod of acknowledgment.

Courtney had Alice recap the whole story, injecting declarations of bravery whenever she could before letting the kid get back into her movie.

"Any idea how long they want to keep her?" Courtney asked. Her voice had lost whatever frustration or hostility it'd had on the phone. Maybe it was just because their daughter lay between them.

"They are basically just keeping an eye on her at this point. The doctor said a few hours."

Courtney looked around the room and saw the whiteboard with provider names written on it. "Is she coming back soon?"

"The nurse is fairly regular to check in," Craig said. "The doctor hasn't been in since I first talked to her, but I assume she'll be back before we get discharged."

Courtney looked back at the doorway. "Maybe I'll ask the nurse if she'd send her by for a second."

Eventually Dr. Russi returned to check on Alice and introduce herself to Courtney. She patiently answered the same questions Craig had asked an hour ago and estimated another hour or two before they could leave—depending on how Alice was feeling.

When she left again, an awkward silence settled over the sound from Alice's movie and the general din of the emergency department beyond the gray curtain that served as a door to their little bay. There was a little utilitarian chat between Courtney and Craig, but she didn't ask any more questions.

Courtney apparently had all the answers she wanted.

But Craig didn't, and the answers he wanted wouldn't be found at the hospital. He used the awkward silence as a chance to go back and review the morning, to poke holes in every possible theory he had come up with as to what had happened. He'd thought a clear head and fresh start would show him a path out of the forest of paranoia that kept telling him one thing.

Levi had done this.

The kid had been in his house, but Craig had never conceived Levi would take things this far. But he had been there that morning, out back watching the house just before Alice had had her reaction. Craig wanted another explanation. Desperately wanted one, because being paranoid was easier to deal with than a neighborhood kid whose behavior had crossed the line from worrisome to psychotic.

So he sat by his daughter's hospital bed, across from his wife, and searched for another answer.

He hadn't come up with one by the time Dr. Russi returned to discharge them. She gave them prescriptions for a few days' worth of oral steroids and another EpiPen. Courtney didn't give Craig any type of look while the doctor handed them to her, nor did she say they already knew the importance of keeping an EpiPen readily accessible when Dr. Russi reexplained it like it was the first time. Instead, she listened and nodded.

They were able to fill the prescriptions at the hospital pharmacy before heading home. Alice was in her back seat booster, voice still a little scratchy, while Courtney followed them home in her car.

Craig could see their garage door open from the end of the block, a casualty of the speed with which they'd left, but he could be forgiven for haste with his daughter fighting to breathe.

He pulled their SUV into the open garage and killed the ignition. Alice was uncharacteristically quiet, which wasn't surprising, considering what she'd gone through, so the ticking of the cooling engine was the only sound. It made the garage feel emptier, more vulnerable. The door across the way was closed but had been exposed to anyone who'd passed the entire time they'd been gone.

Craig got out and helped Alice from her booster seat. He glanced out toward the street for his wife's car, but she must have hit some traffic.

"Can I watch TV?"

Craig followed Alice inside. "Yeah, honey, that's fine. Why don't you go downstairs and rest?"

Felix sauntered in from the living room and followed Alice down into the basement, but Craig stayed in the kitchen. It felt weird. Things were scattered about, abandoned when he'd carried his daughter out to the car. It felt like an ancient home dug up in Pompeii, buried exactly how it had been when the ash froze it in time.

The feeling of running around the marble island, tearing through drawers for lifesaving medicine, came back and hit hard. He didn't know why, but he walked over to the EpiPen drawer. Unlike the garage door, he'd apparently remembered to close this one. He stared at it for a second, not exactly sure what he was trying to prove, then pulled it open.

Two EpiPens lay side by side in their spot.

Craig stood, dumbfounded. His brain tried to make sense of it, but it spun on stripped gears. He picked one up and stared at it like it was a hundred-dollar bill on the sidewalk. Yellow cap on one end, orange push trigger on the other, prescription type wrapped around the middle cylinder, his name at the top. He grabbed the other one and examined it. Exactly the same, except for Alice's name in place of his.

He went over to the sink and looked out toward the woods. Nobody was there.

Craig looked back at the EpiPens in his hand. There was no way, outside reality-bending metaphysics, he could have missed them in that drawer. Even in pure panic mode with his daughter asphyxiating behind him, he would have seen them. They were eight inches long with bright colors at each end. Between the two of them, they filled the front of the drawer. The drawer was dedicated to them. There was literally nowhere for them to hide.

But they *hadn't* been there. He'd bet his daughter's life on that fact.

He looked out back again.

The door from the garage opened and shut in the back hall, announcing Courtney's return. Craig stared at the EpiPens in his hands. The ones that 100 percent hadn't been there when he'd needed them, but now were.

Footsteps on the hardwood approached the kitchen, and Craig's mind spun. He shoved the EpiPens in the back of his jeans and pulled his shirt over them as Courtney came in.

"Where's Alice?"

He stared at Courtney from across the kitchen, plastic digging into the small of his back. Courtney's voice was neutral, but her look couldn't hide the impatience.

"Downstairs." Craig leaned back against the counter and felt one of the EpiPens shift. He pressed back harder into the marble countertop so it wouldn't slip out. If he thought he'd have a hard time explaining finding the EpiPens in the drawer, it wouldn't compare to him trying to explain hiding them from her. "I said she could watch TV and just rest on the couch."

Courtney gave a little nod and turned down the stairs.

When she disappeared, Craig reached behind himself and grabbed the EpiPens. The new one was in a white bag on the kitchen table, ready to be put in its permanent spot, but he didn't know what to do with these. Courtney couldn't see them, because she'd think he'd completely lost it, but he didn't want to throw them away because what if the new one disappeared too?

He reached up and pulled open one of the square cabinets above the refrigerator. It was mostly empty, with just a box of filters and an oversize water pitcher they never used.

Craig put the EpiPens inside and closed the door. They never really used those cabinets, because he was the only one tall enough to reach the doors. Now if they ever needed an EpiPen, he had a few hidden away. Part of him said he was paranoid, but he didn't care. None of this made sense yet, so he'd rather be paranoid and prepared at that point.

Courtney's footsteps came back up from the basement behind him, and he sucked in a steadying breath. She didn't say anything and went over to the kitchen table.

"You just grab this, or has it been out?" She held up the milk Alice had used for her cereal that morning. Her voice was neutral, but Courtney didn't wait for an answer. She carried it over to the sink and dumped it out, then returned to the table and picked up the box of cereal that was still sitting there. Craig watched as she flipped it over and started reading the back.

"I told you, I already checked," Craig said. "Besides, I've eaten that cereal for years. I ate out of that exact box yesterday, and I was fine."

"What else did she have?"

"Nothing," Craig said. "I mean, she had milk with it, but nothing else."

Courtney kept examining the box, as if there were some fine print somewhere that said *Now with 50 percent more tuna*. "Well, she had to get exposed somewhere." She pulled the plastic bag of cereal out and threw it in the trash. She collapsed the cardboard box and stuck it in the recycling bin before heading back downstairs to check on Alice.

Craig stayed against the counter, absently staring at the garbage can as he tried to put the puzzle together. He remembered Alice complaining about the taste just before her reaction started.

He stepped on the foot lever and popped the lid on the trash can, revealing the translucent bag of cinnamon oatmeal squares sitting atop their accumulated garbage. Craig pulled it out and looked for any signs of mold or anything, but everything looked normal.

He opened the top and smelled.

It smelled weird.

He took a few steps away from the garbage and sniffed again.

Same thing. Something was off, but he hadn't noticed anything when he'd eaten it himself the day before. It was a relatively new box—could it have spoiled that quickly? And even if it had, moldy cereal might cause her to puke or something, but there was no reason to think it would set off an allergic reaction.

Craig pulled a bowl from the cabinet and poured the cereal in. He didn't see any mold or anything, but some pieces looked like they were dusted in a pale-pink powder.

He leaned down and sniffed it. The inside of his nose started to tingle.

Craig took a step back from the bowl and sucked in a deep breath as little pinpricks continued to dance inside his sinuses. He stared at the cereal and concentrated on the air flowing to his lungs. His nose itched, but oxygen still flowed.

He reached above the refrigerator and opened the cabinet. His EpiPen sat next to Alice's, right where he'd put them. He closed the door again. Craig felt better knowing they hadn't somehow disappeared.

He closed his eyes and concentrated on breathing, feeling the air move through him.

All good.

His nose continued to itch, however. The bottle of Children's Benadryl sat on the counter where he'd left it this morning. He thought about taking a swig but didn't. He had the real thing upstairs if he needed it.

The bowl of cereal was still on the counter. He wanted to examine it closer but didn't dare. The itchy nose had been a warning shot, and he didn't want to press his luck with whatever was in that cereal.

He moved to the window and searched the woods, expecting Levi's face to pop out from behind every tree he saw.

Chapter Twenty-Nine

Sleep had been hard before, but that night Craig didn't even bother trying. He stared into the dark while every creak and thump he heard tried to convince him Levi had come back. Once Courtney was asleep, he got up and went downstairs to double-check the doors were locked. When they were, he stared out into the backyard, checking the shadows made by the moonlight for a nine-year-old boy.

He snuck back to the bedroom before the sun came up, not because he was finally convinced Levi wasn't coming back but because he didn't want Courtney to know how he'd spent the night.

If she noticed, she didn't say anything when she got up with her alarm twenty minutes later.

Craig must have fallen asleep while she was in the shower, because the next thing he knew, Alice was gently knocking on their bedroom door.

"Daddy?"

He looked up and saw it was already 10:22 a.m.

"Sorry to wake you, but I'm hungry, and I wanted to have breakfast."

Craig sat up and rubbed his eyes. His head was still heavy with sleep. "That's okay, kiddo. Sorry I slept so late. You must be starving."

She offered a shy smile and nodded. "I could have made myself some cereal, but we don't have any of mine and I didn't know which of yours were safe to eat."

He was glad she'd thought of that, because he hadn't. If Levi had slipped something into that box of cereal, who was to say he hadn't contaminated something else? They couldn't trust anything that was already open.

Craig stumbled downstairs and found a granola bar—sealed in its wrapper, so assumedly safe—and gave it to Alice, then pulled a garbage bag from below the sink and carried it back to the pantry. The number of contamination opportunities for someone looking to hurt them was overwhelming.

Two open cereal boxes.

A container of cashews with a screw top lid.

A bag of chips held closed by a clothespin.

He threw them all in the bag, and his eye caught the plastic containers lined up on the third shelf. Flour. Sugar. Levi wouldn't have messed with stuff like that, would he?

Alice's swollen face, struggling to breathe through a kinked hose in her throat, flashed through his mind. He dumped everything into the bag.

Five minutes later, the shelves were as bare as they'd been since they had moved in.

Craig tied up the garbage bag and set it down outside the pantry. Alice was pouring herself a glass of grape juice at the table.

"No!"

His voice echoed through the kitchen and startled Alice so much she dropped the plastic jug with a wet thud. The juice glugged out at her feet, and her initial shock was quickly replaced by tears.

"Oh . . . sorry, kiddo, I didn't mean to yell." Craig snatched a dish towel off the counter and hurried over to mop up the rapidly spreading purple puddle under the table. "I just didn't want you to drink that juice . . ."

His sentence cut off because he didn't know what to say. Craig didn't know how to tell his daughter he thought her old friend was trying to poison them. True or not, the thought was too heavy for a seven-year-old. Luckily, he had the grape juice providing a plausible distraction as he tried to think up something.

"What's wrong with the juice, Daddy?"

Craig wiped the newly purple towel across the floor and put the plastic bottle back on the table, but he still hadn't had enough time to come up with a good excuse.

"Dad?"

He held his left hand under the dripping towel as he carried it to the sink. "Yeah, um, I'm just worried that the juice is old. We'll get some new stuff today at the store."

It was a lame excuse. If Alice were older, she'd probably be insulted he'd even tried it, but she was still a kid whose first instinct was to believe her dad. Even if he didn't make any sense at all.

"Why don't you grab a yogurt drink out of the fridge?" Those were sealed. Safe. But he'd have to go through the refrigerator just like the pantry. Anything open was suspect, and therefore had to go. Once Alice had finished her prepackaged breakfast and gone upstairs to change, Craig filled up another garbage bag. Sour cream. Cottage cheese. A squeeze bottle of chocolate syrup. About half a dozen bottles of salad dressing. Didn't even bother dumping the contents in the sink and recycling the containers. Just tossed them all in the bag.

He tried to rationalize reasons they would be safe, told himself he was being paranoid. But in the end he couldn't take the chance.

Craig hauled the two very full garbage bags out to the garage as Alice came downstairs ready to leave. They'd buckled themselves in the car and pulled halfway out of the driveway before Craig hit the brakes.

They sat for a second, the White Stripes playing through the Bluetooth audio system.

"What's the matter?" Alice asked.

He sat, staring back at the house for another second before giving in.

"I'll be right back. I just have to . . ." Craig trailed off and left the car running in the driveway. He didn't bother taking his shoes off when he got inside, instead hustling downstairs to check the sliding glass door. The lock was in place, just like it had been when he was playing sentry around the house at two in the morning and again that morning when he'd peeked over from the stairway, but he couldn't leave for the grocery store without looking to see it was secure.

He did the same with the patio door upstairs.

And the front door.

All locked.

Craig headed back out through the garage, locking the back-hall door behind him. They never locked that door, figuring nobody would get past the garage door, but those days were over.

Alice was waiting in the back seat for him. He tried a reassuring smile and hit the button to close the garage as soon as he got behind the wheel, but he didn't drive away until he saw it reach the ground. Nothing had accidentally tripped the motion sensor and sent it back up, and nobody had slipped in before it closed.

He slowly backed out, eyes searching around the yard and the side of the house for any signs of homicidal young boys. As they drove out of the neighborhood, Craig found himself staring into the yards as they passed, expecting to see Levi crouched behind a bush or lurking behind a mailbox, waiting for them to leave.

But he wasn't there.

They came home about an hour and a half later, having racked up a monster bill at the grocery store.

Craig carried the first load of plastic bags in—he'd forgotten the reusable shopping bags they kept handy in the back hall—and was unnerved by the quiet of the house. His eyes darted toward every corner, as if Levi would be crouched waiting to fly out at them.

He went out for the second load, and part of him didn't trust it, worried that Levi had done something to the food in the short time he'd been inside. He tried to shake it off but hurried getting the last bags inside and shut the garage door behind him. His eyes roamed to the front door when he got inside and found their way to the patio door when he hit the kitchen.

Both still locked.

Alice was downstairs playing as he put away the new, uncontaminated food. He didn't allow himself to call down and ask her to check the sliding glass door to the backyard.

Craig took the opportunity to rearrange the pantry. Before, it'd had no real order. Stuff Alice needed access to on the bottom, stuff like baking staples at the top, but it'd been mostly chaos on the individual shelves.

Now everything was stacked together neatly. Craig stared at it, then pulled out his phone and took a picture so he'd be able to tell if anything had been messed with.

The doorbell rang. Craig froze.

He peeked around the corner and saw Levi's shadow through the beveled glass of the front door. A spike of anger shot through him.

The *arrogance* of that kid.

He saw himself whipping the door open, staring down at Levi and asking what in the blue fuck he thought he was doing here. Telling him, in a tone he couldn't misinterpret, that he *knew* what he'd done. That if he even saw him within one hundred feet of their house, he'd be *lucky* if he called the cops.

Then he saw Levi telling his mom about it, adding god knows what to the story to make it that much worse. He saw the cops showing up on his doorstep again.

The doorbell rang again. Craig stared at the shape outside. He was afraid Alice would come up and ask what he was doing.

Who it was.

Why he wasn't answering.

After what seemed like an eternity, the shape moved off the front step and disappeared.

Craig looked out the dining room windows as a teenager walked down their driveway and over toward Dan and Kay's house. He opened the door, and a fundraising flyer fluttered down to his feet.

He watched the kid ring the doorbell next door, the fear he'd felt at the sound of his own doorbell still kicking around his system, and realized he couldn't live like this.

—

Craig pulled into a parking spot and killed the engine. He glanced in the rearview mirror and looked at Alice's empty seat. It had been a while since he'd driven anywhere without a steady flow of conversation from the back seat, but he couldn't bring Alice along for this. Luckily for him, Kaitlin had the day off from work and didn't mind coming over to the house for an hour or so.

He'd said he had a dentist appointment.

The city-government complex was a concrete monstrosity, built at a time when architectural aesthetics weren't considered to be as important as cramming all municipal and county departments in one spot.

It was oppressively hot out, so the blast of cold air raised goose bumps on his arms when Craig pulled the door open and stepped through to the polished stone floor. The lobby was spacious and relatively empty. Wooden benches lined the walls on either side, but only one of them was occupied. A reception desk was carved out of the far wall, and the two middle-aged women sitting behind it looked more like bank tellers than he'd expected.

Craig's footsteps echoed off the stone and announced his presence as he approached. The woman on the right gave him a practiced smile and motioned him over.

"Can I help you?"

A door behind their reception desk stood open to the back, where Craig could see cops milling around a room full of desks. Craig buried the hesitation that had threatened to break through on his drive over. It was time to fight fire with fire and stop letting Levi dictate the narrative.

"Yes, I'd like to file a restraining order."

The police receptionist was well practiced and professional. She'd probably seen an unreal amount of craziness come through, but he still heard a hint of doubt in her voice. As if a six-foot adult male would never need protection. Like he should just go out and take care of things himself.

"Okay, well, I can get you the paperwork you need to fill out, or you can download and print the forms yourself, but you'll need to file them over at the courthouse."

Craig had assumed the police would handle this—and shouldn't they? It felt like an unnecessary barrier and cracked the door open for doubt. The receptionist looked across the desk at him, waiting for a response. "Would you like me to get the paperwork for you?" It sounded like a challenge. Like she was calling a bluff.

"Yes, please." He could have gone home and printed it out himself like she'd suggested, but his confidence was leaking, and part of him worried if he left without doing it, it wouldn't get done.

"Just a minute." She gave him a practiced smile, slowly spun out of her chair, and headed back through the open door. The other receptionist sat about ten feet away, head buried in some paperwork of her own but an ear cocked in his direction.

Craig turned away from the desk and surveyed the lobby. Two more people came through the glass entrance, while a stream of cops emptied out from another door to the right. Craig spotted Lieutenant Shaw among them. He was torn between the desire to flag him down for help and the instinct to hide, but the choice was made for him when the cop saw him. Shaw peeled away from his fellow officers and approached the desk with a curious look.

"Mr. Finnigan." His voice was neither concerned nor welcoming, but it was obvious he wondered what the hell Craig was doing there.

"Hello, Lieutenant Shaw." He struggled for a tone of nonchalance that had been unattainable for weeks.

Shaw glanced back behind the reception desk casually. "You need any help?"

Before he could answer, the receptionist emerged from the back with a handful of papers. "Okay, here you go, sir. Fill these out to the best of your ability, and take them to the courthouse. They can explain the next steps over there."

Craig felt Lieutenant Shaw's gaze on the back of his neck as he took hold of the forms. "Thank you."

He turned around and read the question on the officer's face, so Craig didn't wait.

"I'm filing a restraining order."

"I see." Lieutenant Shaw's tone was neutral, probably the same voice he used when a motorist told him he fully intended to fight the ticket he'd just been handed. Shaw looked over Craig's shoulder toward the back, then nodded that way. "Can we talk for a minute?"

He didn't want to, but was afraid to say no. He'd talked to Shaw twice, and absolutely nothing had come out of it. If the cop had been willing to actually listen, Craig wouldn't be here. But it was easier to bend toward the loudest voice in the room than figure out what was actually happening, so here they were. If Craig had to get a court order to make somebody listen to him, then that's what he would do.

Shaw ushered him toward a side door, back into a large room with two lines of desks. A dozen uniformed police officers milled around, drinking coffee and filling out paperwork. No scruffy-looking perps were handcuffed to chairs, nor did any captain come storming out of his office to yell at a play-by-his-own-rules cop.

It looked more like an office than what Craig had always seen on TV.

Lieutenant Shaw sat at the second desk on the left and motioned for Craig to sit in the chair next to it. The desk was empty aside from a computer monitor and a cup full of pencils. It looked like a shared space for cops to sit and fill out forms as opposed to an assigned work space.

"I want to start by saying you are free to do whatever you want. I'm not telling you what to do or anything like that. Understand?" Shaw looked across the desk, waiting for him to acknowledge his disclaimer, but Craig was through talking. He nodded.

"Good." Shaw leaned forward and folded his arms on the table. "That said, I would suggest you think long and hard about what you're trying to accomplish here."

The cop spoke as if Craig were off on some petty revenge, fucking with someone he didn't like out of spite just because he was home all day and didn't have anything better to do.

"Like I've told you, I want Levi Ryan out of my life." Craig looked around the room, uncomfortable talking about this with so many others within earshot, but none of the cops buzzing around seemed to be paying any attention to them. "I've told him repeatedly. I've told his mother. I've told *you*. But he won't leave us alone, and at this point I don't know what else to do."

"He's a kid."

"That kid put my daughter in the emergency room yesterday."

That got his attention. For a brief second, there was concern on his face, but it was just as quickly washed away by doubt. Almost as if—for a second—he'd forgotten that Craig was supposed to be the bad guy, not to be believed no matter what happened. But then he remembered who he worked for. "What are you talking about?"

"My daughter, Alice, has a fish allergy, just like me. Yesterday morning during breakfast she had a severe reaction. But here's the thing, I ate that exact same cereal the day before, and nothing happened."

Lieutenant Shaw looked at him, a little confused. "Okay."

Craig waited for him to catch up, to figure out what he was saying before he had to say it, but it wasn't happening.

"I think Levi put something in the cereal."

The statement slapped down on the desk between them like a dead cat. Even though the room kept bustling around them, to Craig it felt like a record had scratched and every cop had stopped to stare at him, all waiting for Lieutenant Shaw's reaction before moving on.

For his part, Shaw tried to remain professional. To listen the way a cop is supposed to and take seriously any accusation from a member of the public he was sworn to protect.

But incredulity seeped into his voice no matter how hard he tried.

"You think Levi Ryan snuck into your house and poisoned your daughter?"

Craig answered fast and defensively. "I didn't say poisoned, but, yes, I think he put something in the cereal that made her react. But I think he was trying for me."

The cop leaned back in his chair as if whatever crazy he assumed Craig had brought in would jump across to him. "You think he was trying to poison *you*?"

"Not *poison*, he . . ." Craig took a deep breath. Shaw probably already thought he was unbalanced, and frustration wasn't his friend. "The cereal wasn't sugary kid stuff. It's oatmeal squares . . . you know, adult stuff, so he probably assumed I would be the one eating it, not her. He knew I had a fish allergy because Alice told him all about it that day we . . ."

The look on Shaw's face told him bringing up the first time they met probably wasn't the winning strategy Craig thought it was.

"So your daughter had an allergic reaction. Why is your first assumption that Levi Ryan is responsible? Seems to me you're looking to blame that kid for everything that happens in your life, when there could be a lot of much more realistic ways that could've happened. My nephew is allergic to peanuts, and my sister is always checking labels because sometimes things get in at the factory."

Shaw spoke as if Craig hadn't been managing their fish allergy his whole life. As if cross contamination was somehow a new concept and not something he'd dealt with every day.

"I check every single label before I buy it. And like I said, I ate from the exact same box the day before and nothing, so something had to have changed from when I ate it to when Alice did." A flash came back to Craig. Things had happened so fast that day, forgotten memories would still randomly shake out. "She said it tasted bad, and it *did* smell weird. There was this pink dust, and my nose was tingling when—" The realization struck hard and stopped him in his tracks. His brain had been so scrambled from the fear, anxiety, and lack of sleep that he hadn't put it together.

"Those fucking bonito flakes." Craig kicked himself. He'd seen the bag the day before, but assumed it was what Levi was using to trap those squirrels. While those thoughts bounced around Craig's head, Shaw stared at him like he was having a stroke.

"Mr. Finnigan?"

Craig looked back at the doubt in the cop's face. He'd already taken him out to Levi's fort, and everything was gone. It had done nothing but cement the cop's perception of him as a whack job.

Kind of like he was doing then.

"It wasn't just the cereal. The EpiPens were gone. When I realized what was happening, I went to get one, but it wasn't there."

At this point, Craig didn't care if the cop thought he was crazy or not. He plowed forward. "You don't understand. Those pens have been in the exact same spot since we moved in—one for her, one for me.

Everyone in the family knows it, because in an emergency they have to be instantly available. This is something I have dealt with not only Alice's whole life, but mine. It's not something I'd mess up. Not that. The only way they'd be gone is if someone took them."

Shaw couldn't hide the eye roll. "So you think Levi stole your daughter's EpiPen?"

"It's literally the only explanation. Nobody touches them unless they are needed. That's the rule, so we know exactly where they are at all times. It's been that way forever. But when I went to get it—the *one* time they were needed—they weren't there. You think that's a coincidence? I had to rush her to the emergency room. She could have *died*."

He put all the emotion he could on that last word so Shaw would understand the gravity of the situation. This wasn't some little mix-up; it was life and death, and not a mistake he was capable of making. Levi taking the pens was literally the only explanation. Craig stopped talking as a pair of cops walked past behind Shaw. They were preoccupied with whatever they were talking about and didn't seem to be interested in what he was saying. A guy pleading his case to a cop probably wasn't a rare sight back here. Lieutenant Shaw's voice brought him back to the conversation.

"I believe you couldn't find them, but couldn't you have moved them and forgotten to put them back? Maybe your wife was cleaning or something? Or your daughter was messing around and wanted to take them to show-and-tell or something?"

Shaw was either incapable of understanding or willingly choosing not to, and the frustration that caused boiled over.

"No, because when we got home, I went to put a new EpiPen in the drawer, and they were back."

"Wait . . . what?" His professional patience was gone, and Craig saw the cop shut down. He was no longer listening; he was placating. "You're telling me you found them in the drawer where they belong when you got home?"

"Yes, I mean . . ." Sweat broke out down his back as he fought for a way to make Shaw understand. His thoughts were a jumbled mess of bees, buzzing all over each other in a swirling ball. "I tore that drawer apart. It's not like you can miss them. They're big and have these bright-orange caps on the end. There's literally no way they were there before, but when I got home, they were back. Somebody *had* to have taken them, then replaced them while we were at the hospital."

He was flailing and knew it.

"The house was wide open while we were gone. Like I said, she was *dying*, so there was no time to lock the back door and . . . the garage door was open. He could have easily gone in and put them back."

Lieutenant Shaw stared across the desk. If the look on his face weren't enough, his arms were folded across his broad chest and he'd leaned back in his chair. Another cop came up and asked if he had a second to talk.

"Yeah, we're done here." Shaw never took his doubting eyes off Craig. "Just let me walk Mr. Finnigan out, and I'll come find you."

He pushed himself up from behind the desk and looked down at Craig. "Let's go."

"But . . ." Craig stared up at him, desperation swirling around inside him. He'd managed to take a bad situation and make it worse, as was his custom. Like he'd been walking through a field of rakes since they'd moved up here.

"Come on." Shaw jerked his head toward the door but waited for Craig to stand.

His legs felt weak, the pit in his gut draining the strength from him. He looked at Shaw and imagined him calling Stephen Ryan, warning him of what Craig was saying about his family.

Patience gone, Lieutenant Shaw reached out toward him, but Craig pulled his arm away and started toward the door. He wasn't going to let Shaw force him into a scene at the police station. Craig imagined Shaw twisting his arm behind his back and shoving him to the floor, the other cops piling on top of him like an elementary dogpile.

He kept walking, the cop a step behind. The door to the lobby was closed, and Craig had to wait for Shaw to buzz him out.

"I know how it sounds, but you've got to believe me." Craig tried to collect himself. Swallow his desperation. To make himself believable any way he could. "I wouldn't be here unless I was sure. There's literally no other explanation."

"I don't know what happened, Mr. Finnigan, but honestly it seems to me that there are a lot of possible explanations." They stood by the door, away from the bustle of the police workroom they'd just left. Shaw's voice was firm, but with a bit of concern. He sounded like a teacher giving one last piece of life advice. "As I told you before, I can't tell you what to do in regards to this restraining order you want. If you want to file paperwork, that's your choice, but understand that you have to stand in front of a judge and provide evidence as to why it's necessary. Do you have that? Because I can tell you whatever you just told me . . . that ain't it. So unless you have some real proof you're sitting on, I would think long and hard about putting the Ryan family, and your own, on the public record."

Craig glanced back and realized he'd left the forms back on the desk, but made no move to go get them.

"You don't need a court order to stay away from a kid, and that's what I would recommend. Just stay away." Shaw buzzed the door open and held it for Craig. "Don't forget what the appropriate boundaries are with someone else's kid. Just stay away."

That warning rattled around in Craig's head as he walked out.

Chapter Thirty

Courtney's coffee steeped in the French press, but the warm, roasty aroma of fresh ground beans that usually filled the kitchen wasn't there. All Craig's nose could find were the bitter, acrid notes as he sat at the kitchen table looking at his phone, ostensibly reading the news but mostly spacing out while thoughts pinballed around his head. The screen blurred into pixels, floating apart, then reforming into words he couldn't understand. He might have slept that night, but he couldn't tell because exhaustion was the only thing he knew anymore. It was a weighted blanket smothering his mind, his body, his entire world, and a couple of hours of sleep wouldn't get him out from under it.

Courtney plunged her coffee and carried it over to the table with a bowl of Greek yogurt and granola. She sat at the other end without a word and pulled out her own phone. They still hadn't spoken. Or they *had*, but it was just utilitarian banter like *excuse me*—ingrained politeness that didn't count as actual conversation. She wasn't *not* speaking to him, but she wasn't going out of her way to talk either.

She didn't know he'd gone to the police station.

They hadn't had many rocky patches in their fifteen years together, so he didn't have much of a map for navigating choppy waters.

After a minute he realized he was staring at her, yet she hadn't even noticed.

"I'm going to call and get the security system set up."

Courtney gave a slight nod without looking up from what she was reading. She'd asked about setting it up back when they'd moved in—the system was already installed but inactive after the previous owners moved out—but Craig had figured they didn't need it. Their Realtor had said if they ever changed their minds, call HomeTech Alarm, and they'd flip a switch to activate it, easy peasy.

"What do you think?"

She still didn't look up from her phone. "That's fine."

"I'll call today."

Courtney continued to eat her breakfast in silence. The minutes stretched on, and the sense of awkwardness that settled over the table refused to burn away. Craig tried to think of something to say—something funny or useful or banal or anything—but the file was empty. His thoughts had simmered down to one thing, and he knew it wasn't something that would help to talk about.

She finally glanced up from her phone and noticed Craig was still staring across the table. "Are you going to be okay this weekend?"

He blinked against his dry eyes and the fog behind them. Anxiety and sleep deprivation mixed a potent cocktail, and the hangover was tough to push through.

"Did you even remember?" Her lips tightened as her eyes begged him for an answer. "I'm leaving for San Francisco this afternoon? To give the presentation I've been working on pretty much every night for the past I don't know how long? Jesus, it's been on the calendar for over a month."

Craig glanced over at the calendar that hung in the corner and saw *AACR—SF* written in his wife's hand with black Sharpie, then a line stretching from Friday to Sunday. He looked back in time to see Courtney close her eyes.

"No . . . I mean, yeah . . ."

Courtney stabbed the bowl of yogurt in front of her, and the spoon clanked against the edge. "Craig, I'm going to be honest here. I'm really fucking nervous leaving you home alone right now."

"I'm—" He couldn't even get the denial out before she was on him.

"You are *not* fine. I don't know if you're depressed or if it's something else, but you are absolutely not fine. I know you aren't sleeping, and it's absolutely affecting your behavior and judgment. And if you can't see that, well . . . I'm scared something could happen to you. To Alice."

The room blurred into an odd sort of tunnel vision as Craig hit rock bottom with the force of a pilot looking at a faulty altimeter. He wanted to peel himself off the concrete, but his own wife didn't trust him with their daughter, and he didn't know how to come back from that. But could he blame her? When they'd uprooted their lives to move to Minnesota, Craig had taken on a whole new array of responsibilities, and it was finally clear that he had unquestionably failed at every one. His book was gone. His daughter had been to the hospital twice. Now his wife had finally run out of patience with him.

"You have to talk to someone. If you won't do it, I'll find somebody for you, because we can't go on like this." They had never even approached a problem that was unsolvable, and the realization that they were close to that cliff's edge was a shock to the system. What Craig had thought of as another conversation had become an intervention. He turned on whatever charm he had left inside. Assured her he was fine, softened his voice, and agreed with what she'd said. He'd been struggling. The pressure from his book and staying at home with their daughter while trying to integrate into a new town had been too much to handle on his own, but he realized that now.

He was convincing, but Courtney wasn't buying it anymore.

"I'm serious. I want you to have made an appointment with someone by the time I get back. You have to do it not only for yourself, but for *us*. If you won't do that . . . I don't know. You have to."

A series of thumps from the front stairs cut off any response he had, but Courtney held his eyes as Alice bounded into the room. "Good morning, Allie cat."

Craig watched the gravity on Courtney's face fade away into a morning greeting for her daughter. A little girl she was afraid to leave alone with her father.

Alice trotted over and gave her mom a big hug. She untangled from Courtney's arms and beamed a smile across the table.

"Morning, Daddy."

Craig stared through them, eyes blank and focused back inside himself.

"Daddy?"

He shook his head back into the moment. "Yeah, sorry, kiddo. I'm just tired."

"Dad was up late last night." Something inside him knew Courtney's concern came from love, but his addled brain couldn't hear it. "Maybe you can make sure he takes a nap this afternoon."

"Can I watch TV?"

Courtney looked back at her with a smile. "As long as you are quiet so Dad can sleep. He *really* needs some rest, so if he forgets, you need to remind him. That's your job today, okay, sweetie?"

Alice promised, and Craig excused himself to flip the laundry while Courtney enjoyed breakfast with their daughter.

Unsure how to process his wife's ultimatum, he busied himself with chores until Courtney left for work. Alice's presence shielded him from descending into an argument, but it did nothing to ease the tension hanging over the house. As soon as Courtney was out the door, Craig headed to their bedroom and broke down, too exhausted to hold the tears back. He lay on the bed as emotion crashed over him, lacking the strength to keep himself from being whisked out into the deep waters.

He stayed there long enough to realize that Courtney was right. He couldn't go on like this. He'd allowed things to spiral, unable or unwilling to do what was needed to fix them. He wanted to push himself up, try and dust himself off, but he felt a boot on his back. The same one that had tripped him in the first place.

He had to find a way to fix this.

Eventually he pulled himself together as best he could and emerged from his room. Alice was down in the basement, playing with her dollhouse from the sound of it, and he ended up staring out over the backyard.

It was empty, but he couldn't take his eyes off the woods. If he didn't feel safe in his own home, he'd never get better.

He grabbed his phone off the table and looked up the number for HomeTech Alarm. They had to send a tech out, but someone had canceled an install, and they'd be able to come out that afternoon.

—

Craig puttered around the house as he waited for the alarm technician to show up, keeping busy without actually accomplishing anything.

But he had to do something. The look on Courtney's face that morning had been a stark warning that if things didn't change in a hurry, she was at least considering drastic next steps. And he would do anything in his power to avoid that.

The doorbell rang, and Craig froze. He peeked around the corner to confirm an adult-size shadow loomed outside before heading over to open the front door.

"Hello." The tech was an older guy named Ron who gave the *o*'s in his speech the love only a born-and-raised Minnesotan could. "I'm here to get yer alarm system up and running."

Ron's blue-and-white HomeTech van sat parked in front of their house. Craig swept his eyes around the cul-de-sac, convinced he'd see Levi scootering around.

"I'll have to start inside . . ."

"Yeah . . ." Craig focused on the man in front of him and ushered him through the door. "No problem."

Ron went into a friendly but overly long explanation of what he needed to do to get their system started up again. Mostly checking contacts and testing connections, but some of the old hardware needed to be updated, and he'd have to test the alarm a few times.

"These things are as loud as all get-out, so you and your little one may want to head outside till I'm done."

He wasn't kidding. After the first blast, Craig and Alice went out back to the swing set. It had been a while since they'd played in the backyard, but it felt even longer. He scanned the woods constantly. Couldn't help it. At every rustle, he snapped his head back, expecting to see Levi duck behind a tree.

The alarm inside went off again as Alice climbed onto her swing.

"That is *soooo* loud." She sounded more impressed than scared of the piercing sound.

Craig glanced into the woods behind them and stepped up to give her a push. "It's got to be to scare away anyone who isn't supposed to be here."

"Who's not supposed to be here?"

He caught a whiff of concern in her question and tried to make his voice as casual as possible. "Nobody. I mean, if someone tried to break into our house when we were on vacation, this would scare them away." Craig looked back into the woods again, and Alice noticed. "But you don't have anything to worry about. It's just for us to be super careful. And they will put little stickers on the windows that say we have a security system, so anyone who thinks they can get in will see that and not even try. It's really not anything to worry about."

The sliding glass door under the deck slid open, and Ron started fiddling with some new sensors he'd installed. Craig continued to push Alice and eventually pulled a few squeals of delight out of her.

It was a sound he'd missed.

Ron opened and closed the door a few times behind them. Craig looked back to see him examining the door handle. The old man grabbed a screwdriver and started digging around in the mechanism and muttered something to himself.

Craig left Alice swinging and headed toward the basement door. Ron held something up with two fingers.

"What is it?" Craig asked.

"A penny." Ron handed it over to Craig as if he were paying a debt. "Jammed up there in the strike plate."

Craig stared down at the coin, flipped it over and over in his palm as if it were some sort of clue. "How did it get in there?"

Ron chuckled. "Oh, kids like to play around with this kind of stuff, ya know? It's crazy the things we find out here. This one house I was at had Play-Doh mushed into every lock in the place. No way we're cleaning that out, so we had to replace the whole lot. Every single one. And that ain't cheap neither, so you're pretty lucky there. It's a good thing I found it, though, 'cause it was keeping the latch from catching."

Craig stared at the penny in his hand. "No . . . I check that door every night."

"You give it a tug or just look?" He reached inside and flipped the lock on the door, then pushed on the hook that popped out. It didn't hold its spot, just slid back into the door. "See, you can flip it and it looks locked, but if something's in there, it don't catch. The latches on these sliders aren't worth a darn, to be honest. What you need to do is get a piece of wooden dowel cut to about this long that you can lay down in the track behind it. That way even if the latch don't work, the dowel keeps it shut."

Craig felt terrified and validated at the same time. His laptop. His USB drive. Pete. The cereal. He fought the urge to bring that penny down to the police station and slap it onto Shaw's desk, even if he knew he'd never admit Craig was right. He half wanted to tell the old man to put it back; that way the next time Levi tried to get in, the cavalry would come running.

Then again, the alarm would scare him off long before the cops got there, and once again there would be no proof of what that little shit had done.

"Anyway, this all looks good now, and I just gotta put in the new lock on the front door."

"New lock?"

"They're pretty slick," Ron said. "Got a keypad that unlocks the door and disarms the system. It's nice 'cause you don't have to hustle over and punch in your code on the panel before the alarm goes off. But you'll need to think up a four-digit code for me."

Craig looked back at Alice, who'd managed to keep her momentum by pumping her legs back and forth. "Okay."

Ron dug up a pen and a Post-it Note from his tool bag. "If you write her down here, I can program it in when I get it all installed."

Craig thought for a minute before writing something down.

"Two five nine seven," Ron said. "Sounds good. That something everybody can remember easy?"

"It's our old address in Iowa City."

"I thought it was the year that little one was gonna graduate from college." Ron laughed and slapped Craig on the shoulder. "I'll get that installed, and you'll be good to go."

Craig headed back over toward the swing set, scanning the woods the entire way, afraid to see Levi duck back into the underbrush or pop out from behind a tree. Every creak and bump he'd heard while staring at his bedroom ceiling slipped back into his head. His lungs begged for more oxygen and started working harder, breath coming quicker and shallower. Alice called something over to him, but it sounded like it had come from far away.

Somewhere back in the woods.

The edges of his vision blurred, and Alice swung at the end of a long tunnel. The sky seemed so high above, and the trees stretched up like the iron bars of a cell, but the cell offered no protection because Levi could come and go as he pleased. It only served to keep Craig from escaping.

Craig closed his eyes and fought the crushing weight of imprisonment that was settling down on him like ash. He kept trying desperately to pull his emotions back in and pack them away.

He waited until his breath settled into a tenable rhythm and eventually risked opening his eyes again.

Alice watched from the play set, whatever momentum she had kept on the swing gone. She hung, barely swaying in the breeze, eyes a mess of concern. He forced the closest thing to a smile he could and walked over to her on legs that felt like they belonged on a marionette.

The security system was supposed to help his peace of mind, but it was little more than a Band-Aid on what had festered into a gangrenous wound. He could lock all the doors and install every alarm possible, but if the end result was hunkering down inside their house and hiding from a twisted nine-year-old boy, then what was the point?

And if nobody would help him out, he was going to have to find a way to take care of things himself.

Alice wanted to go inside, so Craig obliged. His near panic attack in the backyard had obviously unnerved the poor girl, so he let her do whatever she wanted. They headed up the deck steps and into the kitchen, where Alice asked for a snack. Craig pulled out a fresh box of fruit bars, but just stared at it.

"Daddy?"

They were new. Prepackaged. Fine. But it didn't matter. Logic was no longer welcome at the table of anxiety.

He stood there in front of the pantry, mind spinning, until he felt Alice take the box from his hands. "Yeah . . . sorry. You want some juice?"

The bottle was already on the table.

"Oops. Looks like you got it."

Craig grabbed her a glass out of the cabinet and offered to pour, but she didn't need any help, so he wandered out to the front door and looked for Ron. It was closed, but he could see the repairman's shadow on the other side of the beveled glass, and a muffled voice filtered through as he approached.

The old guy had so many stories, he had to talk to himself.

But as Craig got closer, he noticed a second shadow out on the front step just a few feet past the technician. He froze about five feet from the door. There were enough clear spots in the frosted glass that it was easy to make out Levi's form looming behind Ron as he concentrated on the new doorplate. Craig snuck over along the door and pressed himself against the wall.

Ron was chuckling about something as he put the last of the screws in, his voice seeping in through the door.

"Well, the code is secret. Every family gets to pick out their own so they can remember it easy." His grandfatherly tone was made for explaining things to kids. "Some people use their birthday or their anniversary, but the important thing is only they know what it is."

Craig peeked out one of the bevels in the side window and got a clear view of the front step. Ron's tool bag lay open next to him, their old doorknob sitting atop the clipboard next to it. The neon-yellow Post-it Note was still stuck to the top of his work order, their secret code clearly visible in Craig's familiar scrawl.

When Ron turned back to examine something on their new doorplate, Levi leaned in behind him to see their code.

Craig reached out for the door handle, ready to throw the kid off his property and tell Ron he'd have to reprogram the code, but something stopped him.

An idea. A stupid one. Reckless at best, dangerous at worst, but it was the first one he'd had in a long time.

A way to get rid of Levi.

Craig spun back and rested his head against the wall. It was crazy. He was tangled in a sleep-deprived vortex of anxiety and couldn't be trusted to make good decisions. Literally nothing had gone the way he'd hoped in the past few weeks.

Don't even think about it.

Craig banged the back of his head against the wall, hoping to knock his thoughts into something close to coherence, when the door opened next to him.

Ron stuck his head inside and jumped at the sight of Craig.

"Ope, there you are." If he was disturbed at finding Craig against the wall, he hid it well. "Just finishing up out here."

He stepped into the doorway and nodded back outside. "This little guy came by looking for your daughter, but I think he was more interested in what I was doing with this big ole drill."

Ron pulled the trigger with a *vroosh* and gave Craig a wink to let him know he didn't mind encouraging a little boy's curiosity. He reached down for his clipboard and handed the work order over to Craig. "If you just want to sign at the bottom, they'll send the bill later this week."

Craig stared at the Post-it Note with his code. There was still time to ask Ron to change it. He could tell him he wanted something easier for Alice to remember or he wanted to make the wife happy by using their anniversary. Or he could just be honest and say he saw Levi read it off the note he'd carelessly left out in the open.

He signed on the line and handed the clipboard back. Levi hovered in the background, eyes locked on Craig as if daring him to say something.

"Okay, then, I'll leave you two and be on my way." Ron gave Craig a sturdy handshake and tousled Levi's blond hair before heading back to his van. "Bye now!"

Craig watched the man get into his van and drive away with the last chance to pull back from the ill-conceived idea that had popped up like a toadstool.

Ron drove away and was halfway down the street before Craig said anything.

"We found your penny, so don't bother trying to get in the basement door anymore." He didn't bother making eye contact with Levi, just watched Ron's van drive away, assuming the lack of respect would piss the kid off. "Although if you want to try, I guess, go ahead. The alarm automatically calls the police, and they'll come down and arrest you for breaking and entering. I'm okay with that too."

Silence hung between them like low thunderclouds massing on the horizon. A voice inside begged him to go inside, call HomeTech, and apologize to Ron for bringing him back.

"Either way, no more taking our stuff, wrecking computers, putting fish flakes in my cereal. Of course you screwed that up because I didn't even eat it. All you did was make Alice sick. Hell of a way to treat a friend, eh? Then again you already sent her to the hospital once before, when you hit her with the croquet mallet. What's once more, right?"

"That was an accident." The serpentine tone of his voice pulled Craig's attention down to him. He'd never heard so much anger in a kid before, and it once again made him reconsider. Levi's eyes bore into him with hate. There was so much rage inside that kid, more than he could have ever imagined. Enough to make most people run, but that was the exact reason he had to do something.

"Bull. Shit." He said the words slowly, putting as much condescension into them as would fit. "You think you're so smart, that you've got everybody fooled. Well, not me, pal. I see you. I know what you are, even if no one else does."

Levi's face remained calm, but his eyes burned. Craig stared at him, daring him to say something, then cut him off as soon as he opened his mouth. "Now get the fuck out of here, and never come back."

Silence hung over the cul-de-sac.

"Now, you little shit. Go."

The kid held his gaze for another thirty seconds before turning toward the sidewalk. Craig let him get halfway down their driveway before calling out.

"If you don't like it, why don't you go back to that little fort and cry about it?" It stopped him in his tracks. "Oh, that's right, you don't have it anymore because I found it. You're doing some sick stuff back there, Levi. Glad to get Alice's bunny back, though."

Levi took off down the street.

Chapter Thirty-One

With Courtney on the West Coast and only Alice and him around for dinner, Craig whipped up some macaroni and cheese with chopped-up chicken nuggets mixed in. It was one of his daughter's favorites, but not something one would serve when adults outnumbered kids. When the nuggets were tossed in wing sauce, it was something Craig couldn't deny enjoying either.

It was also easy to make, so Craig could use all available bandwidth to figure out what the hell he was going to do once it got dark out. His big idea was at best a half-baked plan, and those always left an open chair in case doubt appeared.

That Levi would turn up was practically a given.

But what then?

Craig had spent the rest of the afternoon kicking around ways to make this work. Sure, he could be there waiting when Levi came through the front door, but then what? If he wanted it to mean anything, he had to have evidence. The kid had proved more than adept at twisting the situation around to make Craig the bad guy, and he certainly didn't want to get into a he-said, he-said situation.

He needed incontrovertible proof.

A clatter and a thump came from the living room, and Alice let out a burst of laughter. Craig looked over to his right and saw Felix crouched alongside the couch, head down and butt wiggling in anticipation. The cat leaped out from his hiding spot and pounced on something. He tucked around it and rolled into the middle of the floor with a somersault, pulling another squeal of delight from Alice.

"What's he got?" Craig asked.

"It's a feather." Alice struggled to keep the half-chewed bite of cheesy pasta in her mouth as Felix flipped the feather into the air with his mouth, then jumped up and batted it down with his paws.

The two of them watched their cat bound around the living room, catching the feather again and again, filling their house with the sound of laughter for the first time in a long while. For a moment, as Felix bounced around with his feline parkour, Craig felt normal for the first time in weeks. He was having a fun meal with his daughter, giving up entertainment duties to their cat.

Maybe it was that brief clarity that gave him the idea.

—

He waited until Alice was tucked into her bed, Pete snuggled under her chin where he belonged. They said their good nights, and Craig said she could read for ten minutes before turning her light out. She looked so happy, her missing piece back, making her whole. He wanted the same for himself.

Hopefully that night he'd finally get it.

Craig went downstairs to the office. With Courtney's computer and all the papers and files for her presentation gone, the giant desk alongside the far wall looked empty. The orchid pot was still there, but empty. His dead computer stuck on the bottom of the bookshelf, and the Moleskine notebook in which he jotted random story ideas sat ignored in the corner of the desk.

Craig went over to the sideboard along the left wall. It was a nice piece of furniture, perfect for a record player setup. The turntable sat prominently in the middle spot of honor, while his receiver slotted in perfectly on an open shelf below.

There was a cabinet on each side, and the one on the left had become a catchall for random office and electronic junk that had nowhere else to live. Craig dug through a basket of old cords and past an old Wi-Fi router before finding what he wanted buried in the back.

The camera was a white block about five inches tall with a black eyeball jutting out the top. It swiveled on a little base and used a motion sensor to track whatever came into view. They had bought it back in Iowa City when they'd suspected Felix was jumping up on the kitchen counters whenever their backs were turned.

They'd been right, and it wasn't just the counters. The camera, and its surprisingly effective night vision, captured their feline friend doing all kinds of things they'd been certain a good kitty would never dare.

After some corrective training—and the realization that there were some behaviors they were just going to have to accept—they were done, and Craig let Alice play around with the camera. She'd set it up in various places around the house and check in on what else Felix was doing. Alice would place toys and treats around in an attempt to lure him into doing something exceedingly cute for the camera, then watch the videos over and over again on their tablet.

But, as with most things, the novelty wore off, and the camera was put away. After they'd moved in to their new house, it had been stuffed in the office sideboard and forgotten about. Craig wasn't even sure it would sync to his phone anymore.

He set it next to his turntable and plugged it into the wall. The tiny light on the base flashed blue and yellow, and after a few seconds, it panned 180 degrees before focusing its eye on him. Craig pulled out his phone and swiped to the back pages where long-forgotten apps were put out to pasture.

A few taps and there he was, looking back at himself in full color.

He took a few steps to his right, and the camera tracked right along.

He reached over and hit the light switch. The screen went dark, but after a second, the office jumped back onto his screen, cast in a bright-gray hue. He could see himself standing there, eyes glowing like a cat's in the dark.

Craig took a slow step to his left, and the camera followed him. He stifled a smile and turned the lights back on.

His plan just might work.

Chapter Thirty-Two

It was always surprising how much noise a quiet house made in the middle of the night. Creaks, knocks, pops, and moans filtered in from the dark reaches as if trying to confirm the existence of the supernatural.

Craig sat on the floor, back against the wall, just outside the upstairs spare-bedroom door, waiting in the dark. His perch opened up above the entryway of the house like he was playing sniper. The stairway led down to the foyer ahead of him, the securely locked front door just below him to the right. His bedroom door was cracked at the top of the stairs, and he could see the open hall that led to Alice's room through the railing that ran along the edge.

He looked over toward Alice's room. She always left her door ajar so he could peek his head in and check on her before going to bed himself; the glowing butterfly plugged into an outlet next to her bookshelf cast barely enough pink light to see her angelic face. There was no reason to check on her every night, but seeing something that peaceful was calming before going to bed. It filled him with love.

That night, her door was closed.

Craig glanced down at his phone on the ground next to him.

1:13

He had no idea when Levi would show up, only that he would. Craig had invaded his space, taken something from him, then bragged about the security system he'd had installed to keep him out. That was a lot of chum in the water for a little kid with impulse-control issues.

No way he'd be able to resist.

Across the open expanse, Craig could see the outline of the camera looking down at the front door. He'd tested it in a variety of places, and fortunately there was an outlet right in the middle of that upstairs wall because that spot gave it a perfect view of the door and entire front hall.

Whenever Levi came in, he'd better smile because he was going to be on camera.

Craig looked at his phone again, and the time hadn't changed. Presumably Levi had to wait for his parents to go to sleep before sneaking out of the house.

But that didn't mean he'd show up here at that time.

If he does at all.

No, he'd come. He'd have to, just to prove he could. Craig just had to be patient.

The camera jumped to life across the stairs and sent a jolt of anticipation through him even though he hadn't heard anything from the door. It focused down, then slowly panned right along the stairs. A second later, Felix's silhouette popped up from the stairway. The cat padded over toward Craig and gave his leg an affectionate headbutt. Craig reached down and scratched under his ear, and Felix immediately flopped down against his leg. Purrs sounded like a motorcycle engine in the quiet, echoing around the open space over the front hall.

Craig leaned his head back against the wall and yawned. The chaos that kid had dumped into their lives was overwhelming, more destructive than anything he could have imagined. Levi had poisoned his reputation, his marriage, his sense of safety in his own house—with no consequences. Nobody believed that a little nine-year-old boy could be so manipulative and flat-out dangerous, but if Craig could get a recording of him breaking into their house, his parents and the police wouldn't be able to deny it.

The kid would finally be out of their lives for good.

Craig closed his eyes as the guilt of the past month sloshed around inside him. The kid might have walked down through the woods on his own, but it had been Craig who kept him around. First, as a writing tool. He'd practically thrown Alice at him so he could have quiet time to work on his book.

Daddy's writing. Why don't you go outside and play with Levi?

Then, even after the kid started showing his disturbing behavior, Craig decided he would fix him. Bring him down more often. Spend the time with him his parents wouldn't, because something in his brain told him if he helped Levi out, it would make up for not helping Jacob Westerholt.

Not because it had been the right thing to do, but to make himself feel better.

He yawned again and rested his head against the wall behind him. He was a wreck, but maybe he'd always been a wreck who was good at hiding it, and Levi brought it to the surface. Even if this worked and he was able to excise the kid from their lives, Craig realized there was still a lot more he had to fix.

He'd put his own feelings of guilt ahead of his family—his daughter—and it had almost cost him everything. What he'd done—and not done—to Jacob, that was his burden to carry. He couldn't pawn it off on anyone else.

Craig had to own it.

He kept absentmindedly scratching Felix's chin as the purring slowly faded into a breathy snore.

Chapter Thirty-Three

Somewhere buried in the fog of sleep, Craig vaguely felt a sleeping cat jolt upright next to him. Like all felines, Felix was a light sleeper who had evolved to go from sleep to fully awake at the smallest sound.

It was a safety measure to protect them from threats.

Craig had not evolved in such a manner, and his sleep-deprived brain ignored it, fully engrossed in his own rest. His head lolled to the side as he slid back toward the warm nocturnal embrace.

The rattle of the front door reached into the void and hauled him back to a consciousness that hit him almost too quickly to process.

It was dark. He was sitting on the floor, and his head floated in a haze of sleep.

Craig could make out Felix standing in front of him, ears perked and body tense, peering down the stairs.

His body jolted like he'd been hit with a Taser when conscious memory blasted back into his head.

He'd fallen asleep waiting for Levi to show up.

Craig froze again, hoping he hadn't already given away his position. He fought against the weight of residual sleep, straining to hear something from downstairs through the ringing of silence in his ears.

There was nothing. Had that been the door closing? Had he slept through everything? Craig looked over and saw the silhouette of the camera, unable to tell where it was pointed. He could check the feed from his phone, but the light from his screen would give him away. He'd have to trust it had gotten what he needed if he had indeed slept through Levi's trespassing.

The sound of footsteps on the hardwood floor of the entry below drifted up to the open second floor, followed by a quiet click-whir from the camera.

He was still down there, and it was tracking him. The little motor sounded like a jet engine to Craig, but Levi didn't seem to notice as the footsteps eventually disappeared onto the carpet of the living room.

Craig pushed himself into a crouch and leaned toward the spindles in front of him to get a look below. His eyes had adjusted well enough to the scant light filtering in from the streetlight outside that he could tell Levi had indeed moved on from the foyer. In theory he could see a sliver of the living room, but it was nothing but shadows from where he sat, so he had to rely on his ears.

The house stood still for what seemed like an eternity before Craig heard muffled footsteps as Levi's shoes found the hardwood of the kitchen floor.

Felix started down the stairs, and Craig lurched forward, thrusting his arms through the railing in a clumsy attempt to grab the cat before he got out of reach, but only succeeded in spooking him. Felix tore down the steps and landed on the hardwood below with a thud that echoed through the house.

Craig pushed himself back against the wall and held his breath. Levi's footsteps fell silent in the kitchen, and the house paused in an eerie stillness. Craig didn't dare look down for fear the kid would be searching for the source of that noise.

And what if he did?

From his spot upstairs, Craig saw a shadow creep along the wall into the living room. He stared at it, mentally begging Felix to stay away, but it was all he could do. He'd have to trust the cat's instincts if Levi decided a beloved family pet would make a good target.

A shuffle of feet resumed in the kitchen, and Craig debated how far he should let the kid go before confronting him. Was video of him coming in the front door enough, or would he need more? He should have assumed Levi would try to put something in their food again and set up the camera in the kitchen.

But then if he'd tried something else, Craig would have gotten nothing. He looked down to the entryway below and had an idea.

Craig carefully peeled away from the wall and crept toward the top of the stairs, doing whatever he could to keep his footsteps from drifting down toward the kitchen below. He didn't want to spook Levi before he could get in position.

He gingerly lowered his foot down on the first step, terrified of a previously unnoticed squeak blowing his cover. His foot settled onto the carpeted step without a sound, giving him the courage to continue. Craig gripped the railing with one hand as if he could hold the full force of his weight off the stairway and keep his footfalls that much quieter.

He'd made three steps when the camera picked up and swiveled back toward him with another grind of gears. Levi must have been too busy with whatever contamination he was doing to notice, because the faint rustle from the kitchen never stopped. Craig slowed his pace, attempting to keep his feet and the camera as quiet as possible on his way down. Eventually his bare foot went from the worn carpet of the stairs to the cool hardwood of the entryway. Standing where he was, he could get to the kitchen through the living room to his right or go left around the stairs through the dining room.

But Craig didn't want to stop what Levi was doing. A friend who'd worked retail once told him they never confronted a shoplifter until they left the store. Let them do the crime before busting them.

Craig glanced up at the camera on the edge of the walkway above and quietly backed up against the wall. Just to the right of the front door, a coatrack stood in the corner. It was empty except for an old hoodie he'd hung there while cleaning a while back. It wasn't perfect cover, but Craig felt he could blend in with the shadows well enough that Levi wouldn't notice him until he was ready.

He slid behind the coatrack and waited.

His brain tried out a bunch of first lines as if he were shooting an action movie and this was the final scene where the hero steps up and confronts the bad guy with a well-timed zinger.

Don't worry about being cute. Just get the job done.

He'd wait until Levi came back to leave, then step out of the shadows and ask what he was doing there—in perfect frame for the camera above. Craig didn't expect a full confession from the kid—it *wasn't* an action movie, after all—but he was confident whatever he got on video would be enough to prove what he'd been saying all along.

Nerves danced in his stomach like moths around a streetlamp as he waited. His gaze drifted up toward the second floor, and he could barely make out the door to Alice's room. Would she hear him confront Levi? Just like her mother, Alice was a deep sleeper, so he didn't think so, but what if Levi decided to make a scene? Start screaming or something. Surely that would draw her attention.

If so . . . good.

Maybe she needed to see it. Craig had tried to shield her from his worst thoughts about Levi, not wanting to scare her. And, if she did see Levi in their house well after 2:00 a.m., she'd be one more person to corroborate his story.

Craig heard more shuffling coming from the kitchen, then a shadow appeared on the left side of the stairs.

There was a pause; then a thin stream splashed down on the hardwood leading out of the kitchen to the dining room.

The kid was peeing all over their floor. The anger and disgust from such a violation cut through whatever apprehension he'd had and pushed Craig out from behind the coatrack.

"What are you doing here, Levi?"

CHAPTER THIRTY-FOUR

The stream stopped, and something clattered down on the hardwood floor, but the kid didn't turn and run, didn't jump and try to hide against the wall, didn't spit out a dozen lame excuses for why he was in their house in the middle of the night.

He simply turned toward Craig, staring through the dark of the house. It was like the terrain inside the kid's head was too rocky for fear to take root, which was disconcerting because Craig's heart was running like a lawn mower motor. He let silence hang in the entryway, not to intimidate but because his mouth had dried up and he wasn't sure he could speak.

Levi remained rooted where he'd stopped. It was too dark to see much more than the vague shape of his face, but the kid's eyes shone like a cat's in the limited light that came in from the front windows.

The long, thin shadow of a croquet mallet extended from his hand, its head resting on the floor.

All the clever one-liners Craig had concocted scattered like dandelion seeds, leaving him grasping for something resembling a plan.

Craig swallowed hard and forced the words out. "I said, What are you doing, Levi?"

"You made me wreck my fort." The words came out cold and matter of fact. Craig had wrecked his little handmade fort in the woods, so Levi had broken into their house and peed all over the floor. Nothing more than a reaction to an action, proportionality be damned.

"You can't break into people's houses, Levi." He could feel the camera above him, and it helped him keep his voice calm. He couldn't show any sort of threat or anger toward him.

There could only be one bad guy in this movie.

"I didn't break in." The mallet's edge scratched along the hardwood. "I figured out your stupid alarm."

Craig took a step forward, eye warily on the lawn hammer the kid dragged behind himself. "It doesn't matter how you got in—it's illegal to come into somebody's house without permission, and you can get in big trouble."

"I can do what I want." The words came out without hesitation, untainted by doubt. Whether it was his upbringing or something in his brain chemistry, the kid legitimately had no fear of consequences, which meant Craig had no way to predict what he was capable of.

"No, you can't." Craig couldn't resist a glance up at the camera above him. Levi was standing underneath the spot Craig had staked out upstairs—*where he'd fallen asleep*—and was therefore hidden from the camera. He took a step back, hoping the kid would follow him into frame, but Levi didn't move. Hopefully it was still picking up his voice.

Craig made a show of pulling out his phone. "Now you need to leave my house and go home, or I will call the police."

Obviously he was going to call the police no matter what. He'd considered calling them with Levi in the house, and while the cops catching Levi red handed would be ideal, he worried about keeping the kid there until they showed up. No matter what the situation, holding a kid against his will was a hard thing to explain, and Craig was not going to risk opening that can of worms.

The video would have to be enough.

Levi pulled something from his pocket and stepped farther back into the shadows between the dining room and kitchen. He held it out to the side, and three metallic clicks told Craig what it was a split second before he saw the inch-long flame erupt from the tip of the lighter.

"Whoa, what are you doing with a lighter, Levi?" With the boy hidden back by the kitchen, Craig narrated the situation for the camera above. Even if it was just a little flame, introducing fire escalated the situation to a whole other level, and he wanted to be sure the police knew what he'd dealt with when they reviewed all this later. It was unnerving having an unstable boy playing around with fire in his house, but it gave him more justification to act if it became necessary.

Levi didn't say anything, just let the flame dance at the end of his hand. The orange light flickered across his face and revealed a look of unsettling confidence. Levi glared across the room until something between them caught his eye.

Felix crept along the wall between them toward the kitchen, oblivious to the situation unfolding around him.

Craig saw a violent smile cross Levi's face before the lighter went out and threw the room back into darkness.

He didn't need to see Levi raise the mallet to know what was coming, and instinct threw Craig across the room. He knew immediately he wouldn't make it, but the movement spooked Felix, who darted away as Levi swung the mallet down. It slammed with a vicious bang into the wall where the cat had been a split second before.

Craig's foot snagged the edge of the rug below, and his momentum sent him flying headfirst toward Levi. The kid slid to the side, and Craig sailed past. He slammed into the wine rack that stood against the wall between the entrance to the kitchen and the back hall. Pain exploded through his collarbone with a wet snap, and his temple banged against a malbec he'd been saving to celebrate the sale of his book. He rolled over on his back, unable to see anything through the glowing purple pinwheels dancing through his vision.

A high-pitched cackle bounced between the walls and the hardwood as Levi swung the mallet down into Craig's ribs. It felt like he'd fallen on a grenade, and every molecule of air in his lungs shot out into the dark.

Craig rolled to his side and braced for another blow, but it never came.

Just laughter. It wasn't born of humor but was something that sounded like a laugh of obligation. Like a bad actor doing what he thought his role demanded.

His vision slowly cleared, and he tried to prop himself up, only for his shoulder to collapse in pain and send him back to the ground. His head bounced off the same iron leg that had broken his collarbone, a storm of pain rattling his skull. He tried to shake the daze from his head and saw Levi's silhouette lording over him, backlit by the front windows.

Craig fought for control of his breathing, and as his head cleared, he realized the ammonia-tinged smell of urine that he'd expected wasn't there. It was a more pungent odor that told him Levi hadn't been spraying pee all over the floor.

It was lighter fluid.

The smell sent a jolt of panic through him and dumped a year's worth of adrenaline into Craig's bloodstream. He looked up at Levi and saw the orange flicker of flame had returned to his hand.

The fire cleared his addled mind, and he thought of Alice, upstairs in her room. Was she still sleeping, or had she heard his crash into the wine rack? A million other questions flickered through his brain, but were wiped away when Levi bent down and touched the lighter to the rug in front of him.

Chapter Thirty-Five

Blue-tinged flame raced across the floor toward Craig and again lit up Levi's emotionless face. Craig tried to push himself away, but his shoulder crumpled in another burst of pain as the flames swarmed around his legs.

Craig howled and clumsily rolled away from the fire. He pulled himself toward the back hall and rubbed his bare legs with his left hand. The singed hair had pilled up like a low-quality sweater, and he could feel the redness radiating from his skin.

A whoosh came from around the corner as the flames swept across the kitchen floor, quickly followed by the piercing shriek of their smoke alarm. Pungent chemical smoke fought its way into Craig's sinuses, and he covered his nose and mouth like he was stifling a sneeze. He pushed up to his feet and edged back toward the kitchen, where the entire floor was already awash in flame. The table where he and Alice ate breakfast every morning was burning, and fire was already licking at the wooden cabinets by the sink.

A wave of heat forced him to turn away, and Craig leaped over the burning rug separating him from the dining room. The increasing orange glow behind him illuminated the front door, which stood wide open to the night.

He whipped his head around the entryway, but Levi was gone.

The crackle of burning increased behind him as if challenged to match the screams of the smoke alarm, and the heat increased against his back. Smoke rolled over the ceiling above and wafted up to the open air of the entryway, drawing his attention upstairs.

Alice.

Craig tore off toward the stairs and swung himself around the banister with his good arm. The fire had already spread into the living room, where the carpet was ablaze and their swivel chair was burning like a freshly upholstered effigy. If Levi had doused the living room with as much lighter fluid as he had the kitchen, there was a very good chance there would be no way out by the time he got Alice from her bedroom.

He pulled himself up the stairs with his left arm, but the smoke had already built into a thick smog. Through the haze, he could see Alice's bedroom door at the far end of the landing.

Craig coughed and covered his mouth as the continued shriek of the alarm assaulted his eardrums. He lurched toward Alice's door, eyes stinging from the smoke, only to have the doorknob jerked from his hand. He stepped through and almost tripped on his daughter, who was poised on all fours just inside the door, ready to crawl out.

"Alice!" Craig dropped to his knees and pulled her into himself.

"We have to stay low, Daddy." Her voice was calm and hard to hear over the increasing cacophony of the burning house. "Smoke rises."

Craig silently praised whatever firesafety lessons had been drilled into her at school and ducked down beside her. "Right, but we've got to get out as fast as we can, okay? The fire is downstairs, so we're going to get to the steps and head right out the front door, just like we talked about before, remember?" He leaned in close as the smoke continued to thicken. "Can you grab onto my neck and hold on real tight?"

Alice wrapped her arms around him, and he held her tight with his good arm. He briefly lost his balance standing up and braced his right hand against her doorframe, but a wave of pain in his shoulder almost put both of them back on the floor.

Craig got his legs under himself and carried Alice across the landing to the stairs. The smoke around them was thick and black now, and she buried her face into his neck as he tried to hold his breath against the noxious fog.

He fought the instinct to fly down the stairs, instead treading carefully and methodically. With his daughter hanging around his neck and a most certainly broken collarbone, he struggled to not stumble and send them both careening down the stairs into serious injuries.

Craig tried to ignore the fire that had fully engulfed the living room on the left, instead concentrating on the open door in the foyer below. Flames were rapidly spreading into the dining room on the other side, narrowing their only escape route by the second. He could feel Alice's lips moving against his neck as he plodded down the steps and squeezed her tighter.

While the smoke cleared a little with every step down, the air temperature rose dramatically. As soon as his bare foot hit the base of the steps, he hustled his daughter across the unnervingly warm hardwood and out the front door.

Relief hit hard as they ran out into the fresh, cool night air. Craig carried Alice all the way to the street before setting her down and collapsing into a rack of coughs. He fought the smoke he'd inhaled for control of his lungs and knelt down in front of Alice. She looked so little standing in the street, wearing Ms. Marvel pajamas and the bravest face a seven-year-old could muster.

"Are you okay, kiddo?"

She nodded, and he wrapped her in the fiercest hug he'd ever given, pain in his shoulder be damned. When he eventually opened his eyes, he saw their shadow flickering in the street behind them, courtesy of the flames destroying their house.

Craig turned back and stared at the orange glow coming from the door. One of the front windows exploded in a shower of glass and released a stream of thick black smoke into the night. Their new security system was wired into the smoke alarms, so the fire department should be on their way already, but he pulled his phone out to call 911 anyway. The operator confirmed they'd received notice from HomeTech and trucks were en route, which was a relief.

The fire was already well out of any semblance of control, eating away at their house in a way that would never be stopped in time.

But Craig didn't care. Even in the face of such violent destruction, he felt an odd sense of calm as he stood there with Alice. He'd still have everything he needed. His wife was safe in California, Alice was shaken but breathing beside him, and he'd finally gotten the proof he needed to excise Levi from their lives.

Approaching sirens breached the quiet night as Craig pulled out his phone and scrolled through to the WayCam app. Not that he would bother showing the video to the firemen—they'd obviously have more pressing matters—but he needed to see it.

He tapped the icon and pulled up the Recorded Events tab with his left hand while his right arm hung down painfully at his side.

YOUR COMPLIMENTARY WAYCAM PLUS SUBSCRIPTION HAS EXPIRED

Reactivate your subscription to enable cloud storage

He stared at the screen as a black hole opened up inside his gut, pulling in all matter surrounding it. When they'd used the camera to keep an eye on Felix, every video recorded had been automatically uploaded to the cloud and was streamable from the app.

But if it wouldn't upload the videos without a subscription, he'd have no proof of Levi being in their house that night, let alone starting the fire.

He tapped through the notification in a panic.

> Without cloud storage, captured videos can be stored on an optional SD card (sold separately) and transferred via USB.

He'd installed an SD card when they bought it, thinking they needed it to keep videos. He remembered getting pissed when he realized it hadn't been necessary because it sent them all to the cloud.

But apparently only for the first year.

Craig looked back at the door and saw the fire had already spread to the stairs. The camera was still up there, along with all the proof he needed on that mini SD card inside.

But how long before it was nothing but a melted mess of plastic?

"Stay right here, kiddo. I'll be back in a second."

He dropped his phone to the ground and took off toward the house. Alice shouted an objection, but he was already back through the door.

Chapter Thirty-Six

Stepping back through the front door was like climbing into a potter's kiln. The smoky air was sandpaper on Craig's lungs, and trying to look around the entryway felt like staring down the barrel of a hair dryer.

The living room was gone, nothing but a wall of flame, and had pushed the fire onto the base of the stairs ahead of him. Craig squinted up toward the landing above and could barely make out the boxy shape of the camera in the smoke.

Fire covered the bottom five steps ahead of him. Before his brain could tell him no, Craig took two steps and leaped as far as he could up the stairs, landing on the fourth. He ignored the searing pain on the bottom of his foot and lunged toward the top, landing hard on the steps and knocking a huff of smoky breath from himself. His tender ribs moaned, and his shoulder screamed as he reached forward and scrambled up the remaining steps to the second floor.

The entire landing was enveloped in hot, acrid smoke. Standing was impossible. Craig stayed on the floor and grabbed ahold of a railing spindle, dragging himself around the corner. He slithered on his belly through the toxic atmosphere until he could reach out with his left hand and grab hold of the camera.

He yanked the plug from the wall and wormed his way back toward the stairs, staying as low to the floor as possible.

The fire had followed him up the stairs and blocked any hope of getting out with anything less than severe burns. The entire entryway was on fire, and he couldn't even see the front door anymore.

Escape route blocked, Craig crawled over to their master bedroom. He pushed his way inside and closed the door behind himself. The air was slightly better in their bedroom, but a steady stream of smoke wafted in under the door. He yanked the blankets off their bed and frantically wedged them at the base of the door to try and stem the tide.

That done, he lay back and tried to catch his breath. Pain radiated down his right side, but the adrenaline flowing through him helped as much as a handful of ibuprofen would. He ran his left hand along his leg and felt the crispy ends of the little hair that remained, then fingered the blisters already starting to form on his foot.

The smoke alarms stopped wailing. Probably melted.

Craig examined the boxy camera he was apparently willing to die for. It seemed intact, and he flipped it over to confirm there was indeed an SD card inserted.

There was.

The air was clear enough that he stood up and took stock of his options. The entire first floor was engulfed, so there was no going out the way he'd come. He could feel the heat radiating up through the floor, so he knew it was just a matter of time before the entire bedroom broke through to the kitchen below.

There was no waiting to be rescued.

The two windows on the bedside wall opened up over the deck and backyard below, so those weren't options, but the one in the far corner that overlooked the back of the garage was. Craig hurried over and threw up the shade. If he could get onto the roof, he could climb over to the front side and drop down in the flower bed next to the garage. He'd need to be careful not to slide off the back—it was at least a twenty-foot drop onto their limestone retaining wall below—but it was a chance he'd have to take.

Craig cranked the window open and knocked the screen out. It bounced off the edge of the roof and slid down into the darkness below. He held the camera in his bad hand and pulled himself up on the window frame. His grip faltered, and the camera fell out of his hand as he braced himself. The little white box bounced off the windowsill and toppled back into the room.

He stared at it on the floor, waiting for his heart to start beating again before trying to figure out a way to do this safely. He'd need two arms to make that climb, but one was barely functional and contributed nothing but pain. *And* he still had to carry the camera. Without that, he might as well sit down and wait for the flames.

Craig tore open his bedside table and pulled out an old gym sock. He stuffed the camera down into the toe and held it in his teeth as he vaulted himself onto the windowsill again. Sirens from the approaching trucks reverberated through the neighborhood like a late-night alarm clock, and flashes of red and blue light flickered off the treetops down the block.

A loud snap came from somewhere behind him, but Craig swore he'd heard something else. Something high pitched. One leg was already out the window, but he leaned back inside the increasingly smoky room.

"Felix?"

Another faint meow came from the dark. As fast as the fire had spread downstairs, his mental clock insisted it was time to go. The kitchen ceiling below him was burning, which meant the bedroom floor wasn't long for this world. If he was standing on it when it collapsed, neither was he.

Their cat's instincts should have taken him out of the house long ago. Hell, every time Craig opened the front door, Felix bolted for freedom like he was more hostage than house pet.

Another meow, somewhere in the dark, but undeniable.

The clean, cool air outside the window beckoned, but Craig dove back inside and crawled to their bed. The floor was significantly warmer already, and he could picture the flames licking through the wood below him.

Craig pulled up the dust ruffle and saw a pair of shiny eyes stare back from between two flat storage boxes. There was no time to coax a frightened cat out of one of his nine favorite hiding places, so he just reached in and found the scruff of his neck. Felix curled into a ball, and Craig felt two needle-sharp teeth sink into the soft flesh around his wrist as he pulled. The cat's back claws kicked and kicked, raking down his forearm with rivulets of pain. Craig gritted his teeth and kept dragging.

Felix let out a yowl and bucked against his grasp as Craig finally wrested him out from under the bed. If he got away, there'd be no chance to corral him again before the floor gave out, so he held on through the claws and pain. Craig stretched his foot over toward the dresser and snagged the strap of his gym bag. He dumped the cat inside and quickly zipped the top up over him. He stuffed the camera—still inside a sock—in next to him and hoisted the shoulder strap around his neck. Felix thrashed about for a second and then seemed to settle among the shorts and towels.

The floor kept emitting a disturbing number of creaks and crackles, and Craig was sure it would bow out from under them before he could get back to the window.

Somehow it held.

The clean outside air felt downright arctic after the inferno of their house. He swung his feet out and eased down until he felt the rough texture of shingles on the roof. They weren't hot, which was good, but the pitch on the back of the garage was much steeper than he'd realized. Standing wasn't an option, so he sat down and leaned his back against the roof.

With nothing for his bare feet to hold on to, he started slowly sliding down the roof toward the dark expanse below. Panic bloomed as he tried to dig his heels into the roof and reached back with his good arm for anything he could hold on to. His fingers found the windowsill but couldn't get a grasp as gravity pulled him down the roof. Craig rolled onto his broken shoulder to get a better reach, but that only sped his descent.

He flipped onto his back as his feet went over the edge. His heels felt nothing for a second before catching on the rain gutter and stopping his slide. Craig pushed against it and felt the metal bend under his weight. He stayed there, knees bent, feet in the gutter but still on the roof. Felix kicked around the duffel bag next to him as Craig held as still as possible, terrified any movement would break the friction and drop him onto the rocks below.

The crack of collapsing wood from somewhere behind him kicked things back into gear. He slid Felix's bag onto his stomach and started to inch his way across the edge of the roof. The gutter bent every time he put weight on it, but held.

It was like when he and his cousins had gone skating at his uncle's pond. It was too early in the season to trust the ice, but they were dumb and reckless kids. Craig could hear the cracks with every stride but had glided out to the middle of the pond before realizing he could be in real trouble. He'd taken baby steps back, staring at the bank and expecting to crash through into the icy water with every one, before eventually collapsing into a little snowbank on the shore.

He hoped he'd be as lucky this time.

Thankfully, Felix had stopped bucking at every jostle and settled in as he slowly shimmied across the roof. Lights from the fire trucks danced across the woods ahead of him as the sirens cut off. Halfway across he heard another crash from the house—much louder that time—and craned his neck back toward his bedroom. Black smoke poured from the window into the night.

He picked up speed, figuring he'd made it past the retaining wall, meaning the ground was much closer and any potential fall was more limb damaging than life threatening. If he could get to the front side, it would be an even shorter drop, but there was no way he'd be able to make his way over the peak with a busted shoulder and a cat bag slung around his neck, so he kept sliding to his left.

When he ran out of roof, Craig looked over the edge at the ground below. It was about ten feet to the flower bed below, but their huge lilac bush took up almost all his landing area. He laid his head back on the roof and closed his eyes. Shouts came from out front as the firefighters organized whatever they were going to do to a structure that had already been gutted. Hopefully somebody out there would notice Alice and keep an eye on her until he could get down.

A rustle came from below, and Craig saw two fully geared firefighters running around to the backyard.

"HEY!" Yelling must have knocked loose some of the smoke that had settled down in his lungs, because he went into a coughing spasm that almost sent him tumbling off the roof. He held on as the firemen brought back a ladder. By the time he climbed down, orange flames were shooting out his former bedroom's window.

Craig ran around to the front and found Alice standing in the street in the exact spot he'd left her. Kaylene and Dan were with her in shorts and sweatpants, pulled out of their beds by the sirens. He rushed over and dropped to his knees in front of her, and she buried her head in his chest. He ignored the massive fire destroying their home behind them and the pain in his shoulder as he wrapped both arms around her in the tightest embrace he could manage.

Before she could ask, Craig unzipped his gym bag, and Felix poked his head out. Alice squealed in delight and let loose a flood of tears as she attacked her cat with kisses. A fireman came over and checked on them, followed by a paramedic. Broken collarbone or not, Craig insisted they give Alice a once-over before even looking at him.

Kaylene told Alice she'd take Felix over to their house so he wouldn't get scared off by all the commotion. She offered to take Pete the Bunny so he wouldn't get lost, but there was no getting him out of her arms.

As they walked to the ambulance, Craig saw sleepy pockets of his neighbors collecting on the sidewalk. His eyes darted between them as Alice answered the paramedics' questions.

He found Levi relatively quickly, as the orange glow from the fire he'd started invaded the shadows the kid was trying to hide in. The flames danced in his eyes and held him, almost hypnotically. Craig felt no rush of anger—the fact that his house would be nothing more than a smoldering husk within an hour hadn't fully registered yet—and smiled thinking of the camera tucked away in his bag. He'd let Kaylene take Felix, but the gym bag stayed with him. The paramedic ushered him to the back of the ambulance and cautiously lifted it off his shoulder.

"I need to talk to the police."

Chapter Thirty-Seven

The sun briefly slid behind one of the few clouds that dotted the sky, but popped back out the other side to smile down on them. It was another perfect pool day, so he and Alice had made sure to arrive early and snag one of the umbrella chairs.

He put down the paperback he'd been reading and looked around the deck for his daughter. It might take a second to see her, but the pack of girls she traveled in was always easy to locate. Craig had worried she'd be permanently damaged after everything that happened last summer, but his therapist had assured him from the beginning that kids were often tougher than expected. And she'd been right. Once Alice had started at school, she'd found Emma, Sara, and Sophie, and they'd been inseparable ever since. For the first time since they'd moved up from Iowa, Alice had a real sense of belonging, of normalcy.

Friends.

Craig watched the girls climb the stairs of the waterslide and leaned back into his chair when they disappeared down the tube. It had taken him a while to be comfortable back at the Southeast Minnesota Athletic Club, but he thought it was important to be there. It had always been Alice's favorite place, and he was determined that she wouldn't lose anything to that kid, which was why, along with Alice's school, the pool was one of two designated safe spaces in the restraining order where Levi Ryan wasn't allowed.

Ever. No exceptions. He'd be arrested just for showing up.

Levi had avoided juvenile detention, but the judge enrolled him in a program for troubled youth. It hadn't sat well with Craig, even when the DA explained it was the most they could hope for considering his age and the quality of his parents' lawyers.

But as word spread of what had happened, others stepped forward with stories of their own. Kaylene wasn't the only one who'd caught Levi peeping in on them, while others had seen him creeping around when things had gone missing. There were disturbing stories of why his parents had pulled him from a high-priced private school. Eventually the cops found a rat's nest of things in Levi's room. Along with Craig's USB drive, there were stolen family photos, missing underwear, and random knickknacks from all across the neighborhood.

It was blood in the water, and the same group of well-to-do neighbors who'd held their tongue over the years turned on the Ryans in a long-deserved feeding frenzy.

He'd heard the Ryans tried to join the new country club on the other side of town, but their application was denied. A year later, the rumor mill still churned hard enough that even Craig had a hard time telling fact from fiction.

Acquaintances and strangers still asked him about it from time to time, all looking for some inside stories on what had actually happened, but he refused to talk. He'd been working hard with his therapist to sort out all his feelings and emotions from the last year, and both of them agreed that feeding the rumor beast would be counterproductive to moving on.

And that's all he wanted for himself and his family.

It hadn't been an easy road, though. Aside from his therapist, he and Courtney saw a marriage counselor for the first six months after the fire. He wanted to think their rough patch had been brought on by an extreme situation, but Craig learned a lot about his behaviors and emotions that couldn't be pinned on a sociopathic boy from the woods. Levi might have been the spark, but there had been a lot of tinder that had nothing to do with him.

That said, they were healing. They no longer had a standing appointment, and he felt like their relationship had had its cast removed. It was healed enough to hold together, but without that support they'd have to be careful for a while so they didn't reinjure anything.

Alice splashed out of the tube and swam to the side along with her friends. Instead of getting back in line, she dripped over to him.

"Sophie said her mom wants to take us out for ice cream." She pushed back the wet hair that had plastered against her forehead. "Can I go?"

Craig gave Alice an exaggerated look like he was thinking hard about the offer, then broke out into a smile. "Absolutely. Sounds like fun."

He watched her skitter across the wet cement toward her friends, then caught the eye of Sophie's mom and gave a thumbs-up. She smiled and sent back a wave of acknowledgment.

Craig gathered up the rest of his stuff and dropped the book he'd been reading into the bag. He'd really expanded his literary intake over the past year, drifting away from the dark, murdery stuff he usually read and dancing across a wide variety of genres. Historical fiction, science fiction, nonfiction—all the stuff he'd previously ignored opened up like a fresh stretch of wilderness to explore.

He'd stepped away from writing for a good six months after the fire, concentrating on his family, relationships, and his own mental health. He'd sent a note of apology to Jennifer DiAmato for missing their meeting at MinnLit, not getting into any details but simply saying that he didn't have anything for her at that time.

But as things got better and Alice started school, Craig dipped his toe back in the water. Nothing major, no pressure, just getting back to what made him happy about writing.

Before he knew it, he was working on a cozy mystery.

Craig took one last look over at Alice and headed to the car. Heat erupted from inside when he opened the door. As he maneuvered out of the parking lot, the leather seat baked his legs through the towel he'd put down.

He bounced his head along with LCD Soundsystem as he made his way to their new neighborhood. They'd rented for a few months after the fire, but both he and Courtney agreed that quickly finding a permanent home would be good for them. It was a little smaller than their last place and needed a few improvements, but Alice got her own bathroom and was allowed to decorate her new bedroom all by herself, which meant an amount of purple even Prince would have considered over the top.

Craig saw his new neighbors planting flowers next door and waved as he turned in to the driveway. Once again, fate had smiled upon them and delivered great people to live beside. Mark and Sperry were younger—no kids to serve as friends or babysitters—but they'd been friendly and helpful since day one.

Maybe they'll have kids and Alice will be their go-to sitter in a few years?

Craig pulled into the garage and killed the engine. The thought of his daughter growing up enough to take care of others brought a nervous smile to his face.

He popped out of the driver's side and noticed Mark carrying something up their driveway that stopped him cold.

"I found this out back leaning up against that oak tree between our yards."

Craig felt his fingers tighten around the door handle, palms suddenly slick.

"Is it yours?" Mark's voice said he either couldn't see the color leave Craig's face or was too polite to notice. "We don't have a set, so I figured it was Alice's. Don't know who else could have left it back there."

He was too far away to get a good look but didn't need a close examination to recognize a croquet mallet. Craig forced a smile and fought to slow down his heart as Mark held the wooden hammer out to him.

Acknowledgments

As lonely as writing a novel can feel in the moment, it's amazing how many people had a hand in getting this book from first words on my computer to whatever version you are holding in your hands.

First, thank you to my agent, Abby Saul. For being endlessly supportive, for answering every unnecessary and often repetitive question I have, and for not letting me quit on this book when I was staring at a first draft I wanted to throw in a drawer and never look at again.

I want to thank my editor Liz Pearsons for taking a chance on me and working hard to get this book to the finish line. Publishing with the team at Thomas & Mercer has been amazing. Thanks to my production manager Tamara Arellano for shepherding me through the process and getting this all to come together. Big thanks to my copyeditor Alicia Lea and proofreader Elyse Lyon for teaching me how little I actually know about proper grammar and not mocking me for making the same mistakes over and over. Thanks to my author liaison Sarah Shaw for being there to answer any and all questions.

They say you can't judge a book by its cover, but if you want to judge my words based on the amazing cover David Lipman designed, be my guest.

I was lucky enough to work on this with one of the best horror writers out there, Gabino Iglesias, and this book is so much better because of it.

Thanks to Brianna Labuskes, Elle Grawl, and Chris Anderson, who read the early, ugly drafts and pointed me in the right direction.

I mentioned my agent earlier, and with her comes the best stable of writers a scribe could hope to be a part of in the Lark Group. Special shout out to Bri, Elle, Meredith Hambrock, Mindy Carlson, Tara Tai, Jason Powell, Terah Harris, Kris Calvin, Daisy Bateman, Stephanie Thérèse, and Sarah James. You all have kept me sane-ish through this whole thing. #TeamLark for life!

Thanks to my parents, who always gave me money for the Scholastic Book order at school and let me read He-Man books in church (sometimes).

Finally, I want to thank my family. There is no way I could have even attempted writing without the support of my wife, Erin, and I get inspiration from my daughters, Claire and Paige, every day.

But not inspiration for this book. Just kind of in general, you know? Love you guys!

Seriously, none of this book is based on you two.

About the Author

Photo © Grant Hamilton

Tony Wirt was born and raised in Lake Mills, Iowa. A graduate of the University of Iowa, he spent nine years doing media relations in the Hawkeye athletic department before turning his hand toward fiction. He currently lives in Rochester, Minnesota, with his wife and two daughters. His indie thriller *A Necessary Act* was named the 2017 Reader's Choice Novel of the Year by Underground Book Reviews.